John Campbell was born in 1936 in Belfast's York Street district. After leaving school, he worked at Belfast Docks until 1985. He now works for the Queen's University, Belfast, and is a senior shop steward for the Transport & General Workers' Union. A well-known writer and commentator on Belfast working-class life, he has published three individual collections of poetry: *Saturday Night in York Street* (1982), *An Oul Jobbin' Poet* (1989) and *Memories of York Street (1991). The Rose and The Blade: New & Selected Poems 1957-1997* was published by Lagan Press. He is also the author of two novels, *Corner Kingdom* (1996) and *The Disinherited* (2006).

By the same author

Poetry
Saturday Night in York Street
An Oul Jobbin' Poet
Memories of York Street
The Rose and The Blade:
New & Selected Poems 1957-1997

Fiction
Corner Kingdom
The Disinherited

Biography
Tommy Stewart: The Belfast Battler

ONCE THERE WAS A COMMUNITY HERE

Published by
Lagan Press
1A Bryson Street
Belfast BT5 4ES

first published 2001,
reprinted with minor corrections 2009

© John Campbell, 2009

The moral rights of the author have been asserted.

ISBN: 978 1 873687 18 5
Author: Campbell, John
Title: Once there was a Community Here
A Sailortown Miscellany
Format: Paperback
2009

ONCE THERE WAS A COMMUNITY HERE
A Sailortown Miscellany

JOHN CAMPBELL

LAGAN PRESS
BELFAST
2009

*To the memory of the late Tommy McMullen and Tommy Lyttle
—two close and treasured friends who died suddenly
at the beginning of last year. And to all other colleagues and
aquaintances who have died recently.*

Precious links in a priceless chain that stretch to heaven and back again.

ONCE THERE WAS A COMMUNITY HERE

Once there was a community here:
steeped in tradition as old as the sea.
Now wild grass blooms in perpetuity,
growing through the pavements of yesteryear.
The spars of schooners speared the sky,
Dockers worked among crates and bags,
Sailors searched for willing half-door hags,
Beer and flesh were always easy to buy.

Aproned jarvies carted the gentry
from drinking dens to Music Halls,
Carriages swept them to stately balls.
Poor folk starved in the midst of plenty.
The crack of rivet-guns filled the air
as cloth-capped men on shipyard slips
transformed raw steel to majestic ships.
The doomed Titanic germinated there.

Holy war would occasionally flare
when neighbours killed for religious belief,
then nursed each other through times of grief,
Church pews full, and cupboards bare.
Cheek by jowl, in stifled space,
bombed by Hitler, they remained unbowed.
Honestly poor and stubbornly proud.
Hope and optimism filled each face.

The lassies walked with the Allied forces;
fighting men with honeyed tongues
kissed girls with flax or tobacco lungs.
Mills and factories were the deadly sources.
Once there was a community there:
a teeming humanity came and went.
Death could be brutal but heaven-sent
when the burden became too much to bear.

Now commuter trains speed above my head.
Hovercrafts fly with passengers and freight.
Only vermin and birds procreate ...
in a district that's virtually people-dead.
My roots and beginings are in this place.
All that I am, or ever hope to be
was fashioned on ground once home to me;
its premature death, a bureaucratic disgrace.

Keeps it memory alive in the salt of each tear;
Remember each baby, each bridegroom, each bride.
Exalt their existence with reverence and pride.
Never forget: once there was a community here.

CONTENTS

Sailorstown
   A Last Farewell 15
Memories of York Street 18
The Long Shot 27
The Jackie Bell Story 32
A Profile of Davy Whiteside 37
The Mills Bomb 46
Sammy McKee
   Sporting Man 54
The Wino's Story 58
Moby's Story 67
Bitter Crossing 72
Moviehouse Memories 77
Pints & Politics
   A Play in One Act 89
Tommy Stewart
An Uncrowned Champion 117
Halcyon Days
   Henry Street Boys' Amateur Boxing Section 159
Memories of a Forklift Truck Operator 167
The John Hewitt I Knew 174
The Magic Box 180
An Old Hand Goes Back To The Classroom 191
Strangers in the Night 199

SAILORSTOWN
A Last Farewell

In Sailorstown was some good men,
I wish I was back there again ...
No finer souls I've met since then ...
    In Sailorstown.

The great heart of the once vibrant village of Sailorstown is no more. Less than a year ago the last of its inhabitants moved sadly from the areas of Garmoyle Street and Pilot Street. Some settled in the newly erected houses under the shadow of the giant Gallaher Tobacco factory, whilst others moved into the various estates that now surround the city.

Thus ended a sojourn that started in the earliest centuries when humans began to people the mud flats on the side of the river, which is the north-eastern shore of Belfast.

Sailorstown thrived, and soon it began to witness the wooden ships of the fishermen and the longboats of a succession of invaders. Throughout the centuries it acquired a mixed but close-knit community. The narrow streets of kitchen houses bustled with people who toiled on its harbours, quays, shipyards and factories. Others worked in its spinning mill or ploughed the seas in vessels built not more than a stone's-throw from where they lived.

It observed a majestic ocean-going liner, heralded as a floating miracle, steam down Belfast Lough to fulfil its destiny with an iceberg which sent it and quite a few natives of Sailorstown to a watery grave.

It wept at the tragic and heartbreaking religious riots that put neighbour against neighbour and family against family. It sighed as the long queues of emigrants boarded the ships that took them to the promised lands of the New World that offered peace and prosperity.

It smiled when their descendants returned en route to France to engage the forces of the Kaiser in 'a war that was to end all wars'. It saw its narrow streets weep with blood during the fierce, brutal and often merciless war of independence. It saw its people walk in fear along roads corrugated and partitioned against the unbridled hate that seeped from its very cobbles.

It rejoiced as the sons of the emigrants returned to its docks in their large troop-ships, on their way to Europe to once again help liberate the world from tyranny and oppression.

It screamed as the Luftwaffe darkened its skies, before strafing its defenceless streets, raining destruction on it and death and terror on its inhabitants. It watched its bombed-out but unbowed people gather their belongings and move to the outskirts of the city. After the all-clear it saw them return, many to start from scratch.

With the war's end it saw its fighting men come home and bathed in an era of prosperity that had its factories belching smoke, its quays lined with shipping and its streets black with dockers, doffers, spinners, sailors, shipyard men and tobacco workers.

The years flew by and then it witnessed the arrival of the latest invaders. Its great heart ached as the bulldozers and wrecking crews camped arrogantly on its ground. It had sighed with relief when the internecine riots, which had recently gripped other parts of Belfast, had seemingly passed it by.

Now, the new enemy called progress had arrived and as everyone knows, you can't stop progress. It did what the invaders in the longboats couldn't do and what the might of Hitler's air force couldn't do. It drove the people from their homes and the area they had grown to love for all its hardships, real or imagined.

The houses and buildings, filled to the rafters with the priceless memories of countless generations were quickly razed to the ground. Street by street, brick by brick, the once teeming district was reduced to a wasteland of rubble soon to be straddled by an ugly ribbon of concrete now known as the Westlink. Some brave families chose to remain and were eventually re-housed in a newly built area at the foot of the monster. Others, as stated, moved sadly away.

Like Camelot and Brigadoon but without their mystical qualities, it now remains only in the mist-covered memories of its natives. We must ensure that those memories, good and bad, are never neglected. Our bards, poets, singers and taletellers must keep them green and fertile with the moisture of many tellings.

The stories, first-hand or passed down, must be jealously guarded and handed from generation to generation whilst folk can still communicate with each other. The hard times should not be omitted—neither should the good times be forgotten. Only in this way will the area once deeply entrenched in the heartland of York Street be remembered by those who come behind us.

However, I do believe our past is in good hands. With locals and admirers like Denis Smyth, Fred Heatley, Martin Lynch, Sam Mac Aughtry, Sheila McGuinness and others yet unsung who are capable of recording a way of life that will never return.

In Sailorstown a motorway sprawls
where once tough men held sway ...
Where happy children used to play ...
    In Sailorstown.

first published in the *Irish News* (1989)

MEMORIES OF YORK STREET

THIS article contains fleeting childhood accounts of a little boy growing up in wartime York Street in the dockside district of Belfast. As space is limited, I'll glide swiftly from one to the other. At the moment, I'm content to look back fleetingly but lovingly on wartime York Street where I took my first hesitant steps.

The Second World War air-raids on the city had turned the area into a giant adventure playground for we kids. The wasteground or debris where the houses had been reduced to rubble—quickly cleared away by the council—became the scene of many fierce football matches between the boys of the different schools and streets.

Air-raid shelters abounded in the region. Some were large box-like shapes with flat concrete roofs over their red-bricked sides, whilst others were smaller. They looked uncannily like the little wooden houses used in the game called Monopoly. Often, we would gather inside one of these to smoke the cigarette-ends we'd foraged from the pavements on our way home from school. Even during daylight the interiors of these buildings were dark and mysterious. Only the glowing orbs and the wafting acrid smoke gave away our presence. To foil curious parents we would post lookouts at the shelter door. This was commonly known as 'keeping Dick'.

The husks of the bombed-out houses made better hiding places.

Pretending to be soldiers or pirates, we would climb like monkeys through the rafter beams until we'd found a room reasonably intact. Here we would hide from the boring chores of running messages for our mothers or doing homework, or exercises, as it was then known. Sometimes we'd prise up the floorboards looking for money or precious items that the owners or occupiers had hidden when the wail of the siren heralded the approach of the enemy bombers. Needless to add, we were never successful.

On dry days we would make our way to the playground at Henry Street and pass away the hours on the boats, swings and sandpits. Occasionally, when the attendant wasn't around, a man, who, in local parlance, was 'not right in the head' would come into the playground and bully us. There was nothing of a sexual connotation but his behaviour frightened and terrified us.

We had a champion however. Sammy Patterson gathered wastepaper every day on a large hand-cart and pulled it up Little York Street on his way to Cooke's scrap-yard in Great George's Street. Although as big and as strong as a man, Sammy had the mind of a child. Perhaps that was the reason we were never fearful in his company.

Sooner or later we would hear the thunder of the cart's wheels as Sammy pounded hell for leather along the street. When he came within hailing distance, we would yell in unison for help. Immediately, he would slide to a halt. The steel shods would grind along the concrete of the street causing sparks to fly upwards from his feet. When the cart eventually came to a standstill, he would lurch through the gate and hurl himself at our antagonist's throat. As they fell to the ground snarling, growling, punching and biting, we would quickly make our exit, all the time cheering our champion on.

Quite a few characters of that ilk walked the streets of Belfast in those days. Johnny No-Nose, Jimmy Jump, Billy's Weekly Liar (named after the flysheet he sold), Doctor McNabb, Alex The Duck, Corky, and the dreaded Slipper-Foot. As children, we would gather in packs and follow these unfortunate people and chant derisively at them. Often they would turn on us in anguish and anger, causing us to run for our lives in all directions.

Instinct caused us to steer clear in some instances. One was a grim-faced man with no legs who propelled himself around in a little cart. He often visited a house in Trafalgar Street. Some boys said he carried a stick with a poisoned tip with which he killed any dogs that attacked him. If we were in the street swopping comics or calling for friends, we would hide fearfully behind the hall door of the house until he had gone.

The wartime water-tank at the corner of York Street and Earl Street was another way of whiling away the hours. It was about fifty metres square and about six feet high and was filled to the brim with dark, rancid water. It was to be used on buildings in the vicinity, like Gallagher's Tobacco Factory or York Street Spinning Mill in the event of German firebombs. We fished in it, sailed boats and makeshift rafts in it and on hot and humid days, we swam in it. I remember someone found a small revolver and fished it out and on to the pavement. It wasn't long before the police came and took it away.

Another favourite occupation was hopping the horse-drawn carts that trundled up and down Earl Street on their way to the docks. Some carters allowed us to sit on the back as long as we remained quiet and still. Others would immediately dismount and chase us, cracking their long vicious whips for effect. Occasionally, things of value would fall off the backs of these carts. Once I found a pile of coal and quickly carried it into the house where I put it into a fire already glowing in the big range in our kitchen. When I returned to the house, an hour later, I was alarmed to see black smoke billowing from the chimney and through the open door. Rushing up the long hall I was horrified to find my mother, her face and hands covered with soot, trying to stem a flow of thick, black, smoky liquid that almost covered the floor. That was when I learned the difference between lumps of coal and lumps of tar. I received a few clouts around the ear for that mistake.

Horses and ponies also played a part in our growing up. Duncrue Street led to Alec's Bank and the local rubbish dump. It also housed some vegetable and fruit plots owned and cared for by local men. Sometimes we would raid the holdings and carry home fresh lettuce or carrots. Some of the other lads would bring air rifles to shoot the rats that were rife in the rubbish tips. Others would go to the foreshore and paddle or swim if the tide was in.

Some of the gang, like Bouncer Withers and Galloper Thompson, became extremely proficient horsemen over the years. They could often be seen galloping like Indians, riding barebacked, along Nelson Street as they raced to the owner's stables.

The summer holidays would see us making a pilgrimage to the Donegall Quay. We'd wend our way along Garmoyle Street through Great George's Street. The articles or bits lay on the cobbles outside the sheds. We'd spend many hours examining these objects or climbing over them until a Harbour Bulkie chased us from the scene.

I was quite familiar with this part of the city. When dad was returning to his ship at the end of a leave, mum would gather all the children and we'd accompany him to the Heysham boat, which took him to the mainland. Before he'd embark, we'd all be treated to tea and buns in one of the many cafés along the way. Afterwards, it would be tears and hugs and worry until he finally came home for good.

I well remember the day he was demobbed. We were at our breakfast and the house was in its usual state of disarray as mum struggled to get us out to school. None of us heard his footsteps in the hallway. Suddenly, the door opened and he stood in the doorway with a smile so wide we could see his gold teeth. He looked every inch a businessman, with a smart grey suit and matching overcoat, white shirt and blue tie. To top the outfit, a beige paddy hat sat at the back of his head. The whole ensemble was provided with the compliments of the government. Dad called it his 'utility suit'.

We all rushed to him. He and mum embraced whilst we grabbed his suitcase and kit bag and began to forage through them for our presents. Little did we know, having survived the war, he would be dead in less than eighteen months at the age of 42. He would also father another son nine months before his demise.

With the end of the war, the shops in York Street began to receive fruit and vegetables we hadn't seen since the beginning of the hostilities. I first ate a piece of pineapple when my Uncle Billy, then serving in the Royal Navy, came home after three years at sea. He came into our kitchen, plumped the strange looking object on the table, chatted a while, then went off to the pub without mentioning his gift. None of us knew what it was. Mum came to the rescue and within a few moments we were eating the delicious tropical fruit.

As I mentioned, Uncle Billy had been away for over three years. When he arrived at my Granny English's home, he sat on a stool in the middle of the kitchen, whilst his mother and family fussed around him. When asked if there was anything he would like, he rolled his eyes and said for years he'd dreamed of a custard cake out of Bella Wilson's shop. I was immediately detailed to run forth and make this comparatively simple wish come true.

Clutching the sixpence, which was the purchasing price, I ran as fast as I could to the shop, taking a short cut through the wasteground into York Street. Some moments later, I ran proudly into the crowded kitchen. As I reached Uncle Billy, I stumbled over someone's feet and the cake flew from my hands to land in a gooey mess on the front of my uncle's dress uniform, adding a touch more colour to his impressive campaign medals. He laughed heartily as I retreated shamefacedly.

I tasted my first red apple when McCormick's fruit shop at the corner of North Thomas Street received its first post-war consignment from Canada. A girl called Mary Nelson took me by the hand and we joined a queue that had quickly formed. After we'd been served, we stood in the doorway of Wellwood's chemist shop and devoured the whole bagful.

Speaking of apples, one was responsible for the first of many punishments I received at the hands of female teachers. It was during my short stay at the Seamen's school at the bottom of Pilot Street close to the Harbour gates. It was a public elementary school for Protestant children in a predominantly Catholic area.

On the day in question, I was called to the front of the class to spell the word 'apple' by my teacher—a formidable lady called Miss Ferguson. Without hesitation, I shouted out the letters: N.a.p.p.l.e. Silently, she lifted her supple cane and beckoned me to hold out my hand. Two of the best were administered swiftly, but not painlessly, as she informed me through pursed lips the proper way to spell the word. Needless to say, I never spelt it wrongly again.

Schooldays were a terrible hardship for me. I attended many

schools and learned little. When our house in Earl Street was blitzed we were shunted out to many places, including Glengormley and the Lisburn Road in South Belfast. It would be two years before we would return to York Street and a house in our beloved Earl Street. It was number 45, just yards away from the ill-fated 51. I began to attend a new school. This time it was Mountcollyer, which meant a bus journey up the Limestone Road. It was an unhappy period in an impersonal environment. I was ten years old and often preoccupied with my father's safety. He wrote to each of us regularly and once, when I was peeping at one of his letters during class, the teacher asked me a question, which I neglected to hear and therefore answer. Without warning, I was dragged to the front of the class and slapped viciously across the face before being hurled into a corner where I stood in shamefaced silence until the break.

After much of the same, my mother eventually heeded my daily tearful pleas and allowed me to go to Mariner's PES, which was located in Nelson Street close to Whitla Street. All my friends attended this school and for the first time in a long time I was reasonably happy to go out in the mornings.

I managed to stay out of trouble most of the time but other lads weren't so fortunate. Once, when a teacher asked what we knew about the *Titanic*, one boy blurted out: "It went down with two farts and a splash." This enraged the master, who leapt through assorted desks to reach the culprit and punish him with what was known in the vernacular as 'a dig in the gub'. A couple of the masters were Englishmen, recently demobbed. I think they were of the opinion that they had just transferred to another theatre of war.

It was there, however, I began my love affair with the written word. I was not so good in other departments. On my last day, when I got only two out of ten simple addition sums right, the master Mr. Pinkerton studied the results gravely: "Are you finishing today?" he asked quietly. When I nodded in the affirmative, he walked away silently, shaking his head from side to side in baffled disbelief.

Some nights we would sit in Geordie's ice-cream parlour. We'd get the money by tapping Yanks who walked around York Street in droves, looking for a way to kill the boredom. Generally, they were good-natured and kind and would laugh at our antics before throwing us a handful of coins or a few packets of chewing gum.

At weekends, the café would be filled with grim-faced policemen as they waited for the local gig in North Thomas Street to finish. Many of them had old-fashioned Thompson machine guns slung on straps around their necks or from their shoulders. We watched quietly as they stared silently into their tea whilst awaiting the order to move out onto the street. All of them wore large cowboy style revolvers which were set in holsters attached to a broad waist belt.

There was always plenty of drama in those long-ago nights. We'd hide behind the air-raid shelters or climb on top of them and watch wide-eyed as the violence spilled out onto the street. The local men took on Yanks, Limeys, Canadians and Jocks and battle would only cease when Head Constable McKenzie and his machine-gun toting stormtroopers would charge down the street, cracking heads in all directions. He had no favourites—he hated everybody.

Hopping trams was another amusing but dangerous pastime. This was done when we were short of the ha'penny needed to travel legally. We used this means of transport to get to Great Patrick Street on one occasion when we'd heard a young woman had been found murdered on wasteground close to a bar.

We simply sat on the large rear bumper, hidden from the view of the conductor, who was usually too busy galloping up and down the stairs to notice us. It was made of steel and could hold four or five kids.

We also visited an air-raid shelter where the girl-crazy servicemen assaulted a local woman. We didn't remain long at that one. Head McKenzie saw us coming and personally chased us from the area. His face was contorted with rage and anger as he tried, unsuccessfully, to get close enough to belabour us with his trusty blackthorn stick.

But the Yanks didn't do the entire depredation. I remember a large crowd that gathered outside the home of a local man in Meadow Street. He was arrested for the murder of a woman in another area. The court case featured in the local newspapers and was closely followed by the inhabitants of the district.

Another 'university of life' was the street corners where the men gathered to take the night air in those days before television and other such conversation-consuming inventions found their way into people's homes. We were allowed to stand in as long as we didn't speak. Here we learned about such current issues as the Ground Nut scheme, the Iron Curtain, the GI bill and the Berlin Airlift.

The corner raconteur knew a little about everything. Some were natural storytellers and not above exaggeration and plagiarism. We kids would huddle, spellbound, in the dark recess of Crooks' shop doorway, until our mums came and dragged us away or the tired but friendly night cop would move us all on with his predictable growl of: "Have yis no beds to go to?"

Once in bed, we would huddle with our secondhand copies of *The Wizard* or *The Rover* or *The Adventure* or *The Hotspur*. Before the mantle was turned down for the night, we would thrill to the stories of Wilson, the mysterious supernatural athlete or his working-class equal, Alf Tupper, better known as 'The Tough of the Track'. There were also footballers Nick Smith and Baldy Hogan and other characters including the deathless men who fought the ruthless Gestapo.

The yarns fired our already over-ripe imaginations. When it was announced on the radio that a German prisoner of war had escaped from a camp in England, brother Tommy and I solemnly closed and barred the solitary window in our bedroom. It remained closed until he was captured. Many years later, a film was made of his exploits. Even then, I was relieved to note his travels didn't take him anywhere near York Street.

The wireless was our only link to what was happening in the war. At newstime, everyone had to be quiet. Father would brook no noise as he listened to the daily events in the first days of the conflict. Any movement at all would be frozen with a growled *wheesh* and the threat of instant bed.

They weren't good days and they weren't bad days. Like everyone else's childhood memories, it was a mixture of both. Thank God, we escaped the abject poverty and abysmal conditions some families were subject to. When the father of one such family died, the neighbours rallied and gave what little they could spare in the way of milk, tea, bread and butter, whilst the local publican sent round a crate of Guinness.

At the wake, the mourners were pleasantly surprised to find plenty of sandwiches, which they ate hungrily and washed down with the bottles of stout. Later, when asked where she'd got the tasty filler for the sandwiches, she confessed she had cut the bottle corks into thin slices and put them between the rounds of bread. With a little bit of the ingenuity, present in most of the wives and mothers of the era, she'd given her late husband a decent send-off.

These are just a few of my memories of a wonderful period in my life. The trembling vibrant community has gone and can now be recalled only in the recollections of those of us who lived there. The houses that were homes to thousands of people have been bulldozed from the skyline to be replaced by an ugly ribbon of concrete which cuts through the heart of a district that has now become nothing more than a state of mind.

first published in *Memories of York Street* (1991)

THE LONG SHOT

CHARLIE was deeply engrossed in the racing section of the morning paper when his wife called from the small working-kitchen.

"C'mon an' help me put this mangle back in the yard."

Groaning inwardly he rose and walked through the curtain that served as a door into the cramped, steam-filled room.

"Aw, Molly," he moaned with the air of a distressed man, "why don't ye dump that oul thing?"

He glared, malevolently, at the mangle with huge worn rollers in a steel frame that was rusting with age.

"An' how else wud I wring out the clothes?" retorted Molly, without malice as Charlie closed on the mangle and dragged it screeching across the red tiles and into the back yard.

"Don't start that again," he muttered sullenly as he passed her. Judging his mood she did not answer until he returned.

"Thanks, Charlie," she said kindly. He was too breathless to answer and nodded mutely as he returned to his living-room chair.

Molly sighed and pushed back a strand of silver-grey hair with a soap-sudded hand. Every Saturday morning was the same. Charlie hated the ancient mangle. It was the bane of his life.

They lived a reasonably comfortable life in their little kitchen house, close to the Belfast docks. He had never been a big earner but his money was constant. Even so, like many of their neighbours, they lived a hand to mouth existence and necessities, rather than luxuries, took priority.

"What's the boss bettin' today?" she asked, changing the subject in an effort to alter her husband's mood.

"Ack, another donkey by the luk of it. Shure if I had a good pair of slippers on me I cud run quicker myself."

He fumed at the unfairness of it. "He squanders hundreds an' I can't even afford to buy you a decent wringer."

Molly returned to her chores as Charlie continued to scan the racing section. "It's called Ramstam," he shouted, somewhat guilty at being angry with her.

Molly had never once complained, yet, dammit, he muttered to himself, that old mangle is getting too much for her. Even with constant oiling the cogs were difficult to turn and he knew it belonged on the scrap heap.

"Mr. Wandsworth needs his head examined," he continued, "puttin' a hunnert quid on that boneshaker."

"Maybe he got a tip for it," answered Molly, trying to shake him out of his morbid mood.

"Ack, he must pick 'em out with a pin," he replied sulkily. Molly silently agreed with her husband as she hung the washing on the pulley lines. Every Friday night for as long as she could remember Mr. Wandsworth had given Charlie £100 to put on a horse the following day. Sometimes it was well tipped, sometimes a rank outsider. Never had it won. She had long since stopped wondering how a man could squander such an amount every week. Perhaps it was only chicken-feed to Mr. Wandsworth, who had inherited a string of engineering firms from his father.

Charlie was thinking along the same lines. To him, one hundred pounds was a lot of money. If a fellow looked around he might be able to get a reasonable washing machine. Either way, it would make a good deposit.

He chastised himself. His boss had been more than good to him after he'd had the heart-seizure that had compelled him to give up his skilled job. He had retained Charlie, at a lesser wage of course, but still they were able to get by. Except for that damn mangle. He folded the paper resolutely and put on his jacket.

"I'd better move along an' git that bet done."

Molly watched as he walked slowly through the hall and into the street, then her eyes returned to the room and she stripped the cushion covers off the settee.

"Ramstam," huffed Charlie bitterly as he slouched along the narrow streets towards the bookmaker's office. Reaching the entrance, he walked toward a paraphernalia of newspapers pasted or pinned around the walls.

After a few moments studying, he realised the experts agreed with him. Ramstam was 33–1 in a five horse, five furlong race, whilst the favourite, Rifle Drill, was even money to win. Still, he thought as he pulled out the pen to write the docket, Mr. Wandsworth never won.

Whilst his mind dwelt on the unspoken remark, Charlie, pen in hand, gazed dumbly at the docket. Turning abruptly he strode quickly out into the sunlight. As he walked aimlessly in no set direction, he knew he was not going to back the horse.

His mind was clear and controlled. The horse was a rank outsider and the favourite looked certain to win. The money would go to a better cause and he'd be able to achieve his life's ambition and dump the rusting mangle.

He was not sure how long he wandered as he discussed the issue with himself. Mr. Wandsworth was a very rich man and would never miss the money. On the other hand if a miracle did occur and the horse won, he could merely state he'd forgotten to back it. It was so simple Charlie wondered why he hadn't been tempted before.

Still arguing with himself, he entered a pub next to the bookies and crowded with punters. Ordering a bottle of Guinness, his eyes moved to the television screen. Course betting flickered across it and his heart took an almighty leap when he saw Ramstam quoted at 5-1 in a field of four with no mention of the favourite.

"What's happened to Rifle Drill?" he gasped to a grimy-capped man who was observing the horses.

"Lamed itself comin' outa the paddock," he hissed through tobacco stained teeth.

Charlie stiffened as yet another quotation flashed across the screen making Ramstam 2–1 joint favourite with Easel.

"But it was 33–1 in the papers," he confided to no-one in particular.

"Some dough goin' on it now. Must be a hot tip with Rifle Drill outa the race," countered Grimy Cap with the air of a man who knew his horses.

"I'd better back it," croaked Charlie as his shaking hands searched his pockets for the hundred pounds. It wasn't there. A cold wave of panic gripped him as he realised it was still in the pocket of his overalls which were hanging on the back of his bedroom door.

He rubbed a grubby handkerchief numbly across the perspiration that soaked his forehead. The starting gates opened and a final betting flash quoted Ramstam as even money favourite.

Moving backwards, he flopped into a chair, unable to look at the picture as the four horses dashed into a five furlong sprint. He couldn't close his ears to the loud enthusiastic tones of the commentator.

"They're off at a fast clip," he droned, "with Ramstam and Easel slightly ahead of Cupid and Regal. Ramstam going easily the best at this moment. Quite a good gallop with Ramstam on the rails at the two furlong marker. It's Ramstam drawing away from Regal and two lengths clear of Cupid who is taking closer order. Just over a furlong left and it's Ramstam being chased by Cupid with Regal tracking and Easel the back marker ... One hundred yards to go and there's nothing in it between Ramstam and Cupid ... At the line it's Ramstam and Cupid neck to neck. A photo-finish between Ramstam and Cupid with Regal two lengths away third!"

As the occupants of the pub burst into noisy debate, Charlie walked dumbly to the bar.

"Givus a bottle," he croaked, scraping loose change onto the counter. He watched the television screen as it showed the finish in slow motion.

"Ramstam luks a cert," voiced Grimy Cap before lowering a pint of beer. Charlie glared at him as he returned to his seat. The wait seemed like hours but in reality it was only a few minutes before Cupid was declared the winner.

Finishing his drink with a flourish, he hurled a triumphant leer at Grimy Cap before hurrying through the front door.

"I've done it," he thought as he ran into the sunlight, "For the first time in my life I've done the right thing." Filled with exuberance he dashed into a nearby hardware store and emerged with a handful of washing-machine brochures.

He began to run and didn't stop until he was in the living room of his little house. He leaned on the mantelpiece and waited for his breathing to return to normal. Molly pushed through the curtained doorway, holding his sodden, mangled overalls in front of her. Her eyes were critical as she said matter-of-factly. "That oul boiler-suit's about done, Charlie."

She began to laugh at the stricken look that crossed his perplexed features.

"Don't worry: I found the money an' the horse's name in yer back pocket. I got wee Jimmy Steenson to run round and put it on ... The docket's on the table," she concluded as she swished back into the working kitchen.

Charlie stared into the fire for a moment, then silently tossed the brochures one by one into the heart of the flames. After they had burned into unrecognisable embers he walked slowly into the little room and put his arm around Molly's neat waist.

"What's for supper, girl?" he asked, choking back a tear.

first published in the *Belfast Telegraph* (1981)

THE JACKIE BELL STORY

EVEN though the story I am about to relate took place over thirty-five years ago, I think it would be prudent if I didn't reveal the real names of the people concerned or that of the village involved. The reason for this will become plain as the story progresses.

The setting is a little place on the outskirts of Derry. Picturesque and quaint, it was literally owned by a local businessman, who supplied work for almost all of its inhabitants. The main industry was the crops of potatoes that grew in abundance in the fields, for as far as the eye could see. The locals were paid to plant, pick, bag and transport the finished product to either Londonderry or Belfast, to be shipped all over the world as the finest seed or ware potatoes.

I worked in a transit shed with a squad of casual dock-labourers and we unloaded the lorries when they arrived at Belfast Dock. The spud season, as we called it, usually began in the September of every year and ended around the following May. The drivers and their helpers literally worked around the clock during this period, starting at 4 a.m., every morning, to load their vehicles, before making the long haul to Belfast, twice a day. This was before the improved driving conditions that came with new motorways and flyovers.

My uncle, Davy English, was the foreman of the gang and over the years he had formed friendships with many of the country men, who arrived at the docks each day from the hamlets and townlands of Northern Ireland. He was known as Big Davy to all and sundry and if I'm breaking a confidence by revealing his real name, it's because he's been dead for quite a while. I know the RUC has a reputation for securing convictions but I'm quite sure he's now in a no-go area where extradition is unheard of.

During that particular year he expressed a desire to visit the village in particular and asked if I'd accompany him. I agreed, after one of the drivers stated he'd be quite happy to put us up for the weekend in his home. On the Friday night, after a few beers in the American Bar, we crushed into the cab beside the driver and his helper and made the long journey.

The crack was good on the way down. During the inevitable banter we learned our soon-to-be host had been married ten years and was still without an offspring of either sex. Davy pretended to be worried about this and stated that his sexual aura was so strong that even his presence in the house might produce a happy event.

After stopping at a few more watering holes along the way, we eventually reached our destination about nine in the evening. After a typical meal of meat, fresh vegetables and of course, potatoes, we freshened up and headed for the solitary public house, which was also owned by the businessman who owned everything else.

The bar itself was no larger than the thatched cottages that surrounded it. It was packed to capacity. A large open fireplace was heaped high with turf and gave off a warm, friendly glow. The clientele sat around the huge grate on high-backed chairs, absently sucking their long-stemmed briar pipes or sipping their drinks.

A cloud of hazy tobacco smoke hovered in the rafters of the low ceiling.

Drinks were quietly placed in our hands and seats were provided for us, close to the fire, as we were introduced to the company. Pleasantries were exchanged and soon the conversation turned to the one industry not owned or controlled by the man who possessed everything else. The voices dropped a decibel lower as the drinkers knew the publican to be a member of the B-Specials.

In guarded whispers, each man praised the quality of the local moonshine, and Davy, who liked a drop of the pure stuff, asked if he could purchase a few bottles to take home.

One of the men nodded vaguely in the direction of an old fellow dozing in the heat of the chimneybreast. He was slightly built and wore a pair of tan-coloured bib-and-brace overalls, which were too big for him. Despite the heat, he wore a thick corduroy jacket and a woollen scarf was knotted tightly around his scrawny neck. A black cloth-cap, with a large tassel, was pulled down over his ears and covered a mass of thick white hair. Waking from his nap, he grinned knowingly as Davy whispered in his ear.

After a moment or two of thought, he ran his tongue over discoloured teeth and rolled his eyes heavenward.

"We'd need to go and see Jackie Bell," he muttered, rising with a quickness that belied his years. He turned his coat collar up and reached behind his chair for a blackthorn walking stick.

"Jackie Bell will fix ye up," he repeated, moving in the direction of the pub door. Davy and I followed and found ourselves outside on a night that was as black as soot in a street that boasted no lamps. Our eyes gradually became accustomed to the gloom and we followed the old man, aided by the sound of his stick as it scraped against the cobbles.

After about five hundred yards, Davy spoke, still in a whisper. "Is it much further?" The old fellow grunted, inaudibly and continued walking. We followed warily, guided by the sound of his stick and the harshness of his breathing.

Some minutes later, he stopped and we heard him fumbling at the side of the road. A few seconds later, a welcome jet of light flamed from a hurricane lamp, he had foraged from a hedgerow.

Holding the lamp high, with one hand, he stooped again and began to probe the bushes with his free hand. Suddenly, it withdrew clutching a whiskey bottle which at first glance, in the lamplight, appeared to be empty. On closer inspection it was seen to be half-full of liquid which was as clear as water.

"Is that it?" asked Davy.

"Naw," answered our companion, gazing lovingly at the bottle, "But we'll have a few swigs to warm the road till Jackie Bell." He withdrew the cork and the bottle was duly passed round. It was my first drink of poteen that didn't contain a mixer to make it more palatable to my young untrained throat. Being a boy among men, I overdid it and almost choked as the fiery concoction seared its way through my system. The old fellow clucked disapprovingly as he replaced the cork and put the bottle back into the hedgerow.

The lamp made weird shadows as we moved on into the night. "Is it much further?" moaned Davy who was beginning to regret leaving the warmth and safety of the bar-room.

"Just a wee bit more," grunted our companion as he slouched on into the darkness. Some fifteen minutes later, he again halted at a large hedgerow and knelt to search at its base. Out came another bottle, which he wiped, on the lapels of his jacket before removing the stopper. He reached the bottle to Davy and began to chant in a singsong voice.

Mountain dew, mountain dew,
Puts a sparkle in her eyes of blue.

Davy looked at him, fearfully, before gulping hurriedly at the bottle. When it reached me I drank slowly and sparingly, feeling the flame of the moonshine spread all through my cold body.

As we began to move again, a dog howled mournfully in the distance. Davy gripped my sleeve in fright.

"Maybe we shud go back to the bar," he shouted in the direction of the light. "Yer man Jackie Bell might be out or in bed" he added desperately.

"I'll be surprised if he isn't in his bed," giggled the old man loudly. "It's not too far now," he added soberly. After two more halts for strategically placed bottles, we stopped at a large steel-barred gate. Davy was now wheezing as loudly as the old fellow was and every time the dog howled he would almost jump into my arms.

He peered closely at the nameplate on the gate as our companion pushed it open. "It's a graveyard," he muttered fearfully. "I'm not goin' in there." He was not a coward in the physical sense but entering a graveyard in the dead of night was a different matter.

"Come on," I said with more confidence than I felt as the light danced forward eerily. "We'll have to stay with him. We'd never make it back without the lamp. Jackie Bell must be the caretaker," I added.

Almost whimpering with fear he held tightly onto my arm as we followed the dancing light through the rows of crosses and tombstones. Suddenly the old man stopped. Placing the lantern on the grass he knelt at the side of a grave and pushed both hands down through the soft topsoil.

"Say hello to Jackie Bell," he cackled, nodding at the name inscribed on the gravestone. As we watched in horror and disbelief he removed two bottles from the foot of the grave.

"Jackie says how many do ye want? Two or twenty-two?"

Shivers raced down my spine as Davy struggled to speak. His business acumen remained intact, despite the fear of his surroundings.

"I'll take half-a-dozen if they're chape enuff," he stuttered.

Four more bottles were drawn from the soil before the old man rose to his feet. He touched his cap in the direction of the headstone.

"We'll take our leave now Jackie and bid ye good night." He turned to Davy and grinned like a demon in the dancing light. "Didn't I tell ye. He loves his bed an' never leaves it."

Davy blanched and tore the lantern from his hand. Roaring with fear, he half-stumbled half-ran from our midst, as the old man cackled uncontrollably.

He was sitting at the gate when we arrived. Without a word the old man took the lamp and led us to the home of the lorry driver.

Davy was comforted by the driver's wife and eventually regained his composure. The humour of the event gradually got to him and after a shot or two of the excellent poteen, he became his usual self. The low price asked for the lethal brew also had a hand in settling his nerves.

Two days later we left. The entire clientele of the bar, including our midnight colleague, came to see us off. We never returned to the village and never again referred to the moonshine as poteen. From that fearful night in the graveyard, until the day he died, Davy always asked the drivers to bring him back some Jackie Bell. Incidentally, the driver's wife presented her astonished but delighted husband with twins the following year. One of each.

A PROFILE OF DAVY WHITESIDE

AT first glance Davy Whiteside was every inch the archetypal stage-Irishman the rest of the world loves to caricature and ridicule. The stud on the peak of his flat cap often came adrift from its retainer, leaving a mouth-like gap between the peak and the top of the cap.

Like most dockworkers of his age, he wore a scarf tied with a Carter's knot that sat like a cloth walnut between the collars of his khaki-coloured shirt. The two ends disappeared into the opposite sides of the vee in his waistcoat.

A heavy, double-breasted, serge overcoat with shiny black buttons and frayed sleeves fell just short of his ankles, almost covering his blue dungarees. His feet were shod with black waterboots, which he wore with the tops turned down in the fashion favoured by fishermen. A stalk of corn at the corner of the mouth, so beloved by all stage Irishmen, was the only prop missing.

He was well over sixty when we became acquainted. I was helping to unload sacks of potatoes from lorries in one of the dock sheds when I observed him gazing quizzically at me through small, rounded, national health spectacles. His right-hand was clenched loosely in a fist and held close to his mouth, whilst his left hand crossed his body to cup and support the right elbow.

As I watched I saw smoke filtering hazily through his fingers and realised the fist was concealing a tobacco pipe with a small stem. Smoking was strictly forbidden in the cargo sheds and the harbour police were not slow to prosecute any they caught.

It was his eyes that fascinated me. Or, rather, his one eye, for the other had been lost in some long-forgotten incident and replaced with a glass substitute, which brooded unseen behind a broken lens.

Later, when I got to know him better, that solitary eye would blaze like the inside of a furnace as he pontificated heatedly on some subject. Far from being a thick clod-hopping Paddy, Whitey, as he was affectionately known, was a silver-tongued autodidact. Intellectually, he was head and shoulders above those with whom he worked and socialised.

He possessed a brain that was capable of storing for future reference almost everything he read or heard. Music, literature, the arts and theories of everyone from Euclid to Darwin and Einstein fought for space in that vast storeroom of knowledge alongside humorous anecdotes, smutty stories and raunchy barrack-room ballads. Most pleasing to me was his love of poetry.

Sensing my interest, he took me under his wing. I listened with pleasure as he recited from memory poems written by such diverse talents as Yeats, Shelly, Masefield, Service, Moore and Byron. At the drop of a hat he would launch into a rendition of 'Dangerous Dan McGrew' or 'The Cremation of Sam McGee' and immediately transform a noisy barroom into a quiet, listening centre.

Often, with devilish glee, he would switch to corrupt versions learned during service with the British army, just before the First World War. Eskimo Nell and a host of equally filthy monologues would flow as easily from his lips as would some of Shakespeare's most beautiful love sonnets.

A love of literature and an almost daily pilgrimage to the Belfast Central Library—the *only* shrine he worshipped at—made him irresistible company to relax with in front of a coal fire in a cosy dockland pub. I sat, entranced, as he argued and debated with, amongst others, John Nicolson, a well-read Scotsman, when we adjourned to Cullen's Bar after a hard day's work. To be fair, both were hardheaded opinionists and usually agreed to disagree. This verbal sparring was a valuable education to a boy in a man's world.

There were other strings to his bow. Mrs. Peggy Courtney, with whom I conversed when this article was being written, talked of Whitey with something close to hero-worship in her voice. She described him as a working-class genius. Fine words for a man whose formal education ended when he was put to work at the age of 12.

She revealed to me that Whitey was an advanced mathematician who helped her to successfully conquer duo decimals, which is a system of numbers in which each denomination is twelve times the next, instead of ten, as in ordinary decimal arithmetic. On top of this he was an expert at algebra. This is a means of calculating symbols by using letters employed to represent quantities and signs to represent their relation, thus forming a kind of generalised arithmetic. Last, but by no means least, he was well-versed in geometry, having studied the assumptions of Euclid, a geometrician in Alexandria.

No big deal perhaps, in this the age of the computer and calculator but quite an achievement for a man whose early tuition amounted to almost nothing. Proof, perhaps, of the old adage that the only educated man is a self-educated man!

His valuable instruction in all these subjects enabled Peggy, who was the daughter of his closest friend, to have the distinction of being one of the first two working-class girls to become State Registered Nurses, in the Royal Victoria Hospital, in Belfast. In those days, only the daughters of professional men, like doctors and solicitors, nursed in the Royal. Thanks to Whitey, Peggy was able to break that tradition. When I spoke to her, she was still active in hospital administration.

She told me, Davy and her father met through having adjoining vegetable plots on the Old Westland Road during the 30s. Both became flautists in the Duncairn Flute Band, which more than once won first prize for style and ability.

Anyone would think a man blessed with so many gifts would be grateful to God. In Davy's case nothing was further from the truth. He was a confirmed and unshakable atheist, who refused to acknowledge God's existence, never mind give Him credit for anything. When asked to thank God for a wonderful harvest in his plot, he refused point-blank. Nature and the elements he would grudgingly concede to but not Heaven.

The only time he entered a church was when he was forced to, during army service. Even then he took a fiendish delight in twisting the words of the hymns they were ordered to sing. One example was the corruption of the words to a well-known hymn:

This is my story, this is my song.
I've been a good girl, too f***ing long!

His favourite memory of army life was having his boots cleaned by a boy-soldier, who turned out to be the Prince of Wales and later King of Great Britain, Ireland and the British Empire, before abdicating the throne to marry a divorced woman.

Whitey constantly ridiculed Christianity and attacked it at every opportunity. He likened the Bible to a comic book and his interpretation of the Immaculate Conception would have given a minister or a priest a severe cardiac arrest.

He refused to have his children christened, declaring that registration was all that was required by law. His wife, however, differed on this issue and quietly did the right thing.

He believed in Darwin's theory of evolution and would chortle gleefully as he told us of a minister's wife on a visit to a museum questioning a professor's claim that a fossil was over two million years old.

Whitey did a fair impersonation of the outraged lady. "But that was before Christianity!" he mimicked. His voice changed as he assumed the authoritative manner of the professor. "Madam," he thundered. "I'm talking about fact ... not fiction!"

"If you want a God to worship," he would continue seriously, "worship nature". Given the right conditions, he would argue, life could be created anywhere. His explanation to this devastating statement was simple. A shovel full of red-hot ashes taken from a furnace and thrown into a corner would sooner or later be thriving with a species of micro-organism, if it were exposed to the rain and air for a period of time.

He compared the earth at the beginning to a burnt-out cinder and was fairly confident this was how mankind evolved. From microbe to homo sapiens. He also brought in his formidable knowledge of astronomy (garnered whilst studying the night skies from his vegetable plot during the depression years) when debating the Old Testament claim that the Lord created the universe in six days. Those of us in the know would watch as Davy went into his party piece.

I was so impressed by his argument that I memorised it word for word and later wrote it down. At the time it sounded like a foreign language to me.

He would silence his dissenters with a wave of his hand and begin to speak, like a lecturer addressing a class of dim students.

"For a long time it was thought by astronomers that our galaxy represented the whole of the universe, or creation, if you like. But around 1925 it was learned there were other galaxies out there, some of them as large as our own. In fact it's almost impossible to imagine the size and extent of the universe we now know exists."

Taking a piece of chalk from his waistcoat pocket, he would stoop to the floor of the shed and draw a circle about six feet in diameter. In the centre of the circle he made a small dot. Raising his glasses to his forehead, as he always did when reading or drawing, he pointed to the dot.

"Imagine from there to the outer rim of the circle is ten million light-years in distance." He smiled at the blank faces. "In other words, to go from one end of the universe to the other would take a space traveller ten million light-years." Rubbing his head, he studied the circle.

"I'll break that down for ye," he said, almost apologetically. "It's estimated that light travels at the speed of one hundred and eighty-six thousand miles per second ... So a light-year equals a distance of three million, one hundred and forty-four thousand, nine hundred and sixty miles. That's one light-year: now think of that figure multiplied ten million times. It's reckoned the furthest point of the universe is six thousand million million miles away from the earth."

He then picked up a small seed potato and held it between his finger and thumb. "Picture this as the Sun. Actually, it's a star. It partakes a galactic rotation travelling round the centre of the Galaxy, moving about one hundred and fifty miles per second, every two hundred million years."

He selects more potatoes and places them in the circle naming each as he does. "Next the Moon, Mercury, Venus, Earth, Mars, Jupiter, Saturn, Uranus, Neptune and Pluto. That's the galaxy we live in. Outside of that there are millions of other galaxies comparable to our own. The nearest is over two hundred million miles away. The furthest, Ursa Minor, is estimated to be one thousand million light-years away. Some of the furthest away stars observed are reckoned to be eighteen hundred million light-years in space. The whole Galaxy is believed to be one hundred thousand light-years across."

He paused for breath as we who'd seen it all before waited for the punch-line. "An' you mean to tell me somebody made all that in six days?" Then with a howl of derision he would kick the potatoes across the shed floor.

Another of his pet idiosyncrasies which boiled over was when anyone asked him for the correct time. We, being aware of this, would often send an unsuspecting lorry driver to ask him that very question. His face would contort with anger as he launched into a diatribe about the measure of duration, World Standard Time, Greenwich Mean Time, Official British summer time and the passage of time. With this all said, he would allow the one eye to glare fiercely at the inquirer before saying, almost angrily, "I can give you the approximate time. I certainly can't give you the correct time. Nobody can, as I've just pointed out." The driver, who'd stood mutely through this walked away with the air of a shell-shocked man.

His politics were working-class. "Why vote for the bosses?" he would often say, but like the majority of Protestants, regardless of class, he was violently against Home Rule. Religion had nothing to do with this stand. As stated, he was violently opposed to that as well.

One night, he told of an incident in which he was concerned, which, had he succeeded, would have changed the face of history and perhaps the world as well.

Winston Leonard Spencer Churchill came to Belfast to speak in favour of Home Rule. As he spoke from a hansom cab, a section of the crowd began to riot. His one eye blazed like a laser as Whitey recalled the scene.

"They were tryin' to overturn the cab. I had a Webley but no bullets for it! I was runnin' through the crowd tryin' to find someone with bullets that would fit the gun when the police came and got him away."

Churchill survived to fight a greater battle. When he died in the 60s, his funeral was shown all over the nation. Whitey was viewing in a public house in Princes' Dock Street, when a young barman decided to switch off the television and listen to rock and roll on the bar's record player. The incensed old-timer finished his pint and hurled the empty glass at the gramophone. He scored a direct hit as he most surely would have, had someone provided him with the proper ammunition, on that long-ago night.

His explanation for the political turn around was that Churchill had changed his tune and paid many glowing tributes to the tenacity and loyalty of the people of Northern Ireland during the Second World War.

I could go on forever about the man. He would regale us with smutty stories from Chaucer's *Canterbury Tales* and Boccaccio's *Decameron* and often stated there were more 'dirty' books in the Central Library than there were in Smithfield Market. The trick was knowing where to find them. Had he been born to a family of means he would probably have been a professional man. In an earlier century, he would most likely have been a ditch or hedgerow schoolteacher. In fact, when Oliver Goldsmith described the schoolmaster in his poem, 'The Deserted Village', he might well have been describing Davy Whiteside.

> The love he bore to learning was in fault;
> The village all declared how much he knew;
> 'Twas certain he could write and cipher too;
> Lands he could measure, times and tides presage,
> And e'en the story ran that he could gauge.
> In arguing too, the Parson owned his skill,
> For e'en though vanquished, he could argue still;
> While words of learned length and thund'ring sound
> Amazed the gazing rustics ranged around,
> And still they gazed and still the wonder grew,
> That such a small head could carry all he knew.

The destruction of York Street forced Whitey to leave the district. I helped him to flit and was amazed at the articles he had unearthed during the years of cultivating his garden plot, in what is now the Westland Road. Stone axe heads, bronze arrowheads and other such relics of an ancient way of life, were packed in cupboards and long forgotten.

Like most of his age, the change of environment took a lot of wind from his sails. Steady drinking over a long period had begun to take its toll. When I last visited him he was abed, surrounded, as ever, by his beloved tomes.

He greeted me warmly. "Jack," he said, rising on one elbow, as I'd seen him do so many times when he lay in the little single bed, in the Chapel Shed, surrounded by thousands of bags of potatoes. He was the only person ever to call me Jack. I learned later that his friend from the plots who had passed on earlier had been called Jack.

"I've a present for you," he continued. He reached me a small hardbacked book. It was coloured green with gold lettering on its front and spine.

"The second poem on page 153. Read it to me, Jack." I flipped the pages and found it was a poem by Lord Byron—'We'll Go No More Aroving'.

So we'll go no more aroving
So late into the night,
Though the heart be still as loving,
And the moon be still as bright.

For the sword outwears its sheath,
And the soul outwears the breast,
And the heart must pause to breathe,
And love itself have rest.

Though the night was made for loving
And the day returns too soon,
So we'll go no more aroving,
By the light of the moon.

I still possess the book and often read from it. Whitey died sometime after that visit. If I have helped keep some of his wit and knowledge alive, then perhaps the void left by his death won't be as large.

One final anecdote, to show the breadth of the man's irascible humour. On a long-ago evening, in a now demolished public house (were we ever anywhere else?) Whitey listened, with a smile, as a young bunch of whippersnappers bragged about the various positions of copulation. One fellow, who had sailed around the world more than once, was convinced he'd done it every way possible.

"Not so," murmured Whitey warming to the discussion. "I'll tell you a way you haven't done it," he replied.

"Tell me! Tell me!" cried the other.

Whitey's one eye closed as he roared with laughter.

"Standin' up in a hammock," he yelled.

Not really original, perhaps but as the saying goes: "In the land of the blind, the one-eyed man is King." Davy Whiteside was a King to many of us who worked and played in York Street. Sadly, we have let many of his kind pass on without a word about the dreams they had and the talents they possessed.

FOOTNOTE
This article was originally written for *Dockworker*, a small booklet. I was held to a word count and couldn't say all I wanted to about this great old character.

Sometime later, I wrote a one-act play from a short story I'd based on Davy. It is called *Pints and Politics*. The planets story is also used in this project, as are many of Davy's interesting theories.

first published in *Dockworker* (1984)

THE MILLS BOMB

THE day itself was exceptional. A warm, muggy July afternoon with temperatures in the high eighties. The card-school at the corner of Nelson Street and Earl Street had just broken up and the winners were counting their coppers whilst the losers slouched off to a dry and boring Saturday evening at home. The period was the late 50s and in most cases they hadn't even the consolation of a black and white television to while away the long night.

As one of the lucky ones, I had no such problem. Tommy McMullen, my closest and best friend, had also come out in front. It had been a long, hard slog, kneeling in a crouched position for hours, keeping one eye peeled for cycling policemen and the other on the look-out for crooked dealers.

One regular in the school had to be watched constantly. When it was his turn to deal, no matter how many times the cards were shuffled, cut or thrown up in the air, he managed to give himself a winning hand. No one could ever catch him at it, so, when his turn came to deal, everybody, except those who didn't know him, threw in their hands, leaving him only pennies to pick up.

As the crowd dispersed, Mac suggested we go for a few beers before dinner. I heartily agreed. The area abounded with pubs but we settled for the Rotterdam. It had a good dartboard and was usually deserted at that time of day.

Three other participants of the card-school fell into step with us as we began to amble down Earl Street toward Pilot Street. Two of these were seamen. One was lightly built with a mass of thick, black, curly hair and known, not unnaturally, as Curley. He was currently employed as a cabin boy on the Heysham boat, which travelled nightly with passengers from Belfast. Beside him walked a small but heavily-muscled blond lad called Albert Blair. He was a trainee cook in the Royal Navy and was enjoying his summer leave. A decent enough lad but somewhat moody and aggressive when he had drink taken. Another reason for misgivings was the fact that he loved a fight and was forever bantering Tommy Mac, who gave as good as he got.

The third traveller was something of a mystery. Although he lived close by we did not know him too well. We knew him to be an amateur boxer of some note who hit hard and fast with both hands. These doubtful talents were hidden behind a cheerful grin and a mild-mannered nature. He was generally known to be harmless and quiet outside the square ring. One thing we didn't know and would learn, to our regret, much later that evening, was the fact that the first drink he swallowed that day was the first alcohol he had ever consumed in his life.

We were unaware of this ticking time bomb called Mills as we bantered our way past The Bunch of Grapes and across Garmoyle Street. The Magic Bar beckoned as did The Inside Inn with the wonderful legend from Omar Khayam: 'I often wonder what the Vintner buys half as precious as the goods he sells', emblazoned above the front door. However, we continued right down to the dock gates where sat the popular bar owned by Joseph Donnelly and known as The Rotterdam Bar.

When we entered the low-ceilinged and atmospheric public house, I immediately ordered the first round of drinks. The rest of the group rescued the dartboard from a basin of water in which it had been soaking from the previous night.

The bar was practically deserted, except for a few merchant seamen hugging their pints and staring into space. They were soon raised out of their reverie by our boyish exuberance as we began ordering drinks and shouting out scores.

Some time later, Millsy began to change. He said the first two or three pints had caused his legs to go dizzy. We laughed at this but failed to detect the devil emerging from the back of his smiling eyes. A lop-sided grin hung on his cherubic features, which were the colour of chalk but he stayed with us gamely matching drink for drink.

The trainee cook began his usual game of tormenting Tommy Mac by pointedly refusing to notice when it became his turn to buy a round. He giggled sarcastically and blatantly ignored Tommy Mac's none too subtle reminder that everyone's tumbler was empty and it was his turn to hook on. He had earlier enraged the normally placid Tommy when he had ordered an exotic drink costing about three times more than anyone else's when it was Mac's turn to buy. Continuing to giggle, he rose and walked to the toilet. Returning a few moments later he grinned smugly when he saw a round had been bought in his absence.

"Shure if yid waited till I came back I wuda decorated the mahogany," he smirked.

"Ya did," leered Mac, toasting him with a glass of whiskey. Like most sailors Blair had left his change and cigarettes on the table. Mac had simply taken the necessary cash and ordered the drink. Anger contorted the fighting cook's face as he glared at McMullen's triumphant grin. In reality, Albert, which was his Christian name, was not given to being tight-fisted. On the contrary, he was known for his good nature and was constantly giving to the boys at the corner whenever he came home on leave. He just enjoyed playing the game of annoying Tommy Mac.

At this point, Curley, the galley boy, looked at the clock and gasped with surprise. "Lookit the time," he wailed. "I'm supposed to be aboard in half-an-hour." Although about the same age as the rest of us he was already a seasoned drinker and could tipple with the best. He looked almost sober as he moved from the table. He lived only a stone's throw from the bar and was foolish enough to return a half-an-hour later to say goodbye. Like most merchant seamen, he travelled light and his only baggage was a pair of white overalls under his arm.

"One for the road," we cried in drunken unison and dragged his unwilling body up to the bar. Millsy, who was by this time doing a passable imitation of Groucho Marx acting out Dr. Jekyll's famous transformation into Mr. Hyde, bumped accidentally into another customer.

Before the drunken youth could get his tongue around words suitable for an apology, the man leapt from his barstool and dropped into a fighting pose.

"I must warn you I am the ju-jitsu champion of New South Wales," he hissed, through clenched teeth, to Millsy, who was swaying placidly to the music of an orchestra only he could hear. Unimpressed by these credentials, he lifted his leg lazily and placed the boot at the end of it between the man's upper thighs.

"Ju-ju that," he smirked as the man groaned loudly and fell to his knees. Blair moved forward menacingly to finish the agonised seaman off but Joe the owner stopped him in his tracks.

"Git out all of yis, or I'm callin' the cops," he roared. This declaration caused Millsy to upend a table and challenge every man-jack in the bar to a fair go. He began to shadow box, dancing wildly around the bar-room, whilst the rest of us watched with a mixture of fear and amusement. At a signal from myself, Tommy Mac grabbed him in a bear hug from behind and lifted him bodily out the door. As the rest of us followed gladly, I looked back at Joe to apologise.

"Don't come back!" he snapped, as he stooped to shovel broken glass into a bucket. "Yis are all barred, " he added, grimly.

Outside, we tried to talk the normally placid Millsy out of accompanying Curley to the Heysham boat. Completely out of control he was skipping along the cobbles like an inebriated werewolf. The ugly episode had sobered Mac and myself and Curley was looking decidedly worried. The events that unfolded later proved his misgivings to be justified.

Blair was, as usual, in complete control, grinning impishly as Millsy continued to lose all proportion. The alcohol was driving him forward like a motor car filled with high propane fuel.

Reluctantly, we picked our way through the general cargo strewn outside the transit shed and managed to lurch in a bunch through the open doors. Curley clutched his white overalls as he climbed the gangplank. The rest of us clambered, Indian file, behind him. He was at the top when the ship's security officer, a uniformed commissioner, with an impressive row of campaign ribbons on his tunic, stepped forward to aid him. Without warning, Millsy, who was behind the galley-boy, leaned over and knocked the guard down and out with a wild swinging right hook. As Curley turned to chastise his drink-crazed companion, he himself was hit with a left, then a right. Both punches flew with the speed of light and connected with cracks like thunder. The ferocity of the blows drove him over the body of the inert commissioner and into the arms of two of his shipmates, who tried to drag him into an adjacent cabin out of harm's way. This act galvanised Blair into action. With a leap Douglas Fairbanks would have been proud of, he landed on the ship's deck and began belabouring the crewmen holding Curley.

Mac grabbed at Millsy, who, in a vain effort to avoid capture by the bigger and heavier man, lost his footing and slid off the narrow gangplank. I closed my eyes in horror and waited for the splash, but he grabbed drunkenly onto the bottom rope and grinned up sheepishly at Mac and I for help. As we hoisted him to safety, I noticed Curley's whites drifting down the Lough between the ship's side and the jetty.

Suddenly, a clipped voice with an English accent came booming over the ship's tannoy. "Will someone alert the Harbour Police," it requested, almost apologetically. The sound of authority coming from the bridge brought Blair to his senses. He rushed to the ship's side and almost pushed the rest of us off the gangplank in his effort to get ashore. Mac and I followed, a little slower, trailing Millsy between us. Our last glimpse of Curley saw him spread-eagled on the deck by members of the crew, who must have thought they were witnessing an act of piracy. Miraculously we got off the dock without encountering any of the dreaded Bulkies, who would have arrested us for certain. The incident almost put paid to Curley's career. When the ship returned to harbour the next day, he purposely avoided contact and stayed away from the bars we frequented.

But the nightmare wasn't over, as Millsy's unrelenting campaign of violence continued unabated. As we passed the Gents' Toilets, just outside the transit shed, a fresh-faced holidaymaker emerged from its doorway to breathe deeply of the warm, night air. He was dressed in brown shorts with long matching socks and bright yellow hiking boots. Adjusting the large haversack on his back, he was about to move off when Millsy loped by. The tourist never saw what hit him. He must have thought the sun went down suddenly that night as a long-looping right-hand landed flush on his jaw. Horrified at this unprovoked attack, we tightened our grip on our colleague and raced into Tomb Street. At this point, a barking dog, perhaps sensing a fellow canine, leapt forward to attack or greet him. Breaking from our grip, he fell on all fours and matched the dog bark for bark and snarl for angry snarl. The astonished animal quickly fled, closely followed by its elderly owner, who must have thought he'd encountered a Yeti.

Eventually, we arrived at his home in Trafalgar Street and unceremoniously dumped his almost lifeless body in the hall, before running for our lives. "You shuda let me put him outa the game," puffed McMullen as we trotted down the street.

"Naw—we'da had ta carry him an' that wuda slowed us down," I replied. At that point, his irate mother came to the door and lambasted us in a loud voice for leading an innocent astray. Despite it all, we looked at each other and grinned. "Hitler was more innocent," laughed Mac as we parted company at Little York Street.

But the nightmare had another act to unfold. Hours later, as we stood on the dance-floor of the Whitewell Orange Hall, the door to the ballroom suddenly burst open and a man staggered into the centre of the dance-floor. It was Millsy and he was without a jacket and tie. We were four miles from York Street and how he'd managed to get on and off the bus that brought him remains a mystery.

Blair was also there, dressed in his best naval uniform and grinning widely at the antics of the drunken youth. Millsy grabbed the girl nearest him and staggered onto the floor. The band was playing an orderly foxtrot and the dancers were shuffling around the floor in the prescribed anti-clockwise fashion. This rhythm was greatly disturbed as Millsy dragged his reluctant partner against the flow. As they passed the bandstand, the saxophonist, who fancied himself as a trouble-shooter, dropped lightly from the rostrum to chastise him. Seconds later, he was holding a white handkerchief to his mouth in an effort to stem blood that was flowing freely as the result of a flashing head-butt. He stood in shocked, shamefaced silence as the leader/drummer scolded him: "I tole you before to stay on the stage. Yer no good ta me with busted lips," he snarled.

As Millsy whirled away, minus the girl, two beefy bouncers moved in to cut off his retreat. He must have sensed they would be too much. With one mighty bound he leapt through an open window and into the night, pausing only to acknowledge the applause of the dancers.

Mac and I tried to forget him and enjoy ourselves but minutes later we were on the street looking for him. We found him at the bottom of the Whitewell Road. He was curled up in the doorway of a shop and snoring his head off.

Lifting him bodily, we managed to get him aboard a trolley bus and once more deposited him in the darkened hallway of his home.

This time it was his father's voice cutting through the gloom as we wearily made our way down the silent street.

"Campbell ... McMullen ... Don't think I didn't recognise ye! Yis ought to be ashamed of yerselves leadin' a harmless creature like my Clark astray. Don't be coming near our door again."

"Wud ye put that in writin'," whispered Mac as we parted into the darkness and home.

Naturally, we steered clear of him after that as he continued to drink heavily and wreak havoc. One day, many years later he knocked on my door and invited me out. He'd put on a bit of weight like the rest of us but his hair was still full and dark and that peculiar little light still shone in the back of his eyes.

Seeing my concerned features, he put his arms around me and hugged me warmly, before inviting me to pay a visit with him to a building he was involved with in Little York Street. Taking my coat from the back of the door, I strolled reluctantly along the lane past the engineering works, across Trafalgar Street, by the bag store owned by James McCaughy and across Henry Street. I began to worry as we walked to the children's playground and edged towards The King's Arms at the corner of Nile Street. Clark laughed at my consternation and beckoned me across the street. We stopped at the door of a Gospel Hall. The light in his eyes glowed brightly as he gazed at me. It was then I realised it was a divine light because the former drunken tearaway had given his soul to Christ.

His invite to me was not for a drink but to listen to him preaching the gospel from the pulpit of this very church! Needless to say, I was impressed and proud of the way he had taken hold of his life and changed it for the betterment of himself and his fellow creatures.

Sometime later he told me of the events that led to his sudden and enduring conversion. On what was to be a fateful day in his life, Clark left The London House at the corner of Garmoyle Street and North Thomas Street, in the Sailorstown area of Belfast. It was Saturday afternoon and as usual he was drunk. He had arranged to meet his drinking pals in The Sportsman's Arms and was in the process of heading home for a quick meal and a wash. As he weaved his way unsteadily through the narrow streets, he became aware of the sound of music and found himself drawn inexorably to its source. He called it his road to Damascus.

Eventually, he came across a religious group, preaching the gospel. Normally, he would have walked on by but some unseen presence stopped him in his tracks and he suddenly began to realise how he was wasting his life. The orator's words hit him like rocks thrown by a hostile crowd. When he became uncharacteristically emotional, a member of the gathering walked to him and asked him if he was all right. Clark said he was and began to move away quickly. The man, somewhat alarmed, asked where he was going. He replied, he was running home to tell his wife he was saved!

Sometime later, washed and dressed in his best attire, he joined the group who were now playing and preaching outside the Sportsman's Arms at its side entrance. His former drinking cronies were dumbfounded when he entered the bar, not to buy drinks but to hand each one a Gospel tract. He left just as quickly as each man stared unbelievably at his radiant features and marvelled inwardly at the mysterious ways of the Almighty.

When York Street was decimated, we lost touch with each other for a while but lately I have met and spoken to him at neighbourhood funerals. I believe he is a Deacon with his own church now. Like the rest of us, he has grown older and fatter but still moves like the excellent boxer he once was. I often thank God for turning the little warrior into a soldier of Christ; otherwise we'd be well into World War Three.

SAMMY MCKEE
Sporting Man

SAMMY McKee's story is fascinating and at times intriguing. I'd often planned to record his life in full but never got around to it. Part of the problem was his reluctance to elaborate on the greyhound-racing period of his life. The anecdotes, which contained the juice of scandal, were told only when I solemnly promised not to put them in writing. I was a little saddened but not distressed by this principled stand.

Sam was simply being loyal to a colourful fraternity, which is still pulling the wool over the punters' eyes. However, he'd paid his dues and was entitled to his views.

In 1929, after a spell on the out-door relief, his father borrowed some money and went to Manchester to purchase a hobbyhorse cart. Returning home, he hitched a horse to the four-wheeled vehicle and travelled to various parts of the city, charging one halfpenny per person for a ride on the wooden horses that circled the cart when the handle was turned. After school Sam would race barefooted to whatever district his father was working in. At the pre-arranged spot his dad would leave the operation in Sam's hands and go for a well-earned break.

The boy was barely nine years old but even then he had a way with horses and had no trouble negotiating his way through the narrow streets. In those pre-decimal days, it would have taken 480 children to be aboard the carousel for its owner to make one pound.

It held about twenty children and had to be hand-cranked for each ride. Needless to say both the man and boy were exhausted by the time they got home to North Ann Street.

Sam's day began each morning, except for Sunday, at 7.30 a.m. He would run down to Duncrue Street and bring the pony up from the slab-lands where it grazed freely every night on the scrub grass that covered the wasteland close to Belfast Dock. This area was a little piece of the countryside with rivers and meadows. Many of the local men built and tended vegetable plots. It also housed Belfast City dump and was known as Alec's Bank.

Sam would ride the animal to the front of his father's house where it would be harnessed into the hobbyhorse cart. He would then go to school. His day finished when the cart was brought home and the animal was ridden bareback through the side streets to its field. He then made the lonely walk home. In the summer time, he was barely finished before 11 p.m.

During the winter, when the darkness decreed they stop about suppertime, he passed the hours in a boxing club in the Markets area of the city. His idol was Jackie Quinn, an Irish flyweight champion from Pilot Street. Easily approachable and down to earth, the Master boxer advised the nine year old Sam and was in his corner more than once over the years.

Over the next few years Sam fought in halls all over the Province, sharing the ring and the nobbins with boys as tough and ambitious as himself. His record was impressive and at least six of his contests were against Rinty Monaghan, who went on to become an undisputed flyweight champion of the world. He retired undefeated.

Despite the fisticuffs, both men remained firm friends until Rinty's untimely death. Sam carried an autographed photograph of the champion in his wallet.

Because of his stature and his ability to stay on a galloping horse without needing a saddle, his father wrote to English trainers with a view to having him taken on as an apprentice jockey. After a few refusals, a trainer called J.M. Hartigan sent for him.

The lad was three months short of his 14th birthday when he journeyed alone to the stables in England. He was put up and fed by the trainer and paid sixpence per week. He immediately became homesick and cried for weeks. Such was his distress, his mother and father travelled to the site, told him the indentures were signed and explained that he'd have to make the best of it.

He toughed it out and in his first race as an apprentice he lined up at the tapes with racing legends Gordon Richards, Charlie Smirke, Freddie Fox and Harry Wragg. Undaunted by such prestigious company, he finished fourth.

He returned to boxing and became a stable-boy champion at his weight, for four successive years, until the outbreak of the Second World War cancelled the annual event. He was driven to each event by Noel Murless, who went on to train many classic winners and be honoured with a Knighthood.

Named as the outstanding boxer in one event, he was awarded a solid gold medal by Gordon Richards, who went on to become a Knight of the Realm. Judges at some of his fights included such boxing notables as Jimmy Wilde and Len Harvey, champions of the professional ring.

Sammy stayed with Hartigan until the outbreak of the war. The British army commandeered most of the horses and Sammy was detailed to take the rest to the Curragh. There his racing career sadly ended—the advent of the war nipping a handsome career prospect in the bud.

During his days in England, he had sent home, by telegram, some sound information concerning winning horses to his grateful father. He was unaware that his father was sharing his good fortune with the whole of York Street. He was curtly informed of this during the once-a-year fortnight's holiday he was allowed each Christmas. A local bookmaker sent for him and in no uncertain terms told him the tips he was sending home were ruining his business. He made Sam aware that if he continued to send information home to his father, he, in turn, would write to Hartigan and have the lad dismissed.

Sam explained he wasn't aware that his father was giving the tips to the neighbourhood. He agreed to the man's demands and went home. A few moments later, two men he knew to have connections with an illegal organisation turned up at his door and told him to disregard the bookie's threats.

Faced with the greater threat, he reluctantly continued to send home the information. The bookie didn't make good his threat and Sam later learned he had been warned that if he did write to report on the little jockey it would be the last letter he would ever write.

Sam's tips had become a cottage industry for some people in the area. Housewives were known to pawn their shawls and put the money on 'Sammy's Certs' as they were called. His father also passed the tips to influential men who waged large sums. The horse seldom lost and Sam made quite a few men rich in his short career.

When his racing career eventually dried up, he came home, reluctantly, to wartime Belfast from the Curragh and took a job in the shipyard. As he walked down Queen's Road, the first person he met was the bookie he had put out of business. He had returned to his trade and was understandably angry. He cursed the ex-jockey and shouted: "It's all your fault I'm down here working for a living. You cost me a fortune. Only for you I'd be on Easy Street now."

Sam shrugged and replied honestly: "Well I got nothin' out of it and sure I'm in the same boat as yourself."

As both men trudged wearily to their places of employment, each was perhaps reflecting bitterly on what might have been.

Sam's solid information had ruined at least one bookmaker and lifted more than a few in a rags-to-riches scenario. He had just turned twenty and was as poor as the day he'd left for England and J.M. Hartigan.

Unknown to him another exciting period of his life was about to unfold in the Belfast greyhound stadiums called Dunmore and Celtic Park. These were heady days when his younger brother Joe, nicknamed 'The Atom Bomb' would make his mark as a bookmaker in post-war Belfast ... But that's another story.

THE WINO'S STORY

HE held the empty wineglass in a vice-like grip, as if defying anyone to take it from him. The hand that clutched the tumbler was covered with an assortment of cuts and scratches in various stages of bealing and healing. The elbow of his other hand dug into the brown-coloured surface of the round table top. The hand attached to it was likewise covered with superficial injuries. It supported a gaunt unshaven chin that sat beneath two vague and downcast eyes that seemed riveted to the empty glass.

A drab and faded cloth cap clung, precariously, to the side of his grey-haired head. He wore a long dark overcoat that was buttoned to the neck. Despite the heat of the bar, the greasy collars were turned up, hiding whatever else, if anything, he was wearing beneath it. His sad, wan face was locked in a frown that promised ill-will to any foolish enough to disturb him. Unfortunately, the frail body didn't seem capable of carrying through the threat. However, a menace, born of desperation, seemed to hover around him. He reminded me of a wild animal risking a trip into civilization to ease its thirst and being trapped for its pains.

No one in the crowded bar saw fit to sit beside him and all but myself ignored him. He had drawn my attention, some time earlier, when he had wandered in through the doors that looked out into York Street. Walking with an exaggerated swagger that showed he was sober pretending to be drunk, he made straight for the bar and threw a handful of change onto the well-worn surface.

I was unable to hear what he ordered but saw Barney, the host, hesitate for a moment before setting up the drink. His usually cheerful face was a mixture of compassion and sadness as he watched the scarecrow-like figure move slowly towards the deserted table at which he was now seated. The bar was a popular drinking place for dockers and sailors and local natives of York Street, so Barney hadn't much time for reflection before he was called to serve another customer.

My curiosity was aroused. I had met or knew most of the people who lived or worked in the area but had never encountered this man with the air of a tortured creature.

Neither had the waiter, whom I had called to replenish my glass. "New to me," he muttered, taking my order and moving skilfully through the crowd to the counter. When he returned, I paid him and then asked him to bring one for the stranger.

"Barney knows what he's drinking," I whispered. "So do I," snorted the barman, "I kin smell it from here—Tawny wine. You'd drink with anybody," he muttered disgustedly, before moving off.

He returned and placed a Tawney on the table with a bang that shook the occupant out of his reverie. The stranger's eyes took on a look of bewilderment as they crossed the bar, then questioningly at the waiter, who pointed silently in my direction. I met the grudgingly grateful glance and raised my own drink in salute.

His gaze turned from me and focussed on the wine. Discarding the empty glass, with a disdainful shove, he reached over and put the other one to his lips, gulping greedily at its contents. When it was finished, he lowered the glass to the table, clutching it in the same tight grip he had used on its predecessor. Only this time, the crazy eyes were not fixed on the tumbler. They now blazed their mixture of pain and contentment fully into my face. Something intangible, yet appallingly present in the back of them, caused me a sudden apprehension. Not for myself but for him.

By now, my curiosity was stronger than fright. Lifting my drink, I crossed the bar-room to sit beside him. Neither of us exchanged a greeting; speech was at a premium, walled up inside him. Using cruel logic, I matched his stubbornness with my cunning. My inquisitive stare said I would slake his thirst for knowledge, feed habit for information and give nothing for silence and anonymity.

His lips begged to betray his thoughts but his mind would have none of it. With a surly look he turned his eyes to the glass in his hand, as if drawing nourishment from its presence between his fingers and thumb. I hadn't long to wait. His thirst betrayed him, just as I was sure it would and was sure it always had.

His eyes danced hopelessly as he tried, manfully, to keep the telltale tongue honestly employed, licking lips that had become as dry as a desert. He seemed to be listening for an unseen bell that would tell him another unbearable round in his bout with life was coming to an end. His continued despair told me the sound would not come in time. His already weakened morale was surviving on instinct alone.

I remember the sadness in his eyes when he eventually raised them to look at me. Never before or since have I seen such a mixture of sorrow, dejection and grief. I called for another drink and waited. In a mélange of tears and painful silences, the following story unfolded. Only an empty tumbler would cause him to stop.

"The booze has had a grip on me since I was a kid," he whispered predictably. "Can't recollect or remember an hour when I didn't have a glass or a bottle in me, on me, or beside me. Even during the war, when I served on a tanker, I lived in a drink-sodden dream. But I could hold it then. I kept myself clean and presentable and always had a few bob. Maybe it was the war. The danger ... the fear; but other guys served and didn't finish up alcoholic wrecks.

"When I met Matilda, on shore-leave, I was witty, pleasant and well-mannered, but always slightly sozzled. Her ma never liked me though. Saw through me, I suppose. The week before we got married, I lost my job for sleeping on the duty-watch. Her ma wouldn't attend the wedding and cried for weeks after it but brave, loyal Mattie wouldn't hear a word against me. She insisted I would soon get another ship but I didn't. The bad discharge and my bad reputation arrived before me at every company I tried. I'd been a seaman all my life and knew nothing else, but who wants a hand who can't rise from his bunk in an emergency?

"Reluctantly, I took a shore job. I was sacked within a week.

Other jobs followed with the same results. Eventually, Mattie's unfailing loyalty began to flag. Outwardly, she supported me but at home she would sit, humiliated, each time I was carried in or brought back in a taxi for which I couldn't pay. By now, all self-respect had left me. I was prepared to be laughed at, pilloried and ridiculed in exchange for the cheap wine, which my tormentors would eventually provide for me.

"Nothing else in the world mattered. Each morning, I left our wee rented home with only one constructive thought in my pickled brain. To get, by fair means or foul, enough alcohol, in any shape or form, to lessen or countermand the pain and ache its absence left. Only when the likker reached the level of the drunkard's equivalent of a ship's Plimsoll line did I begin to feel even partially alive.

"The coming of our two children didn't change matters. When the first boy was born, I was out for a month wetting the baby's head, as is the tradition around these parts. The second lad came two years later and to my everlasting shame, I don't even remember him being born. I never once visited the hospital during the period Mattie was there. Her mother brought her to her home in a taxi and threw me physically out of the house when I went there full of booze. Needless to say she made plenty of capital out of that episode and who could blame her? But never once, not even once, did my long-suffering wife castigate me. I believe she was of the opinion that one day I would sink as low as a man could and then begin to rise again. I knew that more than once her mother had begged her to leave me. Each time she refused, remaining steadfast, rearing our children and keeping our home clean and tidy. The enormity of her love for me was matched only by my indifference for her and our children.

"And yet it wasn't as if I didn't care for them. Never once in all my drunken escapades was I ever unfaithful to her. I suppose I loved her in some way, but not as much as my body loved the alcohol it schemed, lied and stole to get. I can't remember when I began to thieve from her. At first it was a few shillings out of the housekeeping. Her mother had long since arranged to have my unemployment pay sent to her house, as I was never able to pass the pub with it.

"Only Mattie's pleading saved me from a prison sentence, when an unsympathetic magistrate wanted to jail me for three months. Now, I wish to God he'd been firmer ... maybe things would have been different."

He paused and I used the silence to order another wine. For a moment or two, I thought he wasn't going to drink it—then with a defeated shrug, he tossed it back and continued.

"One day I came home and the house was empty. I was just sober enough to read a note saying she had taken the boys to visit her mum. I'd some drink taken but not enough to fill the dreaded void. My body cried for more and I hunted every nook and cranny for a loose half-crown or a hidden ten bob note.

"I found nothing. Over the years her guile had become the equal of mine. Whatever money she had went with her when she left the house. Whilst she was there it was safe. Despite being a heavy, worthless drinker, I loved her too much to be violent, even when the craving tore my innards apart with an intensity that often caused me to scream in anguish.

"This was such a night and the tiny part of my brain that was still rational was glad she was absent. I couldn't have borne her shame at seeing me do what I did next. I broke into the gas meter—emptied the money into my overcoat pocket like the thief I was. With the cunning of a starving animal, I replaced the lock in such a way that only a close look would show it had been broken.

"I ran as quickly as my legs would take me from the scene of the crime. Reaching the nearest pub, I ordered a large cheap wine. A few hours later, when the craving was contented like a well-fed dog, I began to take stock of my action. Even the dull glow of the drink wouldn't drown the contempt that surfaced from every sip. Try as I might, I couldn't sink that tiny spark of decency. It climbed above the haze like a reef declining to be swallowed up by an angry sea. Beaten and lashed on all sides, it remained unbreachable and refused to let me conceal my shame.

"Rising unsteadily, I ordered another drink. The barman watched with undisguised disgust as I once again went through the ritual of counting out the pennies. 'Have ye robbed the child's money-box, wino?' he roared in a tone that caused the shame in my soul to rise up like the hackles on a cat's back. I slunk to my chair and for the first time in many years looked at my apparel and my appearance. I cringed at my grimy clothes and skin and without a word walked out into the street.

"To be honest, I wanted to cry. The screen I'd built to keep out self-respect had crumbled around me. Now I saw myself for what I was ... for what I'd been all my wasted life. I started to trot home like a little child who'd been lost and suddenly sees a light in the wilderness ... The warm, welcoming light that was coming from the front window of our home.

"She was there when I arrived, standing alone in our small, working-kitchen, washing dishes in the sink. She didn't look up when I rushed in breathless but continued rubbing the dishes. She lifted her eyes and gazed at the small kitchen window that looked out into the whitewashed yard.

"'Mum gave me a pot of stew home for us,' she said, in a voice devoid of feeling. 'It's the flavour the boys love. They couldn't wait to get home to get it heated up. I turned on the gas and their wee eyes lit up when I put the match to the ring. They couldn't understand when it didn't burst into flames, but I did. I knew immediately what you'd done. In my heart I tried to forgive you, like I did when the odd half-a-crown went missing or an ornament or two disappeared. Or the time when you vanished for a week with our dole money leaving us to live on handouts from my ma.'

"She paused and stifled a sob before continuing: 'The boys got their stew ... it was cold, but it was nourishing.'

"The words came out stiffly, like stubborn nails being drawn out by a worn hammer. 'It was their favourite stew and I suppose it didn't matter to them that it was cold ... but it mattered to me. Just now, when you came in, I was washing their dishes in icy water and suddenly realised just how long this has been going on. My poor Da would turn in his grave if he knew what you've put me through.'

"She didn't have to tell me it was finished, but she did. 'When I looked and saw how cleverly you'd concealed the meter-box, I pitied you for your cunning and desperation. Now I hate and despise you ... no more will our children eat someone else's cold left-overs ... no more will I try to wash their dishes in cold water because you stole the money that would have boiled the kettle. I'm leaving with the children tomorrow. My mother will fend for us until I get a job. I never want to see you again.'

"She brushed past me and the bedroom door slammed with a finality that all but sobered me up. Like a thief seeking absolution, I ran to the meter and began putting money back into it. All except the price of a fish supper. I suddenly remembered how I'd gotten round Mattie in the early days. She loved it when I brought in fish and chips, no matter how late it was. I ran out the door and towards the fish and chip shop. A nice warm piece of cod would cheer Mattie up and stop her from leaving me. Then, tomorrow ... tomorrow, I would straighten myself up and start to look after her and our children.

"I'll never forget that moment. I ran down the hill and saw the supper saloon's lights warm and welcoming in the distance. Holding tightly to the money and wheezing with exertion, I forced my flaccid body on. Reaching my destination I threw the pennies onto the counter. I tried to speak but couldn't. The girl was first amused then alarmed at my ashen features and wheezing breath. She screamed when I fell to the floor.

"I woke up in the Mater hospital in a bed close to a window. The ward was alive with the noises of morning and I realised I'd been there all night. Instantly I thought of Mattie.

"'What time is it? What time is it?' I cried in desperation to the occupant of the bed next to me. My own once treasured timepiece, had been sold long ago for the craving.

"The other patient looked at me with the same undisguised disgust I now accepted from everyone.

"'It's breakfast time' he scowled, adding contemptuously, 'Do you know you stink?'

"I ignored him. My main concern was Mattie. Once gone she would never return, especially as I'd been out all night. Naturally she'd think the worst.

"I rose, groggily, from the bed, ignoring the protests of those around me and moved down the ward. Out of nowhere, two nurses grabbed me and began to coax me back to my bed. I fought vainly as their firm efforts gradually pushed me back.

"Defeated, deflated and completely destroyed, I sank my head into the pillow and wept with frustration. About an hour later a doctor bore down on me like a gunboat. He had little to say but the tone of his voice added volumes. His eyes were indifferent as he stared at me through small, steel-rimmed glasses. 'Stop drinking that hideous poison or you'll be dead in six months.'

"They made me bathe before allowing me to leave. I borrowed the bus fare from a sympathetic nurse and prayed Mattie would still be home."

He stopped and sipped from the glass, then looked sideways at me with a pitiful leer he must have thought was a smile.

"When I eventually got there the blinds were still down and the house was in darkness. I heaved a sigh of relief and fumbled for my keys. I was as weak as water and sweating like a navvy. I forced a tired smile onto my features, but it froze when I opened the door. The stench of the gas hit my nostrils immediately, causing me to gasp. I staggered outside and tried to fathom the horror that was unfolding before me like a nightmare. With a wild scream I rushed inside and hurled a chair through the living-room window before charging into the kitchen and opening the back door. I filled my lungs with air in the entry before entering the house again.

"Sobbing uncontrollably I opened the bedroom door and saw them. Innocent in death as in life, Mattie lay serenely peaceful. The children were cuddled against her. The tranquility of their features will never leave me. I stumbled to Mattie and caressed her forehead, which was as cold as marble. 'Peace at last, Mattie' I whispered before collapsing on the bed beside her.

"The neighbours found me just minutes from death. They had heard the window breaking, but were hesitant to come until they heard the sound of my grief.

"At the funeral, everyone was kind, except Mattie's mother. She didn't speak to me once through the long ordeal. She didn't need to ... the hatred leaked from every pore of her body and for once I couldn't blame her. The police were polite and compassionate. They explained gently how it happened. When Mattie had turned on the gas to heat the stew she hadn't turned it off again. Consequently when I put the money back into the meter the gas seeped through the open ring and killed them whilst they slept.

"I never went back to the house or the area. I never saw anything again with clear or dry eyes ... I don't even see you now.

I've told the story to trees, telephone poles, hedges and ditches but never to another living soul. I guess I wanted that drink real bad."

He stroked the empty glass with the tips of his fingers.

"Her head was as cold as a slab of marble," he repeated wistfully. I looked into his sad, miserable face and knew he was telling the truth. The tragedy had been reported in all the local newspapers a few weeks earlier.

"Want another?" I said softly as he continued to caress the glass as if it were Mattie's forehead.

"Naw, I'm balin' out," he sighed.

"Where will you go?" I asked, anxiously, over the noise of the other drinkers. He seemed so haggard, so weary and so vulnerable.

"I'm goin' back to the sea," he answered. "That's my next stop from here. It's the only mother and father I ever knew. The only family I ever had outside of Mattie and the boys. I've got to get back to it."

There was no drive in his voice, no enthusiasm—only apprehension and defeat.

He rose quickly, almost pushing the table over in his haste to be gone. I noticed he was close to tears as he left without a farewell.

Some weeks later, I was working on the deck-cargo of a timber boat at an open berth on the Pollock Dock when the hatch man spotted a body floating in the murky waters. Work was suspended as the harbour police came alongside the ship in a small motor-vessel. They pulled the body to the side of their boat and working gently and carefully, began to wrap a length of tarpaulin around it.

A few moments later, using the motor-boat's lifting equipment, they slowly raised the corpse from the water. The canvas shroud covered most of the body, except for the feet and ankles, which were bare and the features which were pale and frozen in death.

The flesh was soft and flabby and the eyes had been eaten by whatever lived at the bottom of the dock.

I remembered his last words and shuddered. Maybe it is him ... maybe it isn't, I thought as I returned sadly to work. Needless to say, I never saw him again.

first published in *Memories of York Street* (1991)

MOBY'S STORY

THE following episode took place during the 'Outdoor Relief'. For those not familiar with this period of history, it was a time during the 1930s when there was no work and little money for the poorer people of Belfast. Moby, like the rest of his unemployed companions loitering at the corner of Limestone Road and York Road, hadn't even the price of a cigarette. They congregated at that particular point because it housed a bookmaker's office. They lived in hope of someone winning a few quid and spreading a little of it in their general direction.

They resembled wandering Nomads who peopled an arid desert, hanging forlornly around an oasis which had long gone dry, waiting vainly for a breakthrough that would quench their almighty thirst. Speaking of water, drink was also out of reach in those dismal days known as 'the hungry 30s'. Their only luxury was a morning newspaper they had purchased with a few half pennies. It passed slowly between them until the pages were grubby and marked by the huge callused hands left, sadly, with nothing else to employ them.

The talk was of Warnock, Quinn and Stewart. Each man enthused about the local box-fighters in an effort to forget about their own problems. The rumbling stomachs that ached to be filled, or the withdrawal pains in a system that hadn't inhaled a puff of nicotine from last dole day.

To trot out a tired cliché, desperate times create desperate people. They eyed the Post Office a few yards up the Limestone Road and noted it was doing a roaring trade. Soon the good-natured bantering turned to furtive whispers as the men planted the seeds of skullduggery and reaped a foolproof plan to rob the establishment. Within minutes, they were transformed from cloth-capped corner-boys to hardened highwaymen.

Moby—small, dapper—told me this story many years later. No longer short of the price of a drink or a packet of cigarettes, he was a popular ganger on Belfast Docks. He had a cheerful disposition, and despite being saddled with a terrible stammer, was a great yarn-spinner who enjoyed telling stories against himself.

On one occasion, he had entered his favourite bar, which had just taken on a new barman. When the barman who was similarly afflicted, stammered "WWWWhatttt wwwwiiiilllll iiittttt bbbeee?" Moby answered, sympathetically, "AAA hhhaaaallfff aaa ssscccooottcccchh aaaannnnaaaa wwweeee wwwwiiiiillleeeeee dddaaaarrrkkkkk." Seconds later he was running for his life as the barman, convinced Moby was mimicking him, chased him from the bar with a bung-starter.

His mood changed as he continued about the plan to rob the Post Office. After much furtive whispering, an agreed plot was formed. A tall, thinly built man stepped into the tightly knit circle and pulled a heavy .45 calibre revolver from the inside pocket of his jacket. He was rumoured to be, in local parlance, a gunman. It seems he was off duty that particular day and wasn't about to do the job himself. It was agreed the man who drew the short straw would do this.

The matches were produced and each man waited fearfully to see who would be unfortunate enough to draw the job. Moby moved forward stiffly when his turn came and was horrified when he drew the shortest stick. His eyes raised heavenward for help and he refused to look down at the large and heavy lump of black metal that was shoved into his trembling hand.

"Get to it," ordered the gunman, adding elegantly, "Get in ... get out ... an' don't muck about," as he pushed Moby through the door into the Post Office.

The first face he saw was the Postmaster. The giant of a man was not one bit amused when the stricken Moby pointed the gun in the general direction of his ample mid-section. His face was a mixture of derision and scorn as he eyed the would-be robber. Pausing only to pick up a heavily gnarled blackthorn stick, he began to advance.

Moby, frightened for his life raised the weapon to eye level and was shocked to discover the barrel of the gun was pointing to the floor. The owner had rendered it to the safe hand-over position and neglected to inform the luckless dupe. Not that he would have known, as his knowledge of firearms was negligible.

Both combatants stared at each other warily for a few moments, then, with an ear-splitting roar, the Postmaster slashed the empty air and charged at Moby like a demented cavalryman.

The corner-boy took to his heels and left the Post Office at great speed as his erstwhile companions scattered in all directions. Reaching the LMS Railway yard, he tossed the weapon over a high wall before losing himself among the clientele of the Edinburgh Castle.

The irate Postmaster returned to the premises and phoned the police. Moby was arrested that night and detained in the cells. The following morning he was taken to the Petty Sessions in Victoria Street where he was charged with attempted armed robbery. Needless to say he was beyond himself with shame, grief, fear and apprehension. He knew this was an extremely serious charge, which could warrant him a good few years in Crumlin Road prison.

A legal aid solicitor nodded grimly as he tried to prise the details from his client. He lowered his head in embarrassment as the accused stammered and stuttered incoherently, sending specks of spray and saliva all over the table. Eventually, after what seemed a lifetime, the lawyer stopped him and looked up with a new light in his eyes. "Do you always stutter when under stress?" he asked, and watched fascinated as his client tried manfully to answer in the affirmative whist nodding his head vigorously.

Eventually the case came up and the Postmaster was called to the stand. Earlier, he had easily picked Moby from an identity parade and felt confident the upstart would be jailed. The prosecuting District-Inspector also saw it as a formality. An open and shut case, so to speak.

The Postmaster began his evidence. When he came to the part about the position of the gun-barrel, he laughed derisively. "The weapon was in the hands of a useless blackguard," he claimed, with the air of a military man. Moby squirmed as a titter erupted in the crowded courtroom. The judge acted quickly to stifle it as the accused man's solicitor stepped forward slowly to question the witness.

He was brief and to the point. "When the accused approached you, did he say anything?" he asked quietly. The Postmaster thought for a moment before replying. "Yes," he said, "Hands up! ... This is a hold-up!"

The lawyer nodded gravely for a moment, before speaking again. "Is that all he said?"

The Postmaster replied, defensively, "It was enough."

"Is that exactly how he said it?" pursued the solicitor.

"Yes, exactly. Give or take a few words. The threat was definitely there," he added a trifle impatiently.

The council for the defence turned and looked at the body of the courtroom. "Would you say it again sir, precisely as you heard the gunman say it ... give or take a few words."

The Postmaster rose from his chair and addressed the back of the lawyer's head. "Hands up! This is a hold-up!" he bellowed. The solicitor turned his blank gaze to the bored features of the resident magistrate presiding over the court. "Those were the exact words, sir? Give or take a few?" he again repeated.

"His precise words," answered the witness triumphantly.

"Thank you. I've nothing further to ask you," replied the solicitor, courteously. He addressed the magistrate: "Your Worship, could I ask my client to take the stand and utter the words he is alleged to have used?"

The R.M. nodded agreement. The lawyer moved quickly across the courtroom. As Moby rose to take the stand, they both collided. The solicitor's papers fell from his hand and floated beneath the table. As they both knelt down to retrieve them, the lawyer whispered fiercely over the laughter of the audience, "stutter as you've never stuttered before."

The accused rose and walked to the witness stand. It took him five minutes to give the judge his name and address and twenty minutes to take the oath. The pièce-de-résistance came as an anticlimax when he was asked to say, "Hands up! This is a hold-up!"

The courtroom held its collective breath as he stuttered and stammered like a true champion. It raised the rafters when, some fifteen minutes later, with the sentence still unsaid, the judge threw the case out.

Moby stayed away from bad company and was never in trouble again. He gained employment on Belfast Dock as a registered docker and remained there until he retired. When he died, in the 70s, the Dockland lost a loveable character and a raconteur of the highest calibre. Lost also was an abundance of equally amusing stories which, when he told them, were never affected by his stammer.

first published in *Memories of York Street* (1991)

BITTER CROSSING

THE white surf swirled against the dark hull of the cross-channel ferry as it battled its way across a choppy Irish Sea. Some of it was caught by the gale force wind and whipped upwards, in an almost invisible spray that beat against the face of the lone female standing on the deserted main deck.

Clinging grimly to the ship's rail, she ignored the sting of the spray and continued to gaze into the angry sea below her; gazing so intently, she could not have been seeing it. What she was seeing was not in front of her but miles and hours behind her.

Each time a wave crashed into the steamer's heaving bows, the knot in her stomach tightened to a higher intensity. She allowed a wry smile to soften the immobility of her pretty but tired, middle-aged features. The smile, which seemed more of a grimace, did not find its way to her eyes, which were red-rimmed with a mixture of salt-water and tears.

She thought back to the warmth of the young seaman's cabin and shuddered visibly. The smile returned fleetingly but this time it contained a cynical mirth. She knew now it was the natural longing for a human touch and the sound of a friendly voice that had led her to return his cordial greeting.

For a few moments, she had enjoyed the brief flirtation. But that was before the whiskey had died, leaving a void that was now over-brimming with remorse. She couldn't deny he had been charming. His body was young and firm and his features almost god-like. His contagious laughter and almost incessant Irish banter drove the loneliness from her for the first time since the accident.

She was also more than a little flattered by his attention. After all, what woman could remain presentable on the deck of a ship ploughing a rough passage from Liverpool to Belfast?

What was refreshing about the exchanges was what she believed to be his innocence about his almost girl-like beauty.

It was plainly obvious now that his practised eyes had singled her out, sensing she was cold, lonely and thus vulnerable. The tight smile returned as she remembered how she had encouraged him. At that moment as they chatted on deck, he had reminded her of Bob. Sometimes when she looked at him through the needles of flying spray she actually saw Bob. Yet she knew Bob was dead.

The whiskey she had drunk in the ship's bar had double-crossed her. Instead of insulating her against the night air, it had left her feeling tired and empty. Gradually, the coldness of the ship's deck had risen through her unsuitable shoes and numbed the lower part of her body. Otherwise, the offer of warm coffee in his quarters would not have been so readily accepted. With less coaxing than it should have taken, she followed him meekly to his cabin.

It was roomy, and comfortable in a Spartan sort of way. She felt touched at her newly-found companion's concern for her welfare as he took her travelling bag and placed it under a small unmade bed.

A tiny transistor radio blared from the top of a table where it was wedged to stop it moving with the continuous roll of the ship. The strident music bawled loudly in an unequal contest with the monotonous whine of the ship's powerful engines.

She recalled sitting, rather demurely, on the edge of the untidy bed. A remark about the absence of chairs sounded coy, even to her. The moment she made it, he flashed her an old-fashioned look, which she knew now was his innocence about her innocence.

Making sure she was comfortable, he left for the ship's galley and the promised coffee. Alone in the cabin she found herself thinking about Bob. His death had been sudden and tragic. Within seconds, a carefree and happy bachelor driving to his wedding had become a charred corpse in a buckled heap of metal smouldering on the side of a motorway.

The police had been unable to identify him and for four long hours she had waited in the church surrounded by sympathetic guests and thinking Bob had left her in the lurch. When the horrific details were quietly revealed to her, she was understandably distraught. She left alone and in her wedding dress, for her flat in Southport where she spent the entire night weeping.

Two long and lonely weeks later she realised Bob was the only person she knew really well. Their love for each other had been so complete, they had unwittingly shut everyone else out. She had her colleagues in the teaching profession but they had never mixed socially. She and Bob had felt the need for no company other than their own.

Both had been only children. Bob's parents had passed on years earlier and her widowed mother, too frail to attend the wedding, had beseeched her to return to Belfast. She decided to go, hoping the change of surroundings would at least mute her grief.

Every corner of her flat seemed to contain Bob's shadow. She made up her mind suddenly and travelled on the cross-channel steamer. Air travel, which would have been preferable, was unavailable because of an international sporting fixture taking place in Belfast that weekend. All berths had been allocated on the ship and she had been forced to travel steerage.

The return of the young deckhand broke her reverie. He poured the steaming coffee with practised ease into two thick mugs. She grasped the large cup with two hands as he quietly sat down beside her. Sipping gratefully but cautiously, she imagined she detected a slight taste of whiskey. She looked questioningly into his honest features and decided her mouth still retained some of the drink she'd had earlier.

For the next hour the conversation was natural and unstilted. She told him all about herself. Except for Bob. His name was on the tip of her tongue several times but she was unable to say it. Even though the lad had a sympathetic ear, she couldn't share such a personal sorrow.

She accepted a third and fourth cup of coffee and relished the warmth that crept through her entire body. The young man was quite eloquent in his Irish way and soon had tears of nervous laughter coursing down her cheeks. His potted version of his brief time at sea had told her everything about his life but nothing about himself.

She realised, later, she had been laughing too loudly and too long. Her efforts to hide her loneliness had exposed it. She remembered how her heart skipped a beat when his arm tentatively reached out and encircled her shoulder. His boyish features were tense as they searched her face for the slightest sign of rejection.

As their bodies came together, she was conscious of a muted gleam of triumph in his pale-blue eyes. After a moment, flushed and breathless, she allowed him to remove her heavy winter coat. As he fumbled with the buttons of her blouse, she was filled with a drowsiness he acknowledged as consent.

Knowing now the coffee had been laced, she surprisingly felt no animosity towards him and his advances. The aroma of countless perfumes wafted around her head as he laid her gently back onto the bed. As she moved obediently to his whispered suggestions, she thought of Bob and the long years of tender but unproductive coaxing. She saw the white wedding dress; the church and the guests, all of which became interwoven with the mangled remains of a burning automobile, and the painful thrust of his body almost tore her heart to pieces.

Loneliness descended on her. She felt like a flower plucked suddenly from the comfort of the earth and left hanging in its nakedness. Moments later, he moved away from her.

Raising himself on one elbow, he did not bother masking the look of triumph that had returned to his face. She hoped he realised the pitying smile on her features was not for him or for her but for both of them. He even had the audacity to comment snidely about teaching a teacher as he rose and dressed.

He had not taught her anything, she reflected, some hours later, as she clung to the ship's rail. He had simply used her as he had used others before her. She knew neither he nor she would understand why she had given herself so freely.

Other women and girls would undoubtedly chase her image from his mind. It amused her in a bitter way that she could not now recall his features. The face that had attracted her because it looked so much like Bob's was now just a blur of flesh in the folds of her memory. She sobbed suddenly and quietly.

Within herself she knew she could never look lovingly or longingly on another man. Her body shivered in the dawn air. She longed for her beloved Bob to hold her, for his comforting words to ease the pain of betrayal he would never know and she would never forget.

first published in *An Old Jobbin' Poet* (1991)

MOVIEHOUSE MEMORIES

Dad small-talked with some men outside the Edinburgh Castle public house, at the corner of York Street and Canning Street. Mum hovered protectively, whilst I tried to tie a shoelace that had become undone. I succeeded and we moved on up Canning Street.

This is my first recollection of going to the pictures. We were walking to Joe McKibben's, which was also called the Midland. It was around the early years of the Second World War. The film showing was *Alexander's Ragtime Band*, starring Tyrone Power, Alice Faye and Don Ameche. Mum was an ardent fan of Alice Faye.

The Irving Berlin score contained many favourites, including one sang by Miss Faye. It was 'Everybody's Doin' It'. The lyrics were corrupted by the locals who sang:

Everybody's doin' it, doin' it, doin' it.
Pickin' their nose an' chewin' it, chewin it, chewin' it ...

Films played an important part in my growing up. Other films I watched in Joe's, before it became a victim of enemy bombers, included *The Boys From Syracuse* with Alan Jones, a Hollywood tenor, and an early horror film about a werewolf which scared the wits out of me.

I can't remember what the prices were but I'm quite sure Dad supplied cash as opposed to empty jam jars, which reputedly doubled as currency. As stated, the hall was destroyed by enemy action, as was the Queen's at the corner of the Limestone Road. There was a little entry or alley at its side where we queued for admission but I can't recall if there was an entrance at the front.

I remember the first time I went there with an older schoolchum called Harry Barnes. The seating consisted of long, hard, wooden forms. After we sat awhile, I felt the call of nature and asked Harry to indicate the way to the toilet. Removing his glance from the screen for a split second, he pointed silently to the floor. In my innocence, I believed him. Hitching up one leg of my short trousers, I began to urinate.

Harry immediately rose from his seat and yelled at the usher standing nearby. "Luk Mister! He's poolyin' on the flure." The small, but ferocious attendant, who rejoiced in the nickname of 'Hi Ho' Sharkey, charged at me, scattering people like ninepins. With a roar, he grabbed me by the collar of my jersey and yanked me over the back rail of the form in front of me.

I bellowed in fright and continued to trickle as he dragged me to the exit and tossed me out into the entry. I was more embarrassed than hurt as I skulked home, trying to ignore the dampness in my trousers and my friend's treachery.

When I dared to return to that cinema, sometime later, I was with another friend to see *The Charge of the Light Brigade*. Billy Todd's grandfather accompanied us. He said he wanted to see the film as he had taken part in the actual charge. The old man may have been pulling our legs but we believed him at the time. I got in by hiding behind the skirts of his grey overcoat. I was relieved when the sharp-eyed Sharkey paid no attention to the old man tottering along with a walking stick and the two children at his side.

When the hero or the villain appeared on the screen, they were greeted with a 'Ya' or a 'Boo' from the audience. The beam of Sharky's flashlamp danced like a wild thing as he charged up and down the aisles, vainly trying to keep order. The hero was always affectionately known as 'the fella', whilst his comrade or sidekick through thick and thin was 'the wee man'. 'Who's the fella?' or 'Who's the wee man?' were the first questions asked when locals enquired about current films.

Each night, these particular films would be discussed and

dissected at great length by the men as they gathered at the Street corners. Some of them were capable of talking their way through every inch of the footage, acting out each characterisation in turn. Sometimes, these performances were better than the actual film!

Afterwards we got the inside dope on the movies and stars from the corner-boys who, sadly enough, had nothing better to do with their time. That's when I first heard the startling fact that superhero Errol Flynn had lived for a while on the Duncairn Gardens, when his father lectured at Queen's University. One man swore Flynn had hauled a huge grey horse to a stop at the top of the Cavehill Road and paused to pass the time of day with him.

Another told us, in a guarded whisper, that George Brent, a suave leading man of the 40s, had been on the losing side in the Irish Civil War and had fled to America with a price on his head. Arthur Shields, a likeable character, who played a Protestant minister in *The Quiet Man*, was also named by the corner-boys as a Commander in the IRA. I don't know where they got their information from but many of the lads sailed on the Queen Elizabeth and Queen Mary when the stars used these vessels to cross the Atlantic and brought home such titbits of gossip.

A legend which still persists to this day is that the exceptional bar-room brawl between John Wayne and Randolph Scott, in what was the best screen version of Rex Beach's novel *The Spoilers*, was a real scrap between the two screen legends. I wouldn't agree to that, as a close examination of the fight shows two stuntmen taking the falls and swapping the haymakers. Wayne was pretty much what he portrayed on the screen (except in his later years when he became a parody of himself) but Scott was more interested in the stock market than fighting for real and damaging his handsome assets.

The Queen's ran a lot of serials and Gene Autry and his horse Champion, featured in a few of them. We called them Chapters. I remember one in which Gene and his sidekick, who may have been Smiley Burnett, battled extra-terrestrials in a mixture of western and science fiction which was greeted with howls of derision by the adults. It kept us kids on the edge of our seats and we roared when Gene triumphed in the end. I can't recall if they were real spacemen or just some ornery outlaws trying it on.

Roy Rogers was another troubadour of the purple sage who wasn't afraid to put his guitar aside and knock the tar out of four or five baddies at a time. During these furious encounters, Roy's large, ten-gallon Stetson remained spotlessly white and never left his head. After flooring everybody in the immediate vicinity, he would jump onto the ornate silver-tooled saddle on the faithful Trigger's back and launch into a spirited song, without even pausing for breath. Then, out of nowhere would appear Bob Nolan and the Sons of the Pioneers who would fall in behind him. Singing lustily and strumming their guitars, all concerned would ride triumphantly into the sunset as the closing credits rolled across the screen. Leaving the theatre, I would often wonder why the Sons never showed up when Roy was close to getting his malt knocked in.

When Joe's and the Queen's were bombed, I had to travel further afield in pursuit of my cinematic thrills. The Duncairn was a large hall on the Duncairn Gardens, close to North Queen Street. It had a frontage of thick, black glass and its foyer was small but impressive. It boasted a handsome balcony favoured by courting couples but I spent most of my time in the front stalls.

Films were changed every three days, with two houses or showings daily, plus a matinée on Saturday. The fare was usually a short, a feature and the main film. The second show usually started about twenty-past eight and finished promptly, at ten-thirty sharp. No matter what length the main film was, the projectionist would edit it so that you could put the pan on for the closing credits at the exact time stated. Despite the catcalls and cries of "cut short, cut short," the lights would go up and the cinema gradually empty as the crowd left.

The Saturday matinée was generally an actioner and the adults attending would complain bitterly of not being able to hear their ears as hordes of youngsters chased each other noisily up and down the aisles. After a while, the chuckers-out would form a snatch squad and haul the ringleaders to the backdoor, where they were dispatched homewards with a kick up the rear end.

Once, when bored by a tepid version of *The Invisible Man*, I found myself misbehaving with my mates. In next to no time, I was grabbed by no less than the cinema's manager who dragged me into the foyer, where he began to slap me about the head with one hand, whilst retaining a firm grip on my shirt collar with the other.

Suddenly, he let go of me and began crying out in bewilderment and pain as a brightly coloured umbrella, that seemed to wield itself beat a hefty tattoo on his head. For a moment or two, I was convinced that the Invisible Man himself had come to my rescue. Only when the manager turned away in pain and bewilderment, could I see that his assailant was my diminutive and extremely angry mother!

She belaboured his shiny, brylcreemed head, until he retreated like a wounded beast into the darkness of the stalls. When she eventually got her breath back, I was given the rough edge of her tongue and dragged by the ear down Brougham Street.

The Picture House had three emergency exits. One on each side of the cinema in Brougham Street and the other up an entry off North Queen Street. Many kids used these doors to bunk in when they hadn't the price of admission. My older brother Tommy and myself were not above a little larceny ourselves. We would climb onto the rear bumper of a Bellevue or Glengormley tram, when it stopped for passengers at the Gallaher tobacco factory in York Street. We'd hang on like limpets, as it shuddered its way up Brougham Street and jump off just before it clanked to a halt outside the cinema.

Cautiously, we'd check each exit, until we found a door ajar. Some were left open to allow the heavy tobacco smoke, that floated above the heads of the audience, to make its way out. Normally, an usher would be detailed to patrol this area. After a while he usually got bored and headed off to the nearest bar for a quick pint. Once in, we would sneak into the Gents' toilet which was outside the auditorium and then walk back towards the seating area oozing the assured air, of 'paid my way, been to the lavatory' cinemagoers. The next stage was to melt into a seat and pray it didn't belong to someone who had really gone to the toilet. If it were standing room only, we would position ourselves beside adults and act as if we were with them.

There was always a warm ripple of applause through the cinema whenever members of the Royal Family appeared on the screen, mostly on *Movietone* newsreels, which also reported news from the Second World War, accompanied by stirring music. The audience would watch the battle scenes and listen to the bombs and gunfire in silence, as many of them had loved ones serving with the armed forces.

Our parents also liked a trip to the cinema and most Thursday nights we'd go as a family to the Duncairn. Dad would don his demob suit and we'd leave the house in an excited group as we walked through Earl Lane into North Thomas Street, so that Mum could wave to her mother who lived on the corner there. If the weather was good, the old lady would be sitting outside her kitchen window, gossiping with her neighbours.

Moving on, we'd pass the decaying Unionist Hall, where quite a number of men spent their time playing snooker or billiards. We'd cross York Street, go up Spencer Street by way of Meadow Street and Norman Street and stop at Victor Wilson's shop for sweets. He was Mum's cousin and we always got good value, provided she had the required coupons.

After the film, we would hurry home in anticipation of the fish and chips Dad would pay for. One shilling would get two fish suppers in either Nelson's or Crook's Supper saloon, depending on which one was the least crowded. Racing home with the more than generous portion, we would hungrily devour them before being sent off to bed.

Dad was a fan of the musicals, particularly those which featured Nelson Eddy and Jeannette McDonald. He also had a soft spot for a young whippersnapper called Frank Sinatra, whom he'd seen in a film called *Anchor's Aweigh*, whilst in New York, during the war. As a movie buff, he thought he was in for a treat there but as he told us later, he was disappointed to find most of the films on show had already played in Belfast.

Mum liked gangster films and was not above giving advice to the actors, much to our embarrassment and Dad's ill-concealed amusement. She loved James Cagney and detested his on-screen companions, whom she regarded as bad company. Lloyd Nolan, a fine character actor, often bore the brunt of her anger as she vainly warned Jimmy to stay away from him.

When Cagney invariably finished up in jail or full of lead, she put the blame firmly on "That oul Lloyd Nolan" and would solemnly prophesied that he'd "Niver have any luk".

Mum would occasionally take me with her, and one of my favourite memories is sitting with her, in the circle of the Alhambra, watching James Cagney in *Yankee Doodle Dandy*. He was a good guy with not a Lloyd Nolan or Humphrey Bogart in sight.

Perhaps we were naïve to identify with the plots of the films, yet there were times when the movie became real in my childish mind. In the classic *Double Indemnity*, when Fred McMurray, aided and abetted by Barbara Stanwyk, pushed her dead husband off a train in an effort to claim his insurance, I took terrible umbrage at both of them and it was years before I could watch either of them in a film without remembering that terrible deed.

John Wayne was a different animal—every which way, a man who would die before he would do anything dishonourable. Most male cinemagoers squared their shoulders and swelled their chests, as they identified with him, as he hauled Maureen O'Hara across meadow and field. Angry as he was, however, he refused the offer from a kindly female observer of a "stick to beat the good lady with". The scene culminated in an angry and bloody confrontation with her broth of a brother, Squire Danahar, alias Victor McLaglan, who had been foolish enough to cast aspersions on John's masculinity.

In the world of horror movies, a frightening character on screen was *Dracula, The Prince Of Darkness* played by Bela Lugosi. I remember him making a personal appearance in the Hippodrome or the Opera House—I'm not sure which. When he appeared at the end of the show, dressed in character, boys pressed forward to get his autograph. One lad, eager to be first, literally fell into the actor's arms. His eyes danced wildly as he grabbed the boy firmly by the shoulders and held him at arm length. "I only want the book, not the body," he leered in that unmistakable voice that sent shivers down everyone's back.

One movie, which literally scared the pants off me, was the 1938 Technicolour production of *Tom Sawyer*. A few days before, I had received a gift of a pair of long legged trousers from my uncle Ronnie, who was on leave from the Royal Navy. In those days, we wore short trousers until we were about fourteen or fifteen. Graduating to long trousers was a watershed in a boy's life and was known as sliding down the banisters.

From the onset of the film, I was intimidated by the baddie, Injun Joe, played by Victor Jory. When he murdered the doctor in the graveyard and blamed it on Walter Brennan, I knew he was bad medicine. The nightmare episode, wherein Tom and Becky got lost in the cavern, caused me more alarm. The long trousers were of thick corduroy and they made me hot and uncomfortable. With my eyes fixed on the screen I removed them. I had my school short trousers under them so there was no affront to public decency.

When Joe's insanely contorted features filled the screen, I hid behind the seat in front of me and watched the film by peering over it. Only when plucky Tom sent him crashing down a bottomless chasm did I open my eyes and whistle my way down Brougham Street.

Too late, I realised I'd left the trousers behind. I raced back to the cinema but they were gone. Mum boxed my ears when I blamed it on Injun Joe. Sometimes, I wonder what went through the mind of the person who found them.

As I grew older I frequented cinemas like the Gaiety, in Upper North Street and the Alhambra, in Lower North Street. These had been music halls and were down at the heel compared to the Ritz or the Classic but they were cheap and that was an attraction to a young lad with little money. Incidentally, the Ritz became the Cannon, before being demolished and the Classic became the Gaumont and is now the British Home Stores. The Alhambra is an office block and the Gaiety, a Bingo Hall.

Errol Flynn featured a lot in these halls. The packed audiences certainly got their tanner's worth as they cheered him in the role of Irish-American boxer, Gentleman Jim, especially the scene when he took the Heavyweight title from the unbeaten John L. Sullivan, played by Ward Bond. We also cheered to a man when he stood alone, his long blond curls blowing in the heat of the battle, as he defied the might of the Sioux nation in *They Died With Their Boots On*. He was the last man standing at the massacre of the 7th cavalry and when he threw down his empty but still smoking, pearl-handled six-shooters, a hush fell over the audience.

Chief Sitting Bull, by the way, survived into old age, only to be knocked down and killed by an automobile!

In these picture palaces, I saw many classics for the first time: Mickey Rooney as the young Edison, Spencer Tracy as the adult; Greer Garson as Marie Curie; Joel McCrea as the inventor of ether, or laughing gas. These films may have enhanced our knowledge, but sometimes they misled us. Once, in Mariner's, my old public elementary school, when a boy was asked who invented the telephone, he answered without any hesitation, Don Ameche!

The Alhambra was impressive, although the pit had uncomfortable forms for seating. Its horseshoe circle was more comfortable and I remember watching the fights of Joe Louis when he defended his heavyweight title against men like Ezzard Charles or Jersey Joe Walcott. I also cheered for our own and much-loved Rinty Monaghan, from Little Corporation Street, who beat Jackie Paterson to bring the World Flyweight Title back to Belfast. A cheer went up when the referee raised Rinty's hand and he grabbed a microphone with the other and belted out a song called 'Broken Hearted Clown'. The cinema bar was full that night, as it often was, when fights were shown.

The Gaiety was also equipped with wooden forms and we would be squeezed as tight as sardines in a can when the usher flashed his light and demanded that you move along to make room for a few more. There was a continual coming and going of people during the performances and this was met with tuts of disapproval. Occasionally, fights would break out and the usher would act as bouncer, using his long torch as a cudgel to subdue the offenders, before ejecting them to a chorus of approval. Sometimes, he would come off worse and retreat bloodied to await the arrival of reinforcements.

In those times of hardship, many people had no coal at home and willingly paid sixpence to get into the cinema. It was worth it to sit all day in the heat. Some even smuggled sandwiches and tea in with them.

Breast-feeding was common. One day, my pal Albert and I encountered two women suckling their infants. He was so absorbed watching them that he paid no attention to where he was going to sit.

[85]

There was a loud cracking sound and a sticky mess on the seat of his trousers—he had sat on a tray of eggs placed on the form beside the women. They were not pleased.

Queues were another accepted feature of going to the cinema and people would wait good-naturedly in all sorts of weather, even for bad films. Street singers, like Doctor McNabb, would assail this captive audience with his caterwauling until he'd got enough money to go to the pub. Others were genuine entertainers and kept the patrons amused, until the cinema line started moving, sometimes to find the 'House Full' sign up.

Films were always part of our lives. I still associate the birth of my youngest brother with a late 40s B-movie called *Joe Palooka* based on the adventures of a boxer who featured in an American comic-book strip. We raced home to tell dad how much we enjoyed it and were astonished, on stumbling into the bedroom, to find Mum holding a new baby. A film was also instrumental in providing the baby with a Christian name. In 1946, *The Jolson Story* was a big movie and was viewing in Belfast at the time of the birth. Mum decided to call the Baby Alan, after Al Jolson. Although she didn't like it shortened to Al, this is what he became known as. However, when the sequel *Jolson Sings Again* reached Belfast, Dad was dead.

On the day he died, we children were farmed off to relatives to keep us from getting underfoot at home. My cousin, Hugh Bennett took me by trolleybus or tram to the Troxy cinema, on the Shore Road, to see an awful film called *The Egg And I*, which starred Claudette Colbert and Fred McMurray, the guy I wouldn't travel on a train with.

After my father died, money became scarce and I joined forces with some of my schoolmates to gather waste paper, empty jam pots and lemonade bottles. The revenue from this, plus the weekly sixpence from Granny English, allowed me the treat of a movie once or twice a week. After that we would bunk in.

Some nights, my Mum's eldest brother Joe would come round to cheer us up. He told stories about the stars and often re-enacted the plots for us.

Once, whilst reliving a tragic love scene, he, in the role of the hero, clasped his arms around an imaginary heroine and began to sing.

The song turned out to be one of Mum's favourites and as she joined in she forgot for a moment the heartbreak of Dad's passing and the worries of raising her young family. When they finished we clapped and cheered. Joe's one-man cabaret continued until the tea and toast were served. Only when he left did the house feel empty and lonely again.

I often went to the Troxy, which, like so many other cinemas, failed to survive, despite installing a wide screen and stereo sound. It became a theatre until senselessly destroyed by an act of arson, which deprived North Belfast of its only playhouse.

There, I saw the last of the great Hollywood musicals: *Singin' In The Rain* and *It's Always Fair Weather*, starring Gene Kelly; *The Band Wagon*, starring Fred Astaire and *There's No Business Like Show Business*, with a host of stars, including the legendary Broadway star Ethel Merman and Marilyn Monroe.

The Troxy had an usher called 'Torchy' or 'Battery Boy', after a TV character of the time. His ray searched out noisy people and stayed on them until they were shamed into silence. If this didn't work, the beam remained fixed, like a jailhouse spotlight, until one of his henchmen located the offender for a severe talking to.

The Lyceum, at the corner of the New Lodge and the Hallidays Road, also failed to survive but I spent many happy hours there, even though it was nicknamed 'The Fleapit'. It was there I first witnessed the genius of Charlie Chaplin's little tramp. He was a great hero of ours.

It was there too, I saw the newsreel of the atom bomb being dropped on Japan and heard President Truman explain why. Of course, as kids, we believed the Japanese got no more than they deserved. We identified with the American heroes of such flag wavers as *Guadalcanal Diary*, *Bataan*, *Back To Bataan*, and *The Sands of Iwo Jima*—after all we had real GI's on our Streets—and cheered when fanatical kamikaze planes were shot out of the sky, in a flaming ball of fire, by a lone matelot, on the corpse-littered deck of a fighting ship of the US Navy. Sadness engulfed us when a cowardly sniper, hiding in a palm tree on some tropical island, mowed down a lone GI.

The moment of truth came for the watchers, as well as the soldiers, when the sergeant ordered "Fix Bayonets!" The silence was shattered as we leaned forward in our seats, cheering lustily, our eyes following closely the hand-to-hand fighting. The actor's faces would contort in hate as bayonets were pushed into enemy chests, before being disdainfully withdrawn with the aid of a boot or a bullet.

When we asked the American soldiers about the Philippines or islands such as Bataan, we were usually met with cynical laughter, for they knew the horrors of the real war in the Pacific.

Another old cinema, The Lido, was a tuppence-ha'penny trolley-bus ride from home, on the Shore Road, just past Gray's Lane. People still stream through its doors today but for a different reason because it has been converted to a Church.

The coming of television destroyed the cinemas, when cheap black and white sets flooded in. As Sam Goldwyn rightly remarked "who wants to go out and pay to see a lousy film when they can stay at home and see one for free".

Most of us now do our watching at home but it hardly has the magic of going to the cinema: the growl of approval as the hero decks the heavy, who has been asking for it, or the nudges of anticipation from a friend in the next seat, as you await the calamities to be served up by Laurel and Hardy as they attempt to push a piano up an endless row of steps.

How many of us left the moviehouse slapping our backsides as we rode imaginary horses or fired invisible guns at each other, as we portrayed our heroes in their latest productions. Even, as an adult, reading about the lives these people really led, I find it hard to square with what I saw on the screen. It's a long way from the darkness of the front stalls to the reality of the rain-soaked streets.

I hope the new Cinema complex in the Yorkgate centre, in the heart of York Street, will provide a dream-pit for the children of today. Its location is less than a stone's throw away from the sites of The Duncairn, The Midland and The Queen's. Its carpark consists of streets I walked through with my family on our weekly visit to the Duncairn, back in the 40s.

Perhaps, the ghosts from my childhood will float through its plush surroundings and marvel at the modern technology—I know I will!

first published in *Memories of York Street* (1991)

PINTS & POLITICS
A Play in One Act

This is a one act play written originally as a short story. It has nine characters and runs for approximately forty minutes. Despite advice from many professional dramatists and writers, including John Boyd and Chris Fitz-simon, to open it up into a full-blown play, I've decided to keep it as it is, except for a little added dialogue and changes in spelling.

Set in a pub deep in dockland, on the edge of the Belfast Harbour estate during the mid-1960s, the bustling street becomes a cul-de-sac when the harbour gates are closed to both traffic and people each night at 7pm.

CHARACTERS

Jamsie Mulvenna, *a retired dockworker who is now a watchman in a nearby dockshed.*
Paddy Ryan, *a retired merchant seaman who works as a watchman in the same shed.*
Wee Boy, *a trainee barman.*
Peter, *a young local merchant seaman.*
Sean, *a young Southern Irish seaman.*
Tug, *a cockney seaman.*
Sandy, *an English seaman*
Bill, *another English seaman*
Woman, *a Salvation Army worker.*

The curtain lifts on the deserted bar-room of the public house. A lad aged between 16 and 17 years old is slowly brushing up discarded cigarette boxes, empty crisp packets, newspapers, etc—all the paraphernalia of a busy day. He has his back turned to the audience and the bar directly in front of him is covered with dirty glasses and empty bottles.

Above the bar and directly in the centre of the back wall is a large, handwritten sign on cardboard which declares WE NOW SERVE DOUBLE XX DRAUGHT GUINNESS.

To his right is the bar door, with windows on each side. Three or four round tables, each with four or five small stools are placed across the front of the stage, spaced evenly behind him. On the wall to his left is a dartboard and framed photographs of cargo ships, either at sea or loading or unloading cargo. Across the top of the bar on a long, fly-blown, hardboard pelmet are coloured pennants and stickers from various countries. At the back of the bar, above the cash-register, a human skull swings slowly when the door is opened. It hangs sombrely on a piece of string attached to a shelf by a nail.

The boy lifts the filled ashtrays from the tables and deposits the litter on the floor, before giving the table a quick rub with his apron, then brushes all the rubbish on the floor into a neat pile. An unseen clock chimes seven times. He leans on his brush for a moment and listens to the gale-force wind as it lashes torrential rain against the bar windows. He looks at the littered bar-top.

WEE BOY Boys! they musta bin busy the day! Anyway, by the luk of that night I'll have plenty of time to clean up the place. Only an idjit wud be abroad on a night like that. [*Shrugs his shoulders and continues sweeping*]

[*Off-stage noises as the bar door to his right is banged loudly against the wall and the wind blows two capped and overcoated figures into the middle of the pub. The barman scratches his head in exasperation as the mound of rubbish is blown to every corner of the floor.*

Staggering to the bar like survivors of a shipwreck seeking a piece of flotsam, the two men loosen their overcoats and shake the rain from their caps, revealing thick heads of grey hair in the process. The tallest of the two is in his seventies. He stands erect and straight. His flat cap is tweed and his long overcoat is an ex-British army great-coat, dyed black and faded, blue denims and black wellington boots cover his legs and feet.

His companion is a smaller man, dumpy and thick set, wearing a shabby crombie overcoat and a tweed cap, both of which are black with rain. His trousers are blue serge and his laced, brown boots are scuffed and worn.]

JAMSIE [*looking quizzically over his small rounded, stainless steel National Health issue spectacles*]: Where's Francie, weeboy?

WEE BOY [*drops the brush with a defeated gesture and looks at the scattered debris as he walks behind the bar*]: He's aff sick! I'm his relief.

JAMSIE [*To his companion*]: Shure they're hirin' childer nigh Paddy. [*Suspiciously to the boy*] Niver saw you in here before.

WEE BOY [*indifferently*]: I'm from the other bar across the bridge ... The boss says it gits quiet here after six, so he reckoned I cud cope.

PADDY [*surprised*]: Shure yer only a wee boy.

WEE BOY [*mopping the bar impatiently*]: C'mon granda, what do yis want, cos I'm busy!

JAMSIE [*worriedly*]: Will Francie nat be in atall the night?

WEE BOY Naw, he's got a sore stomach. [*Nastily*] I think he wus drunk! [*He looks scornfully around the bar.*] Cudn't blame him anyway. This morgue wud put ye on the juice. It's in the arsehole of nowhere and ta crown it all the bloody TV's broke ...

PADDY [*knowingly*]: Aye. I saw it gittin' tuk away till be repaired.

WEE BOY [*impatiently*]: Right boys—shout it out! Two hot whiskies ... Two hot rums ... Shure yid need nothin' less till brave a night like that.

JAMSIE [*fumbling worriedly in his overcoat pockets*]: Aw ... [*hesitates, looks at* PADDY] Aw ... Two pintsa porter son.

WEE BOY [*pointing at the notice above and behind him*]: Double X only.

JAMSIE [*stuttering*] Where's the porter?

WEE BOY [*hands in pockets*]: I can't draw a pinta Porter

PADDY [*scowling*]: What are ye doin' behin' the bar then?

WEE BOY [*defensively*]: I kin draw a pinta Double X.

JAMSIE [*irritably*]: Shure anybody cud draw a pinta that fizz.

WEE BOY [*smugly, hands still in pockets, looks at the rainlashed windows*] Plentya pubs down the road there ... Yill git all the pintsa porter yis want.

PADDY [*angrily*]: Shure we'd needa bloody boat till git down the road!

WEE BOY [*also raising voice*]: Well, make yer mind up, cos I wanna git the floor swept an' the bar stocked an' I'm nat gonna stan' here forever.

JAMSIE [*humbly, quickly throwing coins onto the counter*]: Two pintsa Double X son.

[*Both men gasp in horror as the barman quickly jets Guinness from a nozzle into two pint tumblers, places them on the counter with a bang, rings in the money and returns to his sweeping. A silence as both men watch froth running down the sides of their tumblers.*]

JAMSIE [*grimacing*]: That's a turn up.

PADDY [*defeatedly*]: The last in a long line a setbacks.

JAMSIE [*defensively*]: How was I ta know Francie wudn't be here tonight?

PADDY [*brightening a little, and nodding hopefully towards the boy*] Maybe he'd givus strap drink if we buttered him up a bit.

JAMSIE [*snorting*]: Ha! by the luk of that wee bugger, he wudn't give a mouse a physic. [*Continuing indignantly*] When I wus his age, I wus in the trenches ...

PADDY [*interupting impatiently*]: Don't be startin' that again! [*Pauses and continues bitterly*] Here we are with nat even the prica two bottlesa Guinness atween us an' yore gonna start about vaultin' the barbed wire at Mons wie a baynet in one han' an' a empty bottle in the other. [*Turns away disgustedly, leaning one elbow on the bar and putting his head into his cupped hand.*]

JAMSIE [*stares at* PADDY, *lifts drink, takes a sip and shudders*]: Least I went ...

PADDY [*swings round quickly, angrily, rushes off bar-stool, puts his face into Mulvenna's and points at his left eye*] There's my reason Mulvenna ... This oversized marble called a glasseye an' I didn't havta go ta France till see the fightin' whot gat me that! Naw I lost it back in 1912 when some of yore boul cronies were sniping down Sussex Street firin' ball-bearings outa catapults. [*Bitterly*] I wus only a wee buck, on me bare feet running till get me da a fish supper.

JAMSIE [*shamefaced, comfortingly*] Aw, no matter what ... past glories won't fill our glasses ... an' one eye or nat ye kin see that wee lad is nat gonna be sympathetic ta the fact that today's yer birthday an' we haven't the necessary till decorate the mahogany ...

PADDY [*sullenly, still angry*]: We wuda had, if you hadn'ta stuck it on that hot favourite.

JAMSIE [*defensively*]: Shure it wus only a pittance an' I wanted till see ye celebrate yer birthday in style.

PADDY [*wearily*]: Ack a knew ye meant well, but these pints, turrible as they are, are nat gonna last too long an' that oul shade's bound till be damp an' coul ... [*Pause*] an' leakin' ... a night like that. [*He places his elbows on the bar, cups his chin in his hands and sighs heavily.*] Me birthday too ... Mandear a coupla halfins an' a wee carry out wuda made my day.

JAMSIE [*producing a briar pipe with half a stem from one of his coat pockets, fumbles again to bring out a bar of tobbacco and a small penknife. Cutting strips from the tobbacco, he thumbs them gently into the pipe bowl. Hopefully*]: Ack ... Sumpthin' 'ill turn up.

PADDY [*sadly, as* JAMSIE *puts a match to his pipe and puffs contentedly*]: Nat tanight Jamsie. That's the dirtiest weather for years, an' nobody's gonna hoof it down that long dark road when they cud nip intil the Yankee or O'Rourkes. Shure ya know yerself this pub is dead after seven.

JAMSIE [*drawing on his pipe philosopically*]: Remember Kipling ... [*Orates as* PADDY *pulls a crumpled cigarette butt from his pocket and lights it*] If you kin keep yer head while all aroun' ye are losin' theirs ...

PADDY [*interrupting*]: Niver mine our heads. How are we gonna keep these pints till closin' time?

[*Silence as* WEE BOY *walks off-stage to the store. Off-stage noises of doors opening and closing, crates scraping and bottles clinking. Both men stare quizzically at each other, then at the Guinness pump on the top of the bar.*]

PADDY [*hoarsley*]: Cud ye wurk it?

JAMSIE [*nervously lifting his tumbler, puts it under the nozzle, glancing quickly along the corridor before grabbing the pump level. Hisses*] Nuthin' beats a try. Watch for 'im.

[PADDY *nods vigorously, turns and stares intently in the direction of the store off-stage. Both men jump visibly as Guinness splatters from the pump and onto Jamsie's coat.*]

PADDY [*desperately*]: Don't fill 'em up Jamsie, don't fill 'em up, or he'll tipple.

JAMSIE [*nods knowingly; fills both tumblers three quarters full, wipes the bar-top with the sleeve of his coat, steps back and takes a long swig, before peeering down the corridor.*]: I wonder does he know about tha store door?

PADDY [*savouring his pint, absently*]: What about it?

JAMSIE [*impatiently*]: Remember last night Francie locked hisself in two or three times an' I hadda go an' let him out? [*Hits* PADDY *with his elbow in an effort to jog his memory*]

PADDY [*vaguely*]: Aye—Y' mean the way the door won't open from the inside?

JAMSIE [*nodding excitedly*]: Yis. Do ya think he knows?

PADDY [*absently, looking at rain flecked windows and puffing dreamily at his cigarette*] It's hard ta tell ... Mebbe they got it fixed.

[*Jamsie walks off-stage towards the store. Sound of door opening.*]

JAMSIE [*Voice from off-stage*]: Hi! Wee boy! Ken I help ye?

WEE BOY [*Voice from off-stage*]: I'm alright. [*Comes out of the corridor with a crate of bottles and proceeds behind the bar where he begins to stack the drink onto a shelf*]

JAMSIE [*winking at* PADDY]: D'ye think this double X 'ill ever catch on?

PADDY [*scornful*]: Nat a chance! [*Spitting some out*] Shure it tastes like soapy water.

JAMSIE [*conversationally, leaning across the bar*]: What d'ye think, wee boy?

WEE BOY [*Turns to them, looks at them sarcastically*]: Arthur Guinness won't git rich they way youse two's nibblin' at it.

PADDY [*nostalgically*]: 'Member oul Joe in the American Bar pullin' a pint ... Man, but he wus an expert. [*He steps back a pace, mimicking a barman holding a pint tumbler*] He worked outa three or four barrelsa porter, some fresh or high, some flat. He'd pour a little drop from each barrel intil yer tumbler until it was overflowing, then he'd wipe the foam off the top with a straight edge [PADDY *mimics the action as he speaks*] then he'd let it sit. [*Puts the tumbler on the bar, places his hands behind his back and paces slowly up and down the bar, stopping now and again to peer closely and critically at the glass*]

PADDY Joe would continue to walk up and down like a dentist

waiting on an anaesthetic to take effect. [*Walking*] Up an' down ... Up an' down ... or, [*laughing*] an' mebbe the pore fella whut ordered it, dyin' of thirst in the meantime ...

JAMSIE [*interupting, laughing*]: Aye! Do ye remember thon bad stutter he had? [*Mimics*] Y've ggggatta wwwait ooon aggggooood pppintt ... [*Laughing heartily*] It tuk him near as long ta git the sentence out as it did ta pull the pint. [*Soberly*] He wus some pup. [*Looking scathingly at the young fellow*] Pity we'll niver see his likes agin. [*Both men laugh at the recollection.*]

PADDY: Nowadays: [*working an imaginary lever*] Blurp blurp, two seconds ... there's yer pint ... all shadowy an' bubbly ... Like a glassa dirty water ... [*soberly*] Yill never need a physic if this thing catches on. An' if it's that easy there'll soon be wimmin behin' the bar, doin' up their faces an' listenin' till what we're saying an' watchin' every move.

PADDY [*shuddering, raising eyes skywards*]: Heaven forbid.

WEE BOY [*yawning*]: All our yisterdays.

JAMSIE [*reciting*]: Yesterday, taday an' tamarra, all our yisterdays on the road till dusty death. [*Puts his pipe in his mouth and nods at* PADDY *knowingly*] That's Shakespeare.

PADDY [*shaking his head sadly*]: Them bloody books is gonna put ye in the nuthouse.

JAMSIE [*steps back sharply, looks at his friend and roars*]: Niver! Niver! The best friend a man has are his books. [*Warmly, leaning closer to* PADDY] My father was continually tellin' me niver till read anythin' I cudn't lern from. Knowledge is chaper than soap he used to say. Nobody has an excuse ta be dirty ... An' there's even less reason till be ignorant. The pages of a book are ever open. Ever willin' till spread their knowledge till those that want it. Just a wee flip a yer finger Pat an' there's the wisdom of the ages. Millions of people kin educate themselves from books an' still lave the pages intact for generations ta come. [*He stabs the air with his pipe-stem.*] An' Paddy ... it's easy carried [*points to his head*] There's no height or depth till the learnin' ye kin cram inta that wee space an' it's all near enuff for free up in the library. If ye kin read atall ... there's a wealth of information an' facts all lyin' up there, waitin' till be harvested.

PADDY [*slowly, sadly*]: If yore so smart, how cum we're in here tryin' till bum drink ... [*disparagingly*] Naw! niver min' the knowledge. It still takes money till buy drink!

JAMSIE [*disregarding*]: Paddy, it's a great place. First time I went up till it I wus so impressed I wrote a wee pome about it ... Do ye wanta hear it?

WEE BOY [*puts his hands on head*]: Aw no!

JAMSIE [*ignores this gesture, takes Paddy's silence for approval, clears his throat loudly and begins to recite.*]: The Belfast Public Librahe, [*self-consciously*] by James Mulvenna. Ghost ta Ghost! It wus a wondrous day. The day I joined the libraeh. The bards of the wurld were in full array ... In the Belfast Public Libraeh!

I wandered aroun' this hallowed hall, lined with tomes on every wall. No finer sight cud I recall then the Belfast Public Libraeh. [*He pauses for effect and takes a swig of Guinness.*] Shelley's side by side with Yates ... Shaw ... O'Casey ... all the greats ... Shakesphere, Byron, Whitman sleeps ... in the Belfast Public Libraeh.

For a mere half-crown I kin rent out three of these books that mean so much to me ... Joyce, O'Neill and Thackeree ... In the Belfast Public Libraeh!

[*He draws pensively on his pipe, relishing the memory.*]

I drink their wurds like a cat laps milk, their poems and prose are honey an' silk. I stud engrossed till the enda day ... In the Belfast Public Libraeh. With this wealth of words in fronta me, I murmur just one heartfelt plea ...

[*Earnestly clasps his hands*]

Let me stay till I'm ninety-three ... In the Belfast Public Libraeh. [*He takes a long, deep draught of Guinness, anticipating applause that doesn't come.*]

WEE BOY [*sarcastically*]: Hi Shakesphere, are ye buyin' anymore drink! If yer any longer over that one yill be lifted for loiterin'.

JAMSIE [*leans over the bar, beckons the lad to come closer, whispers humbly*]: Luk son, it's me mate's birthday an' we thought Francie wuda been here. [*Confiding*] He wud give us drink on tick when we're broke. [*Humbly*] I wus wonderin' if you would care ta carry on the same arrangement?

PADDY [*coaxingly*]: Aye, nuthin' much. Just a wee sumpthin ta help us sleep an' fergit about the rats.

WEE BOY [*absently, looking at the glasses he is washing in the sink*]: Rats?
PADDY [*enthusiastically*]: Shure there's stacks of 'em ... All shapes an' sizes ... The minit the shade pilot lights go out about three in the mornin', they cum up from below the dock ... Hundreds of 'em ... an' when yer sober y'kin hear them crawlin' an' scrapin' all over the place.
WEE BOY [*shuddering*]: Do they go near ye?
JAMSIE [*warmly*]: Aye ... Sometimes ... I remember one night I'd a bara chaclate, I wus keepin' for later ... I wus full. Anyway, next mornin' all I had wus silver paper. Bloody rat gat inta my pocket an' scoffed the lat. [*Takes a small sip from his glass*] Then there wus the one that gnawed its way through the toe of John Doherty's water-boot, through his sock [*incredulously*] till it got clean through till his big toe an' started eatin' it?
WEE BOY [*horrified, stops washing*]: Did he nat feel it?
PADDY [*laughing*]: Lucky fer him it wus his artificial leg. When he woke up the next mornin' the big shiny toe wus stickin' outa his boot.
WEE BOY [*resumes washing: huffily*]: Don't believe it!
JAMSIE [*puffing thoughtfully*]: It's true. Shure there wus one on the run in the big Dufferin for a long time. It wus fifty years old when they finally got it.
WEE BOY [*innocently*]: How'd they know wut age it wus?
JAMSIE [*dancing with merriment*]: It's birth certificate wus stickin' outa its arse!
WEE BOY [*drops washing cloth in sink*]: No tick! [*Resumes stacking bottles.*]
JAMSIE [*face falling, puffs angrily*]: No sensa humer.
PADDY [*in a raging whisper*]: I had him softened, an' y'hadda crack a joke as oul as yer grannie's granda! [*Stands up dejectedly*] C'mon, we might as well finish these pints an' go over till the shade ... We're floggin' a ded horse here.
[WEE BOY *rises from the shelves, lifts the swinging skull and sets it on the bar-top, at Paddy's elbow. He lights a cigarette, takes a long draw and places the lighted end of the cigarette into the mouth of the skull. Two red balls have been wedged into the eye sockets. Soon smoke begins to waft through the open nostrils. A silence ensues, broken only by the howling wind and the rain pelting the windows.*]
PADDY [*eying the skull uncomfortably*]: Mustya put it there?

WEE BOY [*grinning at Paddy's discomfort.*]: Shure it'll do ya no harm.
PADDY [*sharply, indignantly*]: It's lukin' down my throat!
WEE BOY [*derisively*]: Don't talk daft!
JAMSIE [*agreeing*]: Shure how cud it luk down yer throat when it's gat no eyes!
PADDY [*Lifts his drink and turns his back on the skull; scowls*]: It's nat right anyway till keep a thing like that about the place ... It's obscene lukin' ... It shuda bin buried along with the rest of the poor devil it belongs ta.

[JAMSIE, *unseen by* PADDY, *impishly picks up the skull and places it at Paddy's shoulder. He taps Paddy's back softly.* PADDY *turns slowly.*]

JAMSIE [*laughing at Paddy's frozen expression*]: He wants ta buy ye a drink!

[PADDY, *screaming with fright swings his elbow and knocks the skull from Jamsie's hand into the air, and cringes, eyes closed, hands over his ears.* JAMSIE *deftly catches it, retrieves the fallen cigarette, places the skull on the bar and replaces the cigarette.*]

JAMSIE [*mockingly*]: Y'mighta busted his haid.
PADDY [*angrily*]: Bloody blasphemy! How cud a man rest in peace when his mouth's bein' used for an ashtray an' there's wee red balls stuck in his eye sockets. [*Pauses, breathless*] Does any budy even know who he is?
JAMSIE [*grinning sidelong at the barman*]: Aye. He drunk three pintsa his Double X three weeks ago.

[WEE BOY *stares at the rain-swept windows; says nothing*]

PADDY [*after a soul-searching silence*]: It's nat right Jamsie ... Ta keep a man's skull in sucha place ... How cud he rest in pace?
JAMSIE [*exasperated, loudly*]: Rest in pace? [*Waves his pipe in the air*] Where do ya think he is? Sitting up on a cloud somewhere wi' a wee white shroud on 'im an' playin' a harp? [*Excitedly*] Natatall ... Natatall. He's down a hole somewhere, if he's lucky. Rotting away an' nat a bit worried about his skull. [*He cants his head to the side and recites.*] Golden girls an' lads all must, as chimbly sweepers cum ta dust!
WEE BOY [*scornfully, at* JAMSIE]: Yule nat have long till find out.
JAMSIE [*sarcastically*]: If I wus six months ded, I'd be a better man than yew. [*Turns earnestly to* PADDY] I seen better men than him on the business enda my baynet.

PADDY [*worriedly*]: Min' yer blood pressure, Jamsie.

WEE BOY [*still grinning, puts his hand to his chin and pretends to screw it off with exaggerated movement of the hand.*] I'd better put this in me pocket. [*He takes the cigarette from the skull's mouth and puts it in his own, takes a long draw. Expelling the smoke slowly, he speaks mockingly to the old men.*] For two hard drinkin' men yis are sure takin' yer time over them pints ... Yis must be lettin' on till swallow it an' spittin' it back in the glass agin. [*Scratches his head, puzzled*] 'Cos I swear the level is rising in them tumblers.

PADDY [*hastily*] There's no law says we havta hurry our drinks.

[WEE BOY *ignores this and resumes washing glasses.*]

JAMSIE [*softly*]: Shure y'wudn't begrudge us a wee bita hate before we go out inta that. [*Pointing at the window and the weather.* WEE BOY *raises arms and plays an imaginary violin.*]

PADDY [*shrugs lamely, sighs*]: Heaven help us.

[*At that moment, off-stage noises, then door opens and a small dumpy* WOMAN *wearing a clear plastic mac over a Salvation Army uniform, clutching an umbrella in one hand and a collection box in the other is blown into the centre of the bar. The small mound of rubbish is blown around the bar-room.*]

JAMSIE [*glaring at* PADDY]: That wus a quick answer till yer prayer. [*Scowls, whispers to* PADDY] A bloody woman ... That's all we need. [*Gropes in his trouser pocket*] Y'kin refuse a man without feelin' embarrassed.

[WOMAN *moves towards them, smiling.*]

PADDY [*dejectedly*]: If the bloody TV had bin here we cuda ignored her.

WOMAN [*extending collection box*]: Would you care to donate something to help us continue with the work of the Lord?

PADDY [*throws a couple of coins into the box*]: That's mi lot, sister.

JAMSIE [*scowling*]: There's threedee. [*Puzzled*] What brings ye out ona night like that, daughter?

WOMAN [*smiling radiantly up into Jamsie's face*]: The work of the Lord must go on.

JAMSIE [*caringly*]: Shure y'cud git pleurisy.

[WOMAN *shakes the box at the barman who ignores her.*]

WOMAN [*agreeing*]: Yes, it is a savage night, and I'm afraid I haven't furthered the Lord's Cause very much. [*Looks around the bar, shakes her head*] Most of the Dock pubs are empty tonight. [*Smiling*] You gentlemen seem to have come far for your refreshments tonight.

PADDY [*gently*]: We wurk in the shade across the road, mum; we're just nursing these pints so we kin remain a little longer in the hate before we go out inta that. [*Pointing at weather beyond the door.* WEE BOY *mimics playing a violin whilst* JAMSIE *scowls into his pint. The* WOMAN *smiles understandingly, reaches below her pac-a-mac and produces a copy of* The War Cry *which she reaches to* PADDY.]

PADDY [*apologetically*]: No thanks mum, I'm a Catholic.

JAMSIE [*irritably, snatching paper*]: I'll do the crossword in it.

PADDY [*sneering*]: Thought y'were an atheist?

JAMSIE [*defiantly*]: I am!

WOMAN [*shocked*]: Come now, that's a harsh declaration.

PADDY [*helpfully*]: Jamsie, his name's Jamsie.

WOMAN [*looking at* JAMSIE]: Do you read the Bible?

JAMSIE [*defiantly*]: Aye! Inside an' out and back till front. I read it when I want a good laugh! It's better'n *The Beano*.

PADDY [*fearfully*]: That's blasphemy. [*To the* WOMAN] Awk missus, don't start 'im ... He puts the feara God inta me over in that shade some nights.

JAMSIE [*scowling*]: How cud I put the fear a God intil ye when I don't believe in Him? [*Turns to* WOMAN] Missus y'mightn't believe it, but I've got a tea-chest over in the shade an' it's fulla classical literature ... *War and Peace*, *Crime and Punishment*, *Les Misérables*, *Hunchback of Nôtre Dame* an' a whole pile a others besides ... An' the Bible. An' y'know, there's more sense in the comic cuts than there is in that. [*Puts pipe firmly into mouth*]

WOMAN [*softly*]: You must have had a terrible experience to become so bitter.

JAMSIE [*haltingly*]: Missus, did ye ever hear of the battle of the Somme? [WOMAN *nods her head silently.*]

JAMSIE [*reflectively*]: The Somme! The one hell-hole on God's earth where he shuda bin ... [*Bitterly*] But he wasn't. [*Grimly*] Murder ... [*Shaking his head violently as if reliving a nightmare*] It wus murder! [*Defiantly*] Aye! An' I wus doin' soma the murderin'. [*Visibly emotional*] Fight, then pray! It wus death all the way ... At the Battle a the Somme.

WOMAN [*reaches out and holds his arm tenderly. Speaks softly*]: Did you pray hard, Jamsie?

JAMSIE [*sighing*]: Aye! But a foughta damn sight harder ... That's why I'm still here.

PADDY [*thoughtfully*]: A did a lotta prayin' meself ... [*Takes a sip from his pint*]

JAMSIE [*snorting*]: Yew were never at the Somme!

PADDY [*hotly*]: No! An' I tole ye the reasin for that a while ago. But a did a hanful a years on the Russian Convoys during the Second War.

JAMSIE [*disbelievingly*]: Shure yev only one eye an' yida bin too oul.

PADDY [*laughing*]: Jamsie, yew don't need two eyes till shovel coal intil a boiler. I wus about forty-five. [*Seriously*] I ploughed the sea for about thirty years an' the duration of the war.

JAMSIE [*embarrassed*]: A knew ye went ta sea, but a didn't know yid war service.

WEE BOY [*pointedly*]: Nat every body blabbers about it like yew do.

[*All ignore him as the* WOMAN *looks at* PADDY.]

WOMAN It seems you never lost your trust in God.

PADDY [*reflectively*]: No! But I niver saw the carnage he did, nor felt his fear. All I saw was an open furnace scowlin' for coal.

WOMAN [*to* JAMSIE]: It must have been horrible to destroy your faith in the Lord.

JAMSIE [*remembering*]: There wus one hellish July mornin', over three-an'-a-half-thousand men were killed. Seven lads I joined with, we all lived in the same street, are still over there fertilizing the French soil. [*He looks at* PADDY, *then at the skull and grins grimly*] Like yer friend there [*Pointing at the skull*] many were buried in bits and pieces. Some we cud'nt find anythin' of to bury. Other times a gasmask with the head still in it or a boot still containing a foot or a leg. [*Excitedly*] Pieces of burnin' dismembered flesh everywhere. We ran forward too fast ... fought too hard ... covered too much ground. Our flanks fell behind an' exposed us to murderous crossfire. [*Grimly*] We took our objective all right, but there wusn't enuff of us left ta hold it ... [*He raises his tumbler and looks to the floor. Says simply*] Fallen Comrades!

WOMAN [*softly*]: A lot of men found God in the trenches.

JAMSIE [*growling*]: It wusn't for the wanta tryin. I lay for six hours prayin' for death in scorchin' sunlight with an empty waterbottle an' a dead German on tapa me. His baynet was clean through my left side an' inta the mud beneath.

PADDY [*soothingly*]: Tell her that poem y'writ about France.

JAMSIE [*shyly*]: Aye! Alright. [*Screws up his face reflectively*]: Ifakin remember it.

WEE BOY [*rolling his eyes skywards*]: Yew shuda bin on the stage Granda. [*All ignore him.*]

JAMSIE: 'They didn't tell ya Tommy' [*Self-conscious pause*] by James Mulvenna. [*Deep breath*]

Takin' the King's shillin' yew foun' was, oh so thrillin'
an' yew were proud ta wear the khaki grey.
The uniform got glances and many more romances
than those pore blokes whot cud'nt git away.
Enflamed with thoughtsa battle,
yew kin hear the cannons rattle
as yew rush ta git yer teeth inta the Hun. [*Short pause*]
But when y'got till France
an' saw death's indulgent dance ... [*Grimly*]
The only thing yew thought ta do was run!
[*Feelingly*] They didn't tell ya Tommy,
there'd be no place y'cud hide
or put yer weary head in needa sleep.
They didn't tell ya Tommy,
yid have nightmares till y'died ...
with corpses scattered roun'
like slaughtered sheep.
[*Warmly*] 'Goodbye Dolly Gray' was the ballad of the day
as yew marched ta kill a Fritz yid niver seen.
Ya went a lively lad;
fulla fight an' more than glad
of the chance till serve yer country an' yer King.
[*Softly*] They didn't tell ya Tommy,
yid be at the front for weeks
yer face pressed in the mud ta dodge the fire.
They didn't tell ya Tommy, how a shell-torn buddy reeks
as his body decomposes on the wire.

[*Bitterly*] They said yew'd be a hero,
when yew went marchin' home.
They said yew'd be the darlin' of the day.
Yew'd be singin' 'Tipperary'
an' 'Mary. My Sweet Mary' ...
All thoughts af war an' death seemed far away.
[*Softly, slowly and sadly*]
They didn't tell ya Tommy,
how a dum-dum, when it hits,
kin nip a handsome saplin' in the bud ...
They didn't tell ya nuthin' son, about the dirty bits ...
[*Savagely*] Like dyin' in the filthy Mamatz mud!
[*He thumps his tumbler down heavily, obviously moved by bitter memories.*]

WOMAN [*thoughtfully, quietly*]: The wisdom of God surpasses all understanding. We are in the palm of His caring hand. He loves us. For six days He toiled and made the Universe and all that in it is. On the seventh day, He rested. Blessed be the name of the Lord.

JAMSIE [*Looks at her in silence for a moment as if wrestling with his conscience. Sighs heavily and jabs the air with his pipe.*]: Sister, far be it from me ta call yew a liar, but as an atheist, I just cudn't let that statement go unchallenged. Here's a few facts I'd like ye ta hear, [*emphasises*] facts, nat fables. [*Goes on quickly*] This universe yer talkin' about. For a long time it wus thought by astronomers that our galaxy represented the whole of the universe, [*Looks pointedly at the* WOMAN] creation yew wud call it, but aroun' 1925, it wus proved, an' I'll nat go inta details, that there are other huge galaxies out there. [*Waves expansively towards the ceiling*] Some of them are as large as our own. In fact, it's almost impossible ta imagine the size an' extent of the universe we now know exists ...

WOMAN [*interrupting*]: What has this got to do with the Bible?

JAMSIE [*gives her an old-fashioned look, like a schoolmaster chastising a dim pupil*]: Paddy! Git me a bita chalk from that dartboard.
[PADDY *moves slowly to the dart board and returns with a stick of chalk. Gives it to* JAMSIE.]

JAMSIE [*a trifle impatiently*]: Now luk! I'll break it down for yeas simply as I can. [*Hunches down and draws a rough circle about six feet in diameter. In the centre of the circle he places a dot with his chalk.*]

JAMSIE [*peering up at the* WOMAN *and* PADDY *over the rim of his glasses. He points from the outer line of the circle to the dot in the middle.*] From there till there is ten million light-years in distance. In other wurds, till go from there till there [*Pointing*] wud take a space traveller ten million light years. [*He smiles briefly at the blank faces, rubs his jaw thoughtfully and studies the circle.*] Nigh, how can I translate that statement? [*Hesitates, as if doing a quick sum in his head.*] It's estimated that light travels at the speed of one hundred and eighty-six thousand miles per second ... So a light-year equals a distance of three million, one hundred an' forty-four thousand, nine hundred an' sixty miles. That's one light year ... Now think of that figure multiplied ten million times. It's reckoned the furthest point in the universe is six thousand million, million miles away from earth.

PADDY [*looking punch-drunk*]: I wudn't fancy signin' on ta shovel the coal for that trip. How oul is the world anyway Jim?

JAMSIE About ten thousand million years. [*He looks at the* WOMAN *pointedly.*] A bit oulder than Christanity ... Anyway. [*He looks at the barman.*] Givus a handfula tin-taps wee boy.

[*The lad reluctantly hands over the bottle-tops.*]

JAMSIE [*selects one, holds it between his thumb and forefinger, looks at the* WOMAN]: We'll begin with the major planet, if you cud truthfully call it that ... It's actually a star. It partakes a galactic rotation travelling 'roun' the centre of the Galaxy movin' about one hundred an' fifty miles per second every two hundred million years. But that's by the way.

PADDY [*open-mouthed*]: Aye! Go on.

JAMSIE [*places the bottle top, selects another*]: Next, the moon [*Swiftly placing top*] Mercury, Venus, Mars, Jupiter, Saturn, Uranus, Neptune and Pluto, [*as he identifies each planet he places a bottle top in the circle. Stands up, dusts his hands on his coat.*] Right! That's the galaxy we live in. Now outside a that there are millions of galaxies comparable to our own. The nearest to us is the Virgo cluster with over two-and-a-half thousand galaxies similiar to our own, an' over two million miles away ... [*Thumping the air with his pipe, voice raising to a shout*] an' that's the nearest. The furthest is Ursa Major, estimated at one thousand million light-years away.

PADDY [*lamely*]: What's yer point?

JAMSIE [*angrily*]: What's my point? Some of the furthest stars observed are reckoned to be eighteen hundred light years in space [*Shouts*] The whole galaxy is believed to be [*He waves his foot across the circle over the tops*] one hundred thousand light-years across [*looks furiously at the bottle tops*] an' yew mane ta tell me somebody made all that in six days. [*Laughing scornfully, and much to* WEE BOY'S *displeasure, he kicks the bottle tops all over the floor and returns to his pint. A few seconds silence broken only by the roar of the storm and rain.*]

PADDY [*evasively*]: That's all very well. But how are ye gonna prove all that mumbo-jumbo. Shure yew might as well have bin conversin' in double Dutch ... all them big words an' millionsa miles.

JAMSIE [*tiredly and philosophically, looks to the ceiling*]: Oh the curse of the great unwashed.

WOMAN: You surely put forth a good argument, but like all atheists, I believe you are secretly striving to convince yourself of God's existence. Our faith is simple and basic. If the Bible says God did it ... then He did it. Believe that Jamsie and that's the beginning of faith. [JAMSIE *mumbles incoherently under his breath.* WOMAN *looks at the rain-specked windows.*] I must be going now. [*Apologetically*] I won't say a prayer, but if you don't mind I'll leave you with an appropriate hymn. [*Stands erect. Both men doff their caps and stand stiffly, heads bowed, staring self-consciously at the floor.* WOMAN *sings a cappella except for the sound of the wind and rain.*]

Bless this house Oh Lord we pray,
make it safe by night and day.
Bless these walls so firm and stout
keeping want and trouble out.
Bless the roof and chimney tall,
let thy peace lie over all.
Bless this door, that it may be,
ever open to joy and love.

Bless the shining windows bright,
Letting in God's heavenly light.
Bless the hearth ablazing there
with smoke ascending like a prayer.
Bless the folk who dwell within,
keep them free and pure from sin.
Bless us all that we one day,
May dwell Oh Lord with Thee.
[*Repeats second verse. Both men applaud warmly, as* WOMAN *moves to the door,* JAMSIE *takes her arm.*]

JAMSIE [*haltingly*]: Sister ... I know I'm outa order but I'm disprit. It's me mate's birthday and we haven't the pricea another drink. Cud ye sub is a few bob till next week. We'll lave it behin' the bar for ye.

WOMAN [*shaking her head negatively and smiling gently*]: If it was for food I'd be happy, but it would be wrong for me to give you money for alcohol.

JAMSIE [*accepts defeat gracefully, touches his cap in salute*]: I understan' missus.

WOMAN [*softly, as she takes his hand*]: Go back to God, Jamsie [*Looks at the strewn bottle tops*] These parlour games won't help your inadequacy. Don't shut Him out with clever verbiage.

JAMSIE [*humbly*]: Ack, I'm too oul nigh an' I've done too much depredation. It wud be like givin' someone yew luv a bunch a withered fliers.

WOMAN [*moves to door, opens it and turns to the men*]: God loves you ... All of you. [*Door closes as she vanishes into the night.*]

WEE BOY [*scoffing loudly*]: Bate again, granda. Y'haven't wona roun' the night. [*Unbelievably*] Imagine tappin' the Sally Ann Woman. How desperate kin ye git? [*He laughs loudly as he walks around the bar toward the store as* JAMSIE *scowls into his pint.*]

PADDY [*sadly, looking at his almost empty tumbler*]: Nuthin' else for it but ta go over ta the shade.

PADDY [*angrily*]: If yew think I'm gonna let that wee gab-shite git the better a me ... [*He stops in mid-sentence and lifts Paddy's glass to the pump.*] Here! Quick while he's away.

[JAMSIE *is filling the tumblers when off-stage and outside the bar is heard the noise of car doors slamming and men's voices in laughter. In a few seconds five men walk into the centre of the bar-room, look around a second or two before moving to a table under a window and sitting down.* WEE BOY *returns and only his interest in the men prevents him from catching* JAMSIE *red-handed at the Guinness pump. Chairs scrape the floor as the men sit down noisily.*]

PADDY [*wheezing with fear*]: Ack boy a thought ye were caught that time.

JAMSIE [*frantically wiping froth from his coat sleeve*]: Aye! I haven't sweated like that since the last time I toiled in the houl of a tatie boat.

[WEE BOY *goes behind the bar as the men noisily shout out their pleasure to a young man who steps up to the bar. As he arrives a strongly accented Southern Irish brogue calls from the table.*]

SEAN [*loudly*]: Pater! do ye nead a han'?

PETER [*turns and replies in a strong Belfast accent*]: Naw Sean a'm dead-on. [*Turns to speak to the barman*] Givus three double scotch, two double vodkas, five white lemonades and five Tuborg Golds. [*Looks at the old men who are smiling sweetly in his direction. He shyly smiles back before adding to barman*] an' one fer yerself.

[WEE BOY *nods approval and continues to set up the drinks.*]

PETER [*conversationally, to* JAMSIE]: Nat many in.

PADDY [*explaining*]: Aye! It's a docker's pub. Does most of its trade durin' the day.

JAMSIE [*head canted, looks quizzically at the seaman*]: Are ye local son?

PETER [*proudly*]: Aye. Sandy Row. I signed aff the day an' I brought me shipmates down for a farewell drink.

PADDY [*casually, eyeing the drinks being set up*]: Turible night.

PETER [*smiling*]: Aye. We gota taxi till the dure an' we're still soakin'. We tole 'im till cum back about half-ten.

PADDY [*as* WEE BOY *sets up the drinks*]: Shure that ud be time enuff. [*Sighs deeply*] Man I used ta love being a homeward bounder.

PETER [*interested*]: Whor ye a sailer yerself?

PADDY[*shyly*]: Aye!

JAMSIE [*proudly*]: He wus on the Russian convoys durin' the war!

PETER [*shakes his head*]: Boys! I'll bet that wus rough.

PADDY [*remembering*]: Ack it wus grate when ya got home, [*sighs*] but the goin' away was the boyo. We used ta go out via the

Heysham boat. The wife an' the kids used to go with me as far as the shade gates ... [*Pauses, recollecting*] Do ya know when we were walkin' down York Street ... It wuda tuk a tear from a stone. [*Looking at* JAMSIE] Y'know, wondering if yud ever see it or yer family again.

JAMSIE [*nostalgically*]: I know exactly how ya feel. Here's a wee pome I wrote years ago when I wus on a troop ship heading for the Western front. It sorta sums up what yer sayin'. It's called 'Song Of An Exile'.

[WEE BOY *screws his face up as he carries the drinks to the table.* JAMSIE *steps back from the bar and goes straight into the verse.*]

Did ya ever walk down York Street
when the rain is swirlin' down
an' the street is so deserted
yew kin see right inta town.
[*Smiling affectionately*] Yew kin see the Co's big buildin',
Yew kin see the hawker's stall ...
If it wusn't for the rain-clouds
y'cud see the City Hall.
Did yew ever walk down York Street
when the snow is swirlin' down
an' the young lads grab the doffers
an' throw 'em ta the groun',
an' belt 'em all with snowballs
or shove snow down their backs...
When all is white an' covered,
except the trammy-tracks.
Did yew ever walk down York Street
when the sun is shinin' bright,
an' if yer down by Gallahers
an' if the time is right,
The street is filled with lassies
an' every one a queen ...
Lukin' so resplendant
in their smocks of emerald green.
[*Hesitates, then continues sadly*]
Didya ever walk down York Street,
headin' fora ship

an' breathe its air in deeply,
an' feel a tear-drop slip.
I did the day I left it.
Though I've roamed the world I fine ...
In rain or snow or sunshine ... My street is on my mine ...
[PADDY *and* PETER *applaud.*]

PETER [*dreamily*]: Aye! That goes till the heart af it.

JAMSIE [*shyly*]: I'm glad ye liked it. [*Looks pointedly at* PETER *and rubs his throat.*] That declaimin' doesn't half make ye thirsty!

PETER [*warmly, looking at the diminished pints*]: Wud yis like a wee drink yerselves? Somethin' a bit warmer thin coul porter?

JAMSIE [*smiling demurely*]: I wudn't min' a wee rum an' Paddy 'ill hav' a scotch.

PETER: Do yis want a mixer?

JAMSIE [*smiling gratefully*]: Naw, jist a wee drapa water.

PETER [*admiringly*]: Youse are real men. [*To barman who has returned to the back of the bar*] A wee rum an' a scotch.

SEAN [*in a strong southern-Irish brogue from the table*]: Hi Peter I thought you were gonna have a drink wid us?

PETER [*moving backwards*]: Aye mate! I wus just talkin' till the oul-timers.

SEAN [*loudly to barman*]: Set 'im up again son ... [*Pause*] an' one fer yerself.

[WEE BOY *rings in Peter's money and gives him his change. He begins to set up Sean's order. He delivers this and returns to the bar scratching his head.*]

WEE BOY [*to himself*]: I'll need more lemonade.

JAMSIE [*eagerly*]: Shure me an' Paddy'll git it fer ye.

WEE BOY [*sourly*]: I'll git it meself.

JAMSIE [*persuasively*]: Well, I'll help ye. Am goin' down till the bogs anyway.

WEE BOY [*reluctantly*]: Aye! Alright. [JAMSIE *leaves.*]

VOICE FROM THE TABLE:. Same again barman an' one fer yerself...

[WEE BOY *begins to set up the order.* JAMSIE *emerges from the passage with his coat up over his head, pulls it down to normal position and wipes off visible rain.*]

JAMSIE [*enviously eyeing the drink-laden table*]: Has he nat set up our drink yet? [PADDY *shakes his head slowly.*]

JAMSIE [*looks at* WEE BOY, *smiles apologetically, and purrs*]: Did yew fergit our drink wee boy?

WEE BOY [*without looking up*]: Yis! I did!

JAMSIE [*smiling patronisingly*]: Ack shure yew can't think of everythin'. [*Pauses for a second*] I'll hava wee dark rum an' ...

WEE BOY [*abruptly*]: Can't.

PADDY [*impatiently*]: But the sailor ordered them!

WEE BOY [*smugly*]: But he didn't pay for 'em. [*Smiling sarcastically*] I fergat ta take the money for 'em.

JAMSIE [*angrily*]: I bet ye tuk the money fer yer own drink, ye wee bollocks ye.

WEE BOY [*laughing*]: Naturally! [*Looks at their half-filled glasses*] Are youse still on the same pints? [*Points at the seamen*] Them fellas is only in an' they've spilt more than youse hav drunk!

PADDY [*whining; frightened of being slung out into the elements*]:Ack son, we're just tryin' till keep warm an' dry as long as possible.

VOICE FROM THE TABLE: Same again son! An' one fer yerself.

JAMSIE [*scornfully to* PADDY *as the boy starts to set up the seamen's order*] Ball-licker!

PADDY [*angrily*]: No worse than yew. [*Steps back a pace, mimicking*] Aye son! Yis son ... I'll git the lemenade fer ye ... I'll houl the dure fer ye.

JAMSIE [*waits until the lad walks to the table, then grabs* PADDY *by the arms, and places a cautionary finger on his own lips and speaks sternly*] Hush! That's nat ball-lickin'! That's my trump card. The coup de grâce which I wusn't gonna deliver, but that wee upstart is gonna learn he's walkin' on a minefield when he insults Jamsie Mulvenna.

VOICE FROM THE TABLE: Same again son an' yerself.

JAMSIE [*as the lad moves to the table to pick up empties*]: I've bin settin' it up all night Paddy ... I wusn't gonna do it, but now it's him an' me. [*Glaring fiercely at Wee Boy's back*] He won't even let 'em come till the bar nigh, so that manes the boys won't git us a drink, an' if we go over there, he'll throw us out fer moochin'.

PADDY [*moaning, hands on head.*]: Ack we're bate Jamsie. We may go over till the shade 'cause there'll be no livewires in here the night.

JAMSIE [*grinning*] Remember Kiplin': If yew kin meet wid triumph an' disaster an' treat those two imposters just the same.

VOICE FROM THE TABLE: Same again son an' one fer yerself.

PADDY [*enviously*] They're orderin' faster than their drinkin'. All doubles.

JAMSIE [*winking*]: Aye! Shure yew know what sailors are.

[*The barman goes to the table with the order.* JAMSIE *steps lightly to the centre of the bar-room floor.*]

JAMSIE [*to* WEE BOY, *loud enough for the sailors to hear*]: Is it alright if I give a wee number?

[*The barman's negative answer is drowned out by the roar of approval from the table.*]

JAMSIE [*cupping one ear with his right hand begins to sing*]: There wus fiendyins ta the lef' an' fiendyins till the right ...

PADDY [*jumping angrily off his stool*]: I'm nat havin' that ... [*Runs at* JAMSIE.]

WEE BOY [*leaping between them*]: No party songs.

JAMSIE [*raises his fists and looks to the ceiling, shouts*]: Till Hell wid the Republic.

PADDY [*astonished*]: Jamsie! havya taken lave a yer senses? I always thought ye were a good socialist ...

JAMSIE [*viciously to* PADDY]: Shut yer face popehead. It's apity the boyos didn't put the boll-bern' between yer eyes, that 'uda made one less till vote us intil a banana Republic.

[PADDY *walks determinedly to the middle of the room. Facing* JAMSIE *he starts to take his overcoat off.*]

PADDY [*grimly*]: Defend yersel' ya Orange bigot!

[*The barman rushes forward, grabs* PADDY *roughly and begins to bundle him to the door.*]

WEE BOY [*to* PADDY]: Right oul fella, it's out fer yew. Fer the price af two pints yev turned this place intil a doss-house an' a poetry recital. An' nigh, till crown it out yis wanta fight! [*Shakes his head knowingly*] Pints an' politics niver mix.

JAMSIE [*agitated, to barman*]: If I wus a younger man yew wudn't git till trate me mate like that. [*Loudly, towards sailors*] He wus on the Russian convoys, dodgin' subermarines an' icebergs fer longer than that wee shit's bin in long trousers. [*To* PADDY, *quickly, pleadingly*] Paddy ... I'm sorry ... sorry. I wus outa order! [*Tapping his head*] Forgive me mate! I musta had a brainsturm.

SEAN [*rising shakily to his feet, in a slurred voice*]: Lave the oul fella alone.

[111]

WEE BOY [*reasonably*]: He's just an' oul troublemaker Sean.

SEAN [*swaying, staying upright despite efforts by his companions to pull him back to his seat, points to* JAMSIE]: It's that oul Orange bastard ye shud be throwin out.

JAMSIE [*laughing defiantly*]: Aye! Orange an' proud af it!

WEE BOY [*yelling nervously*]: Yore next, granda!

SEAN [*drunkenly*]: Nigh yer talkin'!

PETER [*annoyed, drunkenly*]: Sit down Sean. [*To other seamen*] See if yis kin talk till him lads!

SEAN [*to* PETER, *sarcastically*]: Oh Aye. Sandy Row man stannin' up fer King Billy.

PETER [*heatedly*]: I'm nat stannin' up fer anyone. It's a storm ina tay cup ... Shure the oul lads are buddies ... Pals ... It's nuthin till do wid us.

SEAN [*nastily*]: Youse Prods are all the same! Think yis own the North.

PETER [*rising menacingly*]: We don't think it! We know it! An' youse kulshimucks 'ill niver git yer han's on it.

TUG [*looking woriedly at his other companions, then at* PETER *and* SEAN]: Easy boys.

[*The barman remains still. He continues to hold* PADDY *but is undecided as to what to do.*]

JAMSIE [*rushing forward, waving arms pleadingly*]: Ack lads it wus all my fault. Don't be fightin' among yerselves. Shure yis might niver see each other agin after the night! Shure it wus all my fault. I don't know what kim over ma. [*Holding his head and looking for a clean place to collapse.*]

TUG [*puzzled, strong cockney accent*]: What are yis gettin' upset abaht? It's only a song.

SEAN [*grimfaced*]: Stay outa it foreigner.

PETER [*grimly, shaking his head sadly*]: So he's a foreigner now, after being yer shipmate fer the past two years.

[SEAN, *shamefaced, slumps back into his seat and glares defiantly at* PETER. WEE BOY *releases* PADDY *who slouches over to the bar straightening his clothes.* JAMSIE *walks to* PETER *and* TUG. *He leans over them and wraps an arm affectionately around each man's shoulder.*]

JAMSIE [*stage whispering, looks apprehensively over his shoulder at the barman, who is mopping glasses at the sink. His head is down looking at what he is doing.*]: Ef yis git him any more annoyed he'll ring the peelers an' we'll all be turfed out intil the street an' yis 'ill be soaked till the skin, afore yer taxi cums. [*Earnestly, to* TUG] Why don't yis all go out till the wee store an' settle yer differences quietly an' then come back an' enjoy the rest af the night! [*Pauses, warningly*] Don't be goin' intil the toilet ta talk. It's gat no roof an' yis 'ill be soaked through in an minit er two. [*Whispers*] Use the wee store. It's the first door on the right.

CHORUS OF VOICES FROM THE TABLE: Aye! Sure! Right! That's a good idea!

JAMSIE [*patting shoulders warmly*]: I'll go up nigh an' tell him yis have made up. [*The men rise, arms around each other and move off-stage.* JAMSIE *listens intently for the sound of the door closing. Grins with satisfaction and moves quickly to the bar. Takes a sip from his pint.*]

WEE BOY [*looking up*]: Well! Did ye apologise?

JAMSIE [*Head bowed, nodding humbly*]: Aye ... But I don't think it did any good.

WEE BOY [*alarmed, stops washing glasses*]: I hope they're nat away till the toilet till fight ...

JAMSIE [*innocently*]: Naw. They're away intil the store.

WEE BOY [*horrified*]: The store? The store? It's fulla drink an' them fellas 'ill wrack the place. [*Looks hatefully at the two men, points at the door*] Right! That's it! Git out ... Git out an' don't ever cum back while I'm here. [*His face twists as he loses control.*] I hope yis git soaked an' I hope the rats ates the balls offa yis.

[*He watches as the two old men, heads bowed, shuffle slowly and silently towards the door; he then runs in the direction of the store. The bar is empty and quiet. Then the sound of a door being wrenched open, allowing a babble of voices to be heard. This is cut off with the sound of the door closing. There are a few seconds of silence, then the bar-door opens slowly and quietly as* JAMSIE, *followed by* PADDY *enter and peer around apprehensively.*]

PADDY [*still bristling*]: Jamsie, in all the years I've knowed ye I've never knowed ye till insult me like that.

[JAMSIE *doesn't answer, but puts his finger to his lips and grins broadly.* PADDY *pushes his cap to the back of his head and scratches his head.*]

PADDY [*puzzled*]: Jamsie; if he's went intil the store they'll all be locked in. We'd better let thim out. [*He moves forward, but Jamsie's hand stays him. He looks blankly at Jamsie's impish grin for a second or two before realization shows on his face.*]

PADDY [*hoarsely*]: Yew planned the whole thing. Insulted me till git the fight started till git them at each others throat. Then ya got them intil the store till make up. Then yew woun' that wee idjit up till run intil the store. [*Whistles gleefully*] Holy Mackerel ... But why Jamsie?

JAMSIE [*beaming at the praise*]: First that wee pig needed a pin turned in his nose and secondly—[*He points at the table laden with drink.*]—I promised ye a birthday party.

[*Moving to the table they pore over the selection of drinks.*]

JAMSIE [*sadly*]: I'm sorry I had till insult yer religion mate.

PADDY [*equally sadly*]: Ack shure I called ye a ball-licker.

JAMSIE: Aye it luked that way, but I hadda go down there wid 'im to make shure he didn't tipple to the state a the lock.

PADDY [*empties a glass of whiskey in one go, burps appreciatively and nods.*] He'd a caught it on early and yid a lost the element a surprise. That's why yew kept goin' with 'im. To houl the dour open. [*Fondly, he toasts his comrade.*] Yer a genius.

JAMSIE [*sniffing at a glass of vodka and looking round the table*]: Yid wunder at sailors nat drinkin' rum. Still, beggars can't be choosers. [*Lowers a vodka in one gulp and grins.*] If that cheeky chile cud see us drinkin' nigh. [*Grins mischievously at* PADDY *and begins to sing softly*]

If yer bored an' want a clash/
Clear yer throat an' sing the Sash.
Even better in a pub/
where someone's itchin' fer a rub.

PADDY [*continues in the same key*]:

Pints an' politics niver mix/
fer soon they're followed by stones an' bricks,
till someone's hurt an' the cops cum quick
till break yer skull be yew prod or mick.

JAMSIE [*sinks another drink quickly, wipes his mouth. Reflectively*]: Ack Paddy, it's this country has us the way we are [*Pauses*] an' it's us that has the country the way it is. [*Thoughtfully*] That wee Free-Stater wuda kilt me.

PADDY [*defensively*]: Shure the Peter fella wuda stud up for ye.

JAMSIE [*laughing*]: Aye, a Sandy Row man an' a Free Stater. All the ingredients necessary for an explosion.

PADDY [*sadly*]: Ack Jamsie, the ingredients for the explosion is in all of us. Shure didn't I try till brain ye myself! [*He looks around the table, helps himself to a packet of cigarettes and nods towards the store.*] It must be like the League of Nations in there. Free Stater, Welshman, Englishman and two Ulstermen ...

JAMSIE [*interupting laughingly*]: Aye an' where there's two Ulstermen there's trouble.

PADDY [*sips another drink, muses*]: This cud maybe lead till one of them International incidents yew hear about nigh an' agin on the wireless.

[JAMSIE *chuckles and begins to pour whiskey and vodka into empty lemonade bottles. He picks bottle tops from the floor and recaps some full beer bottles and puts them carefully into the pockets of his greatcoat.*]

PADDY [*beginning to do the same*]: Cud we nat tak a coupla bottles a hard tack from behin' the bar?

JAMSIE [*scoldingly*]: Nigh Pat. We're nat thieves! Justa coupla honest men takin' advantage afa scoundrel, namely the wee upstart.

PADDY [*agreeing*]: Aye, an' as me da always said: a honest man's a pore man.

[*Both men laugh silently.* JAMSIE *leans back contentedly.*]

JAMSIE [*conversationally*]: Y'know Pat there wus only one time I stooped till crime an' it wus back in the hungry 30s. Me an' my mate, Billy Baxter, he's ded nigh, followed a big American sailor one night. He'd bin in the Stalingrade buyin' all the oul dolls drink an' throwin' money away like it had a disease. We jumped him in Pilot Street. I wus a fair till useful scrapper in them days an' Billy wus no slouch either. Anyway I touched fer the big fella wid my sunday punch smack on the button. [*Puts on an astonished look*] He laughed at me. Then he decked me. Billy smacked him from behin' but he still didn't go down. After a few minutes of hectic fightin', we realised we'd picked a real hard case, like Jack Dempsey or John Wayne. It tuk the two af us almost ten minutes af hard fightin' till stun him enuff fer Billy till rifle his pockets. We left him lyin' there still yelling defiance an' ran as fast as we cud till the wee snug in the American Bar. When I got me breath back I ast Billy how much he'd gat. [*Looking intently at* PADDY] Know how much he gat?

PADDY [*deeply interested*]: No! How much?

JAMSIE [*dejectedly*]: A Tanner!

PADDY [*repeating incredously*]: A Tanner?

JAMSIE [*solemnly, with a straight face*]: Aye a Tanner. Good job it wusn't a shillin' or he'd akilt the both af us.

[*Both men laugh silently as the door off-stage begins to rattle.*]

PADDY [*vaguely*]: Do yew hear someone rapping?

JAMSIE [*shaking his head sadly*]: Shure how cuda when I'm nat here; didn't I git throwed out a while ago along wi' yew? [*He lifts the lemonade bottles filled with spirits carefully and stands up.*]

JAMSIE [*to* PADDY]: C'mon it's time we gat the party started. [*Grins impishly*] An' no party songs will be tolerated. [*He walks towards the door.* PADDY *follows, looking off-stage towards the store.*]

PADDY [*worriedly*]: How'll they git out?

JAMSIE [*matter of factly*]: The sailor's taxi-man won't be long till he's here. Failin' that the Harbour Bulkies won't be long notifyin' the RUC if the lights are still on an' the doors still open at eleven. I tell ye Pat thet little boy was tinkerin' wi'oblivion when he picked on yours truly.

PADDY [*staggering a little at the door*]: Pints an' politics do mix.

JAMSIE [*scowling*]: Course they do! Hasn't yore politicans an' my politicians bin doin' well outa oul idjits like us for the past fifty years.

[*Both men move slowly and silently out leaving the door open causing the heap of rubbish to scatter over the floor. The bar is silent except for the sound of the storm and the rain lashing the windows. The off-stage hammering gets louder and voices are heard demanding help. A loud wailing voice from beyond the bar-door begins to sing.*]

JAMSIE [*drunkenly*]: Happy Birthday to you,

Happy Birthday to you ...

Happy birthday dear Patrick ...

The voice fades into silence as the storm itself abates.

TOMMY STEWART
An Uncrowned Champion

A LAND FIT FOR HEROES

Tommy Stewart was born in the shadow of Henry Street Flax Spinning Mill on 22nd February 1915.

The day of his birth was seasonal with snow and showers of sleet. He would most certainly have been born at home with a midwife and doctor in attendance. His father would have piled coal into the bedroom fireplace at the expense of the one in the small downstairs kitchen. With coal at almost two shillings a bag it was more economic for all the family to be based in the bedroom until mother was fit enough to venture downstairs.

As he stared into the firelight and thanked God for the safe delivery of his latest offspring, the father of the house may have reflected on the news from the front. The pages of the *Belfast Telegraph*, were dominated by the Allied successes at Ypres, with news of a German battalion being wiped out.

The war to end all wars was in progress—many of the men of the district had joined the forces and gone to France to take on the army of the Kaiser. The families of the district left behind in the squat mill-owned houses struggled to make ends meet in impoverished conditions.

The mill was the centre of this small universe. It provided employment for thousands of people including children who would be classed as part-timers going to school one day and work the next.

The wages were abysmally low and the health risks high. Many maladies dogged the workers. One condition, 'mill fever', was contracted by beginners, usually children. The symptoms were an inability to breathe and lungs that felt raw and sore. The remedy for this was simple and effective. A sheet of brown wrapping-paper smeared liberally with cooking lard was placed on the bare chest at bedtime. Most patients returned to normal after a day or two blissfully unaware of the painful future that lay ahead for them. Almost every family was affected.

The war finished. Quite a few men never returned to the homes they had set out to defend. Those who did returned to the same frugal conditions they had left. The same hard taskmasters continued to run the roving rooms and spinning rooms with an iron discipline that made army life seem tame. Women and children toiled from dawn to dusk, making the thick black smoke belch vigorously from the giant mill chimney before falling slowly and lethally onto the streets and houses around it.

The filthy residue covered the roofs and pavements; rooms and beds; cupboards and utensils. Every house was affected. No amount of scrubbing by the house-conscious dwellers could completely wipe away the sooty residue that also clung to their exposed bodies. The children were sometimes viciously scrubbed by mothers two or three times a week in a vain effort to keep the constantly falling poison at bay. Washing could not be left on an outside line, and most of the houses had pulley lines attached to the kitchen ceiling in an effort to stop the clothing being polluted by the smoke and dust so painstakingly removed by the woman of the house. Carbolic soap and a scrubbing-board after a long steeping in the family bath were a popular and exhausting way to do the family washing. Needless to say it was every bit as bad in a day or two.

The old adage 'Cleanliness Is Next To Godliness' hung on many a sparse bedroom wall, but there was no advice to protect the inner sanctum as the unsuspecting people filled the lungs designed by their Maker to thrive on clean air with the poison seeping daily and relentlessly from the bowels of the giant smokestack.

'Pouce' was the term used to describe the brown powder that came from flax while it was being turned into Irish linen. Whilst some rooms in the mill had a ventilating system, it was the variety that sucked the dirty dust up from the rooms and through a large mother fan on the roof of the building which in turn hurled the dust into the air. It joined the foul smoke from the chimney and slowly fell on the unsuspecting populace. The pouce that often clogged up the machinery was brushed up by the operators and shovelled into large sacks. These were loaded onto carts and sent through the narrow streets to another factory where it was used in the manufacture of roofing felt.

As the carts trundled noisily along the cobbled streets the fine powder sifted through the coarse sacking, through the cracks in the cart, onto the cobbles where it lay until the wind picked it up and blew it through the open half-doors and into the rooms. The situation was worse in the summer when the hot weather would see the large doors and windows of the mill thrown open to clear the offending dust. It joined with the rest of the filth and slowly settled into nooks and crannies and chests and lungs sowing the seeds of the respiratory ailments that would torment and painfully kill many of those who grew up in its midst.

YOUNG TOMMY

In such an environment was Tommy Stewart reared to manhood. He attended Earl Street school, which was also a church. It sat at the corner of Earl Street and York Street, and was pulled down in the 40s after being damaged in an air raid. (The site is now part of the car park at the Yorkgate shopping centre.)

Leaving school at the age of 13, he started working in the Workman Clark shipbuilding yard. As befits a local legend, it is said that his great nemesis Rinty Monaghan also worked there. Unfortunately for the myth-makers, while they may have both been shipyard men, they could never have worked together—Monaghan would have been eight years old when Stewart began at Workman Clarke.

Like many a Belfast lad from the tough mean streets, Stewart saw the ring as a way to earning extra money.

Stewart trained in the White City Club, situated in Trafalgar Street—conveniently close to the Bowling Green public house. He never boxed as an amateur and was, according to friends, paid in buttons when he started fighting professionally.

The tiny warren of streets was a hive of boxing activity. These back-to-back terraces and alleys housed dozens of clubs and halls where men like Stewart fought in Spartan conditions for purses that ranged from half-a-crown to thirty shillings. The fee would depend on the number of rounds fought and the popularity of the fighter. The fights rarely made the papers. Purses and column inches were for larger venues such as the King's or Ulster Hall.

Like many of his cronies and workmates he took to smoking cigarettes—blissfully unaware that the combination of pouce and tobacco would later play a major part in causing him to miss out on a chance for greatness. His fists were to take him high, but his lungs were to bring him down. Who knows to what heights his boxing would have taken him had he been born in a district free from the fallout of the factory chimney.

He was just turned 18 when he began boxing to supplement a meagre wage working in a timber yard. The first newspaper report is dated Saturday, March 23rd, 1933. The *Belfast Telegraph* headline states: BOXING AT THE RING. PLENTY OF HARD-HITTING CONTESTS.

Further down the page two lines record the start of his career:

Young Stewart knocked out Jim Thomas in the fourth round with the loser being in trouble from the beginning of the bout.

Thus began a short but explosive career that brought fame, heartache and an early death.

His record for 1933 reads: five contests, three wins, and two defeats, all on points. As well as Thomas, Stewart beat Pat Finnegan and Jackie Mussen. His two defeats came at the hands of the highly useful Al Sharpe.

It was a promising beginning for the youngster.

The next year saw him a busy fighter. Not yet fully grown, he stood about five feet high and came to the scales a natural flyweight. In his first fight of the New Year he met and defeated Pat McStravick—a member of the respected boxing family from

New Lodge Road (a stone's throw from Stewart's North Queen Street stomping ground)—on points over six rounds.

Tommy continued his campaign with points wins over Pat Kelly and Ted Rosbottom. Rosbottom had defeated him earlier in the year on points as had Marvin Harte. He boxed a return with Harte, but was unable to reverse the decision. Again the decision was on points over eight rounds.

June 30th saw him fight his first cross-channel opponent—and score his first knockout. The action took place in Seaview Park, home of Crusaders. The fight was scheduled for eight rounds and Tommy must have looked highly impressive when he knocked out Manchester's Jack Harvey in the third round. Three weeks later, he overwhelmed Belfastman Jim Lamont, forcing the referee to stop the scheduled four-rounder in the second. He returned to the open air and opposed Scot Roy Fitzsimmons, whom he knocked out in the fourth round of a scheduled six-rounder. The venue was Grosvenor Park, home of Distillery.

This third stoppage in a row caused the local sportswriters to take an interest. After his disposing of Oldham's Dick Hilditch in a sixth round stoppage and Jackie Saunders with a third round knockout, the *Irish News* noted that Stewart had 'a propensity for knocking out cross-channel opponents.'

The year ended on a down note as he was defeated on points over four rounds by two very experienced Belfast flyweights, Jackie Campbell and Billy Warnock—a member of the famous fighting Warnocks from the Shankill Road, one of whom defeated the legendary Benny Lynch, who was then the world flyweight champion. (Unfortunately the fight was on a non-title basis. It has, however, remained a classic talking point in the clubs and bars where old timers meet to talk about fighters from a bygone age.)

Stewart began 1935 with a hard-fought draw against cross-channel import Jack Stubbs. Stubbs, a tough no-nonsense fighter, was widely seen as a rising prospect and the draw was considered a good result by Stewart's supporters at the Chapel Fields ringside. It is also interesting to note the contest was fought at Bantam, with Stewart giving away weight for what was not the first or last time.

Two clever Bantams, Tommy Stewart from York Street and Jack

Stubbs from Congleton, fought an interesting and exciting six-rounder at a very fast pace. The outcome of all this action was a draw and a very fitting decision without much dispute. The English boy was just a shade superior in the opening rounds, but Stewart soon found his mark and became more aggressive from round four.

In these rounds the York Street Battler brought the fight to his opponent making up for lost ground. In these final rounds the York Street lad shook up the English lad and gave him something to worry about, clearly out-fighting Stubbs bell to bell.

Stewart was in the the Chapel Fields Arena ring again just six days after the Stubbs' fight. He faced Scot Mick McAdam on 19th January. Stewart had just turned flyweight and the Airdrie man never came to terms with the powerful York Streeter who looked positively brilliant.

In the first round Stewart hit the Scot smack on the button with a great right hook which sent his opponent to the canvas for a count of eight. McAdam got to his feet, badly dazed. Stewart moved in for the kill but the Scot was saved by the bell.

In the second Stewart forced the pace and piled on the pressure. McAdam, a very strong opponent, soaked up the heavy punishment and even managed to get a few licks of his own in, catching Stewart with a flurry of left and right hooks and a powerful jab to the head. The third round was a cracker but Stewart proved to be the master and his punches were bang on target. As the fight progressed the Belfast man was the stronger fighter. Durable and confident, he had the Scot on the canvas for a count of eight in the sixth round. He continued to mercilessly pound the Scot until McAdam's corner wisely called it a day.

At the beginning of February Stewart was in action again against Young McManus of Glasgow. A 'Ma Copley' tournament in the Arena, the first round was a dull affair as the two men sussed each other out. In the second the Belfast Battler dropped McManus to the canvas with a peach of a right. The Scot was caught unawares by the clinical punch. He took a count of eight and was lucky to survive the round. Despite a fightback in the third, the durable Stewart kept coming forward. It was just a matter of time before he put McManus away. A combination of heavy punches sent the Scot to the canvas for a knockout.

1935 continued apace with mixed fortunes for Stewart. He beat Paddy Doherty (Glasgow) twice, Jack Mussen (Belfast), Jackie Ryan (Hamilton) and Johnny Burke (Kilmarnock) on points. He knocked out his only Free State opponent Gary Roach from Wexford in five and Joe Bradley from Edinburgh in seven.

On the down side he lost on points to Jim Brady (Dundee) in Dundee over 10 rounds, Freddie Tennant (Dundee) in Dundee over 10 rounds and Joe Hardy (Manchester) over 15 rounds. These cross-channel defeats pointed to the Belfastman being a bad traveller. At home, on 5th December, he lost on points to his old Belfast adversary, Al Sharpe. He fought a draw against Dumbarton's Matt Griffo who gave a good account of himself against the York Street Battler, considering the fact that he took the fight at short notice.

The year which began so brightly finished on a sad note when he was stopped for only the second time in 37 fights by Tut Whalley from Hanley. The venue was in Manchester and the referee ended it in the ninth round of a scheduled 12 rounds. This was no disgrace, as Whalley would go on to be a main challenger for the world flyweight title three or four years after that fight.

It was an indication that Stewart was a fighter from the top drawer.

Stewart's string of knockouts and stoppages against over-the-water boxers caused the *Irish News* to write on 16th March:

> Tommy Stewart's flair for performing against cross-channel fighters is so remarkable that it is interesting to note he meets another visitor, and with a bout between Jack Bernard (Carrick) and Tommy 'Poker' Lyttle, the 'house full' notice will be required at the Thomas Street venue.

Tommy was four days away from his 21st birthday and had reached his full height of 5 foot 2 inches when he pulled on gloves to face Manchester's Tommy Higgins at the Ulster Hall. The drawn fight went the full six rounds and was a sizzler. Both men were rematched for an eight-rounder at the same venue four weeks later. A carbon copy of the first bout, both boxers gave value for money and the crowd was well-pleased, as Stewart and Higgins attempted to gain the upper hand in what was a evenly matched contest. The verdict was again split. Only the most ardent of Stewart fans could disagree with the draw.

That night was a great night in local boxing as Jimmy Warnock, the Irish Flyweight champion, systematically disposed of Jimmy Nash, the London Flyweight champion, in the second round.

Following his epic fights with Higgins, Stewart's next recorded bout was with Jackie Davis on 9th May. A Chapel Fields top liner, the local press noted with satisfaction:

> Tommy Stewart proved beyond a shadow of a doubt that he can hit. This hard-punching boxer from York Street is proving to be a prospect and a force to be reckoned with. He proved far too much for Jackie Davis, a well-built and sturdy lad who was always willing to have a go. But Stewart was just too good, too strong and too hard of a puncher. The constant barrage of punches took its toll and Davis was forced to retire in the sixth round.
>
> Both lads received a great ovation from the ringside fans who declared it a great contest.

Stewart's class and local popularity was confirmed with his next bout—once again at the Chapel Fields—against the canny Charlie Curry. 'STEWART STOPS CURRY' screamed the headlines:

> In the top of the bill at the Chapel Fields on Saturday night, Tommy Stewart the holder of a powerful punch in either hand beat Charlie Curry of Wheatley Hill when he stopped him in the eighth round of a scheduled 10-rounder. Stewart was just too good for the cross-channel visitor and from the first bell came out fighting and ready for action. Curry fought well for the powerful storm that Stewart was lashing at him, and it says much for his courage that he lasted as long as he did.
>
> The cross-channel boxer also proved to be very cautious and this kept him out of any real trouble in the opening rounds whilst

Stewart stalked him like a prey in a jungle. Curry possessed a good left which helped keep the Belfast Battler at bay, but this defence was eventually worn down when Stewart caught Curry with a string of great punches to the head which caused the boxer's nose and mouth to bleed profusely. This affected his breathing, but Curry refused to let his corner throw in the towel. Despite Curry's gameness, Stewart's punching continued to take effect and the referee stopped the contest in round eight. A great fight and a great result for Stewart.

Stewart crossed the channel to Glasgow for his next fight which took place on 23rd June. Local boy Jim Maharg was the opponent and Stewart was beaten on points over 10 rounds, a result which seemed to confirm his inability to produce the goods on an away from home basis.

He was next in action as part of an all-star boxing tournament in the open air of Seaview Park.

Stewart's advisers seemed to be somewhat uncaring for their charge, matching him against Nottingham's George Marsden—a capable featherweight. In the end, Marsden proved too much for the plucky flyweight. For the first four rounds the boxers swapped punches but Stewart was unable to overcome the Englishman's considerable weight advantage and in the latter rounds became a mere chopping block for Marsden. Stewart had a well-deserved reputation for gameness and proved that he could take a punch as well as give one. Several times he tried to get on terms and was severely punished for his trouble. In one exchange he sustained a cut eyebrow but continued to throw punches.

He was as game as a fighting cock and continued to push forward, never once taking a backward step. Marsden had the advantage of a longer reach and Stewart had a lot of trouble trying to get round the long left hand that was picking him off at will with rapier-like precision. He soaked up heavy punches to the head and the body in an effort to land a big punch, but the end came in round four when the referee wisely stepped in to save the courageous Belfast man further punishment. Stewart was not often subject to such drubbings and must have agreed to the mismatch. Nor would it be the last time he would face great physical disadvantages in an effort to perform for Belfast fight buffs.

On 22nd July at the Chapel Fields he again went into overdrive and stopped Mick McAdam from Airdrie in the third round of a bout that was scheduled for 10.

As in the first Stewart-McAdam fight the previous year, the Scot came under intense pressure from the first bell. The York Street Battler quickly got on top of McAdam and piled on the agony with both fists flaying in a series of assaults. The Scotsman was soon in quick retreat as punches came from everywhere onto his body. He really had no answer or defence against the fusillade of power-punching coming from Stewart. The Belfast Battler was powerful and at his most dangerous in the opening rounds and all the Scot could do was cover up. In the second round he was caught with a vicious right to the jaw which clearly staggered him and pushed him back into a corner. In the third round the Scot sustained a damaged eyebrow and an enormous amount of punishment. He seemed utterly defenceless and the referee stepped in at this stage to save the gallant boxer further punishment.

Stewart next tangled with Tommy Bodell of Oldham in an eight-rounder and stopped him in the final round with a knockout punch that seemed to travel from Stewart's feet. From the beginning it seemed the Englishman was in awe of the Stewart reputation for hard punching. He stayed off and seldom mixed it. In the third round his eye was cut by a powerful punch, which proved to be a handicap. He opted to fight on but was cut off by a solid right that sent him down and out.

Stewart was ready to fight the very best ...

THE GREAT KANE

On 27th August Stewart was to take part in a fight that would be talked about for many years to come. Tommy Stewart v Peter Kane took place in the Ulster Hall and was hailed as one of the classic bouts of the York Street man's career.

For the record, as true boxing aficionados know, Kane was undoubtedly a wonderboy, one of the greats of British boxing. His incredible record reads: 102 contests, with 92 wins, two draws, seven defeats and one no-contest.

At the age of only 19, Kane met the incomparable Benny Lynch on the Scot's home ground in Glasgow in October 1938—just over a year after his bout with Stewart. Lynch knocked him out in the 13th round, but later forfeited the title when overweight for a scheduled defence against American Jackie Jurich. Jurich met Kane for the vacant title. Kane won on points to become world champion at the age of 20.

Kane was to relinquish the title in May 1939 owing to weight difficulties. It was suggested the coming fight between Tanner and Paterson should be recognised as a world title fight. In 1943 he tangled with Paterson who was then world champion and was knocked-out in one round. War service in the RAF and an eye injury sustained outside the ring interrupted his career.

But that lay in the future. Kane came to Belfast—a Belfast eagerly awaiting his confrontation with the local hero Stewart—with 18 inside the distance wins under his belt. Local partisanship aside, all knew that the Liverpudlian was a class act.

The Kane-Stewart joust was a battle royal which Stewart would lose on a TKO. But the York Street man was not outclassed. He put up a great fight and at one time it looked as if Stewart was going to stay the distance and finish the bout on his feet.

Kane started in forceful form but at the same time found it hard to hit his mark with any great accuracy, as Stewart was both wily and elusive—belying the 'up-and-at-them' legend. But the Liverpool man had a considerable armoury and bided his time.

Stewart was never prepared to give anything away and made Kane work for his purse. Kane had tenacity and nerve, packing a punch that was as lethal as that of his opponent. The York Street man produced his renowned gameness—even the handicap of a cut eye did not deflect him from the business at hand.

Kane was finding it difficult to land a telling punch and found Stewart to be a clever craftsman, using every inch of the ring to stay out of any real danger, whilst always looking for an opening for a cluster of his own damaging punches.

Kane began the sixth fighting ferociously in an effort to catch Stewart off guard. Stewart continued to dance cleverly out of reach until the moment when Kane caught him with a number of solid rights to the head. The weight and ferocity of the barrage would have sent lesser men to the canvas, but Stewart never flickered an eyebrow, refusing to let Kane know he had hurt him.

In the seventh both fighters clashed violently and almost came through the ropes onto the ring apron.

Stewart made a great rally in the eighth pushing Kane backwards with some very good punches which included a right to the head, a combination to the body and another right to the head. But he was also being picked off by Kane and seemed to be tiring. He weathered the round by calling on every ounce of his courage and stamina, whilst Kane went to his corner looking as strong as ever.

In the ninth round of a contest that had the crowd hoarse from shouting encouragement and constantly brought to its feet by the barnstorming performances of both men, Kane proceeded to take charge of the action by pounding Stewart with a venom that sent the Belfast man to his knees. He survived the round by sheer courage and guts, but it was obvious he could not take much more.

He left his corner for the tenth round almost out on his feet. Pure instinct and a refusal to be second-best kept him in there, but with less than two minutes of the last round left—friends of Stewart still to this day claim it was less than a minute from the end—the referee saved him from himself and stopped the fight with the Belfast man still on his feet protesting violently. Regardless of the ref's decision or the timing, Stewart had every reason to be proud of his wonderful performance in defeat and this must rate as a highlight in a great career.

After such a legendary bout, the rest of 1936, needless to say, was an anti-climax with Tommy losing over six to local boy Pat McStravick and to Bob Bates over 10 rounds.

On the upside, he beat Mancunian Tommy Atherton over 10 rounds and reversed the points decision in a return with Bates. The year finished with a win over Sheffield's Tiger Denton. These contests all took place in Belfast and it is interesting to note all were judged on points with the big punch seemingly slumbering for the time being.

A FIGHT A FORTNIGHT

A hit following his epic with Kane, 1937 saw Tommy Stewart in great demand for boxing venues, all of which took place in his hometown—with the exception of one trip to Liverpool.

Stewart campaigned a staggering 28 times in that year—over one a fortnight. He began with a match against another local boxer Jackie Mussen. This bout was billed as being an eliminator for the Northern Ireland Flyweight title. It was over 10 rounds and Stewart was beaten on points. He continued into the year with points wins over fighters from England and Scotland. Ted Green and Bob Bates and Peter Millar made the boat-train trip in vain, as did John Kelly, Abe Tweedie, Tommy Rose, Tommy Hamilton, Willie Leggat and Joe Tierney.

He also sent Ginger Ebbits packing with a fifth round stoppage. Willie Leggat tried to avenge a points decision and was stopped in three. Al Dyer retired in three as did Tommy McNeilly. He knocked out Lefty McKie twice. Once in round four and in a return bout the Englishman was knocked out in seven.

A few of his old enemies turned the tables on him with points decisions mostly over 10 rounds—Bob Bates, Charlie Curry, Abe Tweedie and Stan Woodburn.

He was disqualified against Tommy Brown of London in round three and was stopped by Willie Leggat when the referee halted their 10-rounder in the third. Most of these battles took place in the Arena, in the Chapel Fields.

It is interesting to note the two bouts with Charlie Curry took place within a fortnight. The first fight on 29th March 1937 took place in the Arena, in what turned out to be a thrilling and exciting exhibition of boxing in which the Londoner won a very narrow points decision. It could well have been a draw according to the Belfast press. Stewart started well and had Curry on the retreat with some vicious punching. Curry evaded any real trouble by using the ring and scoring points with a very efficent left jab. Soon, however, they were toe-to-toe with punches from each man coming down like hailstones. Both were extremely fit and needed to be as they tested out each other's punching power.

Halfway through the fight the score was about level as they

were delivering the goods punch for punch. In the seventh and eighth they were still boxing at top speed with neither showing any signs of exhaustion or fatigue as they vied for supremacy.

The action continued right to the last second and when Curry took it on a narrow margin the fans erupted to show their delight at the wonderful show put on by both men.

The rematch was as thrilling and exciting as the first, taking place in the Arena. It was the main event of the night and was a splendid bout with clean and clever boxing from both men. Not once during the whole contest had the referee to intervene. Curry had the advantage as he was slightly heavier than Stewart and scored well with a snappy left hand, but Stewart remained forceful and was determined not to give anything away. Curry continued to box defensively and was quick to go on the retreat when the York Street man threatened any serious trouble.

In the fifth round Stewart launched a two-fisted attack that caught the visitor off-guard, landing a series of lefts to the jaw and rights to the head. He continued to attack in the sixth and had Curry back-pedalling from a flurry of blows to the body.

Curry absorbed the punches and came back with an attack of his own. The seventh was a real tussle as both men stood toe-to-toe in the centre of the ring and traded heavy punches in an even encounter. The Englishman's advantage in weight gave him a slight edge, but Stewart would not give up. In the final round, with Curry apparently in front, Stewart continued to make a fight of it as he tried desperately to land the big one that would drop his opponent. He was still fighting when the bell sounded for the end of the fight.

The fans repeatedly applauded both boxers as the referee awarded the fight to Curry on what must have been the narrowest of margins. Indeed, the result might have again been different had Stewart not conceded weight to a man who was a very clever boxer and a punishing puncher. Stewart accepted the decision like the sportsman he was.

The crowd saw it as the best bout for many months and one of the most enjoyable nights in Irish boxing.

In September he took on Glaswegian Willie Leggat. The York Street Battler was in great form. His fast, clean punching was prominent in the opening rounds and had the Scot on the run. Unfortunately there was a clash of heads in the third round of a very good fight, and Stewart came out the worst with blood seeping from an ugly gash. Stewart's disappointment was visible to all as the referee called it off and awarded the fight to Leggat on a stoppage.

The cut must have healed quickly for he was back in action barely a fortnight later on 4th October—and this time it was Pat Murphy of Jarrow who suffered a cut eye in the sixth round. Stewart had floored Murphy in the third when the Geordie lad decided to mix it with the Belfast Battler. But Murphy was game and even though he was up against the big guns of Stewart he was still prepared to have a go.

He took some of Stewart's heaviest punches and still came back for more. In the fifth he caught Stewart with a good left hook to the jaw which caused the York Street Battler to throw caution to the wind and put the visitor under pressure.

In the sixth a weary Murphy sustained a cut eye which led to a stoppage.

Stewart followed this with a points win over Al Dyer. It was a 10-rounder with plenty of action. The lad from Wigan gave a good account of himself but was out of his class. November would see him face late substitute Tommy McNeilly. Stewart was in brilliant form and stopped the Middlesborough fighter who retired halfway through the third round.

Sadly, as stated earlier, the last fight of the year was lost on points to Stan Woodburn from Barnsley. The York Street man fought gamely and well but Woodburn had his measure. So ended a year of incredible campaigning that earned him a legion of fans.

1937 saw him engage in 27 contests—a staggering one fight a fortnight throughout the year. While a professional in the truest sense of the word, we should remember that Stewart was employed in a timber yard where he toiled more than eight hours a day doing hard physical work. On fight nights he would hurry home, change and make his way to the venue where he would give of his best on every occasion. Sometimes the next morning would see him cut, hurt and sore, but the work had to be done for his family had to be fed and clothed. He constantly dreamed of the big time as he propelled himself further up the ladder in the fight game.

1938 was an important year in more ways than one. He was continuing to do the business that made promoters rich and kept his fans happy and the record for that year is highly impressive.

He started the year like a rocket. Six straight wins against cross-channel fighters, five of these inside the distance, either by knock-out or intervention by the referee.

The six who fell to his heavy artillery were Joe Skelly (Barnsley) twice; Glasgow's Ginger Ebbits, twice; Mickey Clarke from Rochdale; and Burnley's Tommy Norton.

After such a run, Stewart was ready to have another shot across the water for a bout against the highly useful Kid Tanner.

'BELFAST BOXER UNLUCKY AT LIVERPOOL' was the heading of the ring report of the fight. Stewart was retired by the referee at the end of the seventh in what was described as a very close fight. An eye injury sustained earlier in the bout brought a disappointing end to a fight that promised to be great. A brief report says Stewart took a count of eight in the fourth but fought back splendidly and there was little in it when the referee was called to inspect an eye injury Stewart had sustained earlier in the fight.

Perhaps discouraged by the Tanner defeat, Stewart returned to Belfast and three weeks later he lost on points over 10 rounds to Jim Millar from Leeds. He recovered his form in May beating Young Tully of Manchester on points and Billy Hodgson of Lancaster when the referee stopped it in the sixth round of a fight billed to go 10.

Re-established in his winning-ways, June saw Stewart performing four times—all in Belfast before the crowds that idolised him. He beat Willie Smith of Margate on points over six, lost on points over 10 to Billy Tansey from Middleton, stopped Taffy Jones from St. Helens with a KO in round four and finished the month by beating Artie Smith from Burnley over 10 rounds. His only recorded bout for July of that year saw him beating Colin Warren over the same distance.

PATERSON

On 19th August he faced the second of his opponents destined to become a world flyweight champion. Jackie Paterson came over from Glasgow to face Tommy Stewart.

Paterson was destined for greater boxing glory. Born in Scotland on 5th September 1920, he became British and Empire Flyweight Champion and defeated Peter Kane in the first round to win the World Flyweight title. Fighting at Bantamweight, he took the British, Empire, and European titles.

In 1947, he failed to make the weight for a defence against Dado Marino and was stripped of his World Flyweight title. Rinty Monaghan fought Marino and won the disputed title. Paterson took the BBBC to law and won the right to be matched with Monaghan. Losing the weight to reach the required eight stone is said to have weakened him to a shadow of his former self.

Monaghan did the business and knocked the former champion out in the seventh round. (Although he had won well, the Scottish contingent at the fight were angry at the singing slugger's choice of post-fight song—'Broken Hearted Clown'. Monaghan later apologised saying the song had been an impromptu choice.) Paterson lost his European Bantamweight title to Theo Medina. Paterson retained his Empire crown and lifted the British title, but after that it was all downhill. He retired in 1951 and moved to South Africa where he was knifed to death in a street brawl in 1966. He was 46 years old and had fought 91 known contests with 63 wins, three draws and 25 defeats.

One of the draws was against the York Street Battler.

The venue had been at the recently re-opened Belfast Sports Stadium in Cuba Street. Both men were overcautious from the first bell as the Glaswegian tiptoed round Stewart peppering his face and body with light lefts when the occasion presented itself. The Belfast Battler seemed more intent on avoiding the punch that had floored Rinty and appeared to abandon his usual bustling tactics. His timing seemed badly out.

The exchanges brightened in the fourth but Stewart, scoring with a spearing left failed to get his right across properly, as Paterson was quick on his feet and extremely elusive.

Stewart's eye was cut in the ninth but there was little dividing them going into the last round.

The York Street man's fans cheered wildly as he left his corner, hoping their man would put Rinty's conqueror where he belonged, namely on the seat of his pants. They were disappointed and showed it when the referee declared the contest a draw.

They believed their hero had done enough, voicing their disapproval at the decision. The newspaper dryly reported that Stewart had been beaten by his rival's reputation, but also noted that he had stayed with the Scot a lot longer than Monaghan.

Paterson made sure he never fought Stewart again.

ENTER THE CROONING SLUGGER

John Joseph Monaghan was born not a stone's throw from Stewart's Henry Street. Lancaster Street also looked out onto York Street a little further town-wise in the direction of Royal Avenue. Legend says he acquired the nickname of Rinty whilst racing through the streets every night to deliver the *Belfast Telegraph*. He seemed to be always on the go and the original nickname was Rin-Tin-Tin after the popular canine movie star of the period. This was however shortened to Rinty and he carried this name to the height of fame when he beat Dado Marino in London in 1947 and then knocked out Jackie Paterson from Scotland in the seventh round in 1948 to win the World Flyweight title proper. In 1949, he defeated France's Maurice Sandeyron and found himself holding the World, European, Empire, British and Northern Ireland Flyweight titles.

Not bad for a little man from York Street who, the legend says was taught to box in the backyard of his aunt's house. He would be later taught the finer points by Frank McAloran who steered him to the titles.

But this was all in the far-flung future. He was born on the 21st August 1919 and his first bout is recorded as 1934 which would have put him in the ring at the age of 15. He fought twice that year, the results being a draw against Sam Ramsey and a win against Jim Pedlow. He campaigned with mixed results through 1935 and 1936, but 1937 saw him lose just one bout out of a credited 12. The loss was to the talented Jim Keery, but the rest of the contests were

11 straight wins, six on points and the rest by stoppages. In other words Rinty was demonstrating he was growing into a force to be reckoned with.

When he met Tommy Stewart in September 1938 he had more than endeared himself to fight-crazy Belfast fans. Out of eight contests he'd only been defeated once. That was in July when he had gone right-hand crazy and was knocked out by Jackie Paterson.

Rinty had distinguished himself with the previous seven results which were all stoppages, either by knock-outs or intervention by the referee. This record showed him to be a formidable opponent for his near-neighbour Stewart who was 23 years old.

Rinty was four and a half years younger. Both possessed sledgehammer punching and the match was eagerly awaited by the boxing fraternity of Belfast.

Rinty had not boxed since his setback at the hands of Paterson. This was the 33rd time that he'd fought as a professional. Stewart on the other hand had boxed and fought 96 fights comprising nearly 700 rounds of box-fighting over a period of six years, compared with Rinty's five years campaigning. As stated, both were time-served tacticians although Rinty was prone to go all out and leave himself open. The consensus on the street said he'd be foolish to pursue such a plan with Stewart.

Rinty scaled in at 7 stone 11 ounces and Stewart just shaded him by one ounce. The bout was also billed as a 10 round eliminator for the Northern Ireland Flyweight title.

On Friday, 2nd September at the Oval the York Street men girded for action. They were obviously well trained for the struggle with little between them in weight. Rinty seemed to have the heavier dig and his deliveries were well placed, but Stewart, throughout the fight, fought like a terrier determined to have his bone, and in the finishing rounds did not retreat one step from Rinty's artillery.

Cautious tactics had marked the opening round, but not for long. Monaghan snapped home a whizzing left to the head whilst Stewart delighted his followers with a right to the jaw which staggered Monaghan. Stewart forced the pace in this round and the next landing with both hands. There were many exciting moments in the third when Stewart, neatly blocking his opponent's leads almost forced him through the ropes. Rinty was not out of the picture during these exchanges, but continued to play a waiting game, seeking to land a KO punch of which he'd given Stewart a sampler during the fourth.

Monaghan took control in the fifth rocking Stewart across the ring with a volley of lefts and rights to the jaw. Stewart's unwillingness to backtrack landed him in trouble when a clip to the chin dropped him momentarily to his knees. The sixth saw Monaghan scoring with solid shots to the head, one of which drove Stewart halfway through the ropes, but he was back immediately showing fine spirit by fighting ferociously until the round's end, staggering Rinty with a left swing just before the bell.

The seventh was a ding-dong affair with honours even. Stewart's forcing tactics won him the eighth and Monaghan collected points in the ninth with steady shots one of which tore Stewart's gumshield from his mouth.

The last heat proved the decider. Stewart's extra aggressiveness must have impressed the referee who, after a glance at his scorecard stepped forward and raised Stewart's hand. The decision was a popular one with the spectators, and Monaghan proved to be a good loser when he stepped forward and shook Stewart's hand.

This was Rinty's second defeat after scoring eight stoppages in a row. He would, however, shrug it off and place another eight wins under his belt. He knew—as Stewart knew—they would meet again.

Yet that night belonged to the Henry Street fighter. 'STEWART TRIUMPHS' roared the next morning's headlines.

FLYWEIGHT CHAMPION OF NORTHERN IRELAND

After his win over Rinty, Stewart was now closing in on a title. After disposing of Manchester's Joe Tierney on points in October, his next bout was scheduled against Jim McStravick, the latest from the North Queen Street production line.

This fight took place in the King's Hall and was billed as being for the Northern Ireland Flyweight title.

Both men were evenly matched. The fight itself was also even until the eighth when Stewart punched the other fighter around the ring and only the gong saved him from being knocked out. In the ninth round Stewart again weakened McStravick with heavy punches. In the tenth round McStravick went down for a count of nine and when he rose to his feet he was unable to defend himself.

The referee, the legendary Mr. W.W. Barrington-Dalby, wisely stopped the fight and gave the decision to Stewart, who had accounted for his opponent—who a had given a wonderful display of pluck—in the most workman-like fashion.

17th February saw the new Northern Ireland Flyweight champion back in the ring in his 99th contest. It was against Joey Dixon of Macclesfield over eight rounds which Stewart won comfortably. Two weeks later he would be in the Ulster Hall to box Billy Nash from London over eight rounds on a Nat Joseph bill. Nash was a popular and well-known boxer and a very large crowd had descended on the Bedford Street venue to see Stewart opening up with some of the finest boxing ever produced by a local fighter.

During the second, he launched a vicious flurry, including a hard blow to the stomach followed by a left and right hook which dropped the Londoner to the canvas for a count. Nash came out in the third boxing clever but he came second in the points scoring as Stewart was performing out of his skin, placing neither a foot nor a punch wrong. Nash scored well in the fourth but the York Street Battler continued to better him as he continuously caught the Londoner with some well-placed punches.

Nash made a rally in the fifth and seemed to uncover some reserved energy as he fearlessly traded punches with Stewart. In the sixth Stewart again took control and stalked the Londoner about the ring, catching him with right hooks and left jabs as he ruthlessly piled on the pressure. Stewart staggered Nash with a solid left. This was followed by a left hook which glanced off the side of Nash's head, and would have knocked him out had it connected properly. In the seventh and eighth both men freely mixed it to the delight of the crowd and it says much for their stamina that the rally continued until the end of the eighth round. Nash at times tried to pin the Belfast Battler into the ring corners, but Stewart was far too clever to allow that to happen.

Both boxers gave of their all. Nash was a courageous opponent, worthy of his trade but he came off second best that night as Stewart was awarded the fight on points.

On 3rd March Tommy took the boat-train and showed up in Manchester to take on local boy Pierce Ellis over 10 rounds. Again he did not bring his big punch and was beaten on points after a very hard fight which could have gone either way.

Stewart was back in the ring again on March 28th. The venue was the Ulster Hall and the opponent was the stylish Billy Tansey from Middleton. Stewart was billed as the Northern Ireland champion and out-pointed Tansey. It was a tame affair, not at all like the blood and thunder performances they usually got from the York Street Battler.

Neither boxer produced the goods and both performed well below their best. The fight contained many dull moments. Stewart appeared to be below par, but now and again produced the deadly left hook for which he was famous. Unfortunately, it did not connect and the Northern Ireland champion seemed at times embarrassed by his performance.

Tansey worked well at close quarters and gave Stewart some anxious times as he too tried to land the big one. The fight could have been a draw but Stewart shaded it. A number of Tansey fans disagreed and showed it.

Tommy's indifferent performance should have sounded the warning bells for those who professed to care for him and advise him. The long, hard campaign was wearing him down and the lungs which are the bellows of a fighting man were not blowing strong enough to produce the raw, white heat that had previously fired punches with the deadly velocity of a shot from a gun. Perhaps the residue of inhaled pouce and factory smoke were fouling up the delicate respiratory system and causing him to have breathing difficulties which in turn would hamper his concentration. The power that had previously propelled him was having difficulty finding its way to his great heart.

Whilst the fighting machine was not functioning on all cylinders, his naked courage in refusing to take a backward step began to border on the foolhardy. Those around him should have strenuously advised him to rest and be more selective in his choice of opponent.

They should have seen the symptoms. Tommy Stewart with his one fight a fortnight against all comers was in danger of becoming a burnt-out fighter at 24.

All the signs were there. At an age when most fighters peak, Tommy was finding it hard to concentrate. The fighter/boxer who had bewildered and almost out-boxed Peter Kane was having to dig deep for what had previously come naturally. Some of his contemporaries blame it on his dislike of regular training; other lay the onus squarely on his advisers. "They wuda put him in with King Kong," snarled one man I spoke to, who was a friend of the fighter. Then with a grin he added, "An' Stewarty wuda fought the big monkey if the money was right."

In truth Stewart didn't make a lot of money. He reputedly received £7 for the murderous affair with Kane and the fight a fortnight was not sufficient to allow him to quit his day job.

Nobody saw or wanted to see the warning signs of a fighter in need of better counsel. Many boxers were meal tickets to the unscrupulous promoters and managers of the Hungry 30s. Tommy's alter ego, Rinty Monaghan, was 30 when he wrested the world flyweight title from Paterson. His potential was nursed by Frank McAlorum who steered him in the right direction.

According to many admirers Stewart was as good a prospect as the likeable Rinty and should have reaped more reward from the profession he put his heart and soul into. His unquestioned courage and absolute refusal to take a backward step gave the boxing fraternity of Northern Ireland many nights of good entertainment. These characteristics showed on his proud face and he wore them like medals. They undoubtedly were also responsible for his early retirement and untimely death.

The records available show he had three fights in the month of June. The first was against Willie Smith of Glasgow at the Oval football ground. Stewart scored a points win which didn't go down too well with the fight fans.

The bout was over six rounds, a distance which would normally have seen Stewart at his most lethal. He did apply pressure but in the middle rounds the Scot proved stronger and tried to turn the tables on the York Street man. Stewart's undoubted skill and experience caused him to punish the Scot, but Smith was always prepared to fight it out and did apply some good and effective counter-punching, which caused Stewart some grief.

Less than a week later he shared the ring with Al Sharpe. The fight was over eight rounds and was adjudged a draw.

It was time to step into the ring again with Rinty.

RINTY AGAIN ...

It was a bout that was to go down in Irish boxing history.

Following his previous defeat at Stewart's hands, Rinty was determined to chalk up a victory and even the score. Stewart was equally determined to beat Monaghan for a second time and show the world just who was the best flyweight in York Street.

On the bill advertising the fight, Monaghan was described as 'The Crooning Slugger' but singing was furthest from his mind as the two stood toe to toe.

Both of these flyweights entered the ring with the urge to get this fight over as quickly as possible. Monaghan consistently caught his opponent with a devastating left which he employed like a rapier. Clearly the stronger of the two, he also excelled at defending himself and kept out of range of the useful fists of Stewart.

In the second Rinty caught Stewart with a brilliant right to the jaw, which stopped him in his tracks and sent him crashing to the canvas. The champion rose at the count of eight and ferociously set about defending himself, showing no signs of distress from the knock-down.

Monaghan was in peak condition, forcing a variety of punishing shots through Stewart's defence. By the sixth the Crooning Slugger was so far ahead on points that Stewart's only hope to salvage the fight was to knock his antagonist out. The pace never faltered and Rinty collected a cut eye which seemed to come from a clash of heads. Stewart continued to push forward with the dogged determination he was renowned for, but Rinty was content to pepper him with point-scoring lefts whilst back-pedalling and keeping the injured eye well covered. He gave Stewart no chance and won on points, and no doubt entertained the crowd to a trademark song. Stewart, in turn, was bitterly disappointed by

Monaghan's hit-and-run tactics and also his own inability to corner and destroy the elusive opponent.

The fight was to have a curious afterlife, leaving a legacy of bitterness between the two York Street legends. Some years after the fight, Rinty would write about it in a now defunct cross-channel newspaper and make a disparaging claim against Stewart that would cause friction between the two fighters who had remained friendly up to that time. Legend says the normally placid Stewart met Rinty in the street and threatened to whip him there and then. It was uncharacteristic of the likeable Monaghan to have made such a remark in print about anyone, least of all Stewart whom he liked and admired.

The incident did sour their relationship although Monaghan appeared at Stewart's funeral to pay his respects when the York Street Battler was buried from his home in Henry Street in 1964.

Tommy licked his wounds and took his venom out on his next opponent, one Joe Barret who came all the way from Liverpool to be knocked out in four rounds by a rejuvenated Stewart. The bout, Stewart's last of 1939, had been scheduled for 10 rounds and took place in Belfast on 9th December.

On Saturday, 6th January, in his first fight of 1940, Stewart was again giving away weight when he was matched against Pat O'Toole from Liverpool. The Ulster Flyweight champion scaled 8 stone 8 pounds to his opponent's nine stone. In spite of this the local boy carried the fight to his opponent and penetrated his guard, scoring repeatedly with lefts and rights to the head. In the fourth he launched a ferocious attack which sent the Liverpudlian to the canvas for a count of eight. On rising he was met with a devastating blow which put him down again. At this point the towel came in and Stewart was declared the winner.

... AND AGAIN

The final Stewart v Monaghan fight was on the 4th March in the Ulster Hall. Belfast had been clamouring for the match to take place. The pairing had generated much excitement and rumours abounded that both men had placed personal bets on the outcome.

Since his defeat of Stewart ten months earlier, Rinty had scored points wins against Billy Ashton in Liverpool and the very useful Seaman Chetty in Newcastle. Nineteen forty started badly however with a January points defeat by Paddy Ryan in Newcastle over 10 rounds.

The fight with Stewart was, in boxing parlance, a stinker. This was a shame as the box office had been inundated from the moment the rubber match was announced. All the ringside seats, each selling at ten shillings and sixpence, had gone in the first three days. 'House Full' notices had already been placed in the papers.

The papers agreed that the fight didn't live up to expectations:

> The fight did not provide the excitement that was very much expected and it certainly was not as good as the two previous fights. Both men were over-cautious and boxing clever. They were not prepared to have a go, which was sad, as this was billed as the fight of the year. Monaghan took the result on points over the eight rounds.
>
> As both boxers possessed considerable armoury, it had not been expected to go the distance.

Another report was similar:

> In the flyweight division Tommy Stewart and Rinty Monaghan renewed ring rivalry. The first four rounds saw no action at all as Rinty back-pedalled. At the end of the fourth the referee spoke to both men and the next round brought some serious punching. Stewart landed a few in round seven. The end of the bout came as a relief for the crowd.

A complaint echoed by the last reporter:

> The Flyweight contest between Stewart and Monaghan was bereft of fireworks, a tribute, if anything, to Rinty's elusive tactics. Monaghan got the points, but Stewart deserved a lot of sympathy as he tried to make a fight of it. Tommy undoubtably did all the chasing, but it was Monaghan's left lead that took the score in a very close points decision.

Two-one. Stewart was never to be given the chance to even up the score.

FIGHTING ON

Despite the setback against Rinty, Stewart was soon back in the ring, giving away three pounds weight to a dangerous Scotsman from Dundee called Jim Brady. Brady was the Southern area champion and had recently been matched with Peter Kane in an eliminator for the British Bantamweight title. Kane had earlier relinquished the World Flyweight title as he was unable to make the weight.

Stewart had been originally penned in to meet Kid Tanner, the triple champion of British Guyana, who had narrowly beaten him on a cut eye decision in April 1938. A local newspaper report said Tanner was in line to fight Johnny King for the Empire Bantamweight title. No doubt he was well advised to steer clear of the hard-hitting York Street man before such an important fight.

According to the ring report Stewart fought a great fight although Brady won on points over eight rounds. It was a strenuous affair of hard punching and speedy footwork, fought at a terrific pace even for bantams. Stewart scored cleverly with straight lefts and often made Brady miss. The Scot was clearly behind in the fifth although he fought cleverly and intelligently. Both took a terrific amount of punishment in the sixth in their efforts to gain supremacy.

There was nothing in it at the end of round seven and Stewart left his corner in the last round with a margin of points in his favour. Brady, however, attacked strongly and dropped Stewart with a right to the stomach. Stewart rose quickly and put up a magnificent show before the bell ended the fight, but the knockdown had been enough to send the referee in Brady's direction to give him the decision.

According to the experts, this was Tommy Stewart's last professional fight. There were reports of possible fights with Kid Tanner and useful Glaswegian Billy Comerford. Nothing seems to have happened.

A career that had once promised so much spluttered out.

WHAT MIGHT HAVE BEEN

Boxing, more than most sports, is peppered with 'What Ifs'. And Tommy Stewart had more than a fair shair of 'What Ifs'.

As Stewart's fight career ground to a halt, his old adversaries—Paterson, Tanner, Kane, Brady and Rinty—continued to make the headlines in the efforts to become champions. Their names and—among local aficianados at least—*his* would be forever interlinked.

They fought each other a number of times. Other names, other champions—Lou Salica, Jackie Jurich, Manuel Ortiz—came and went. But boxing—and Stewart's story—was dominated by three great champions—Peter Kane, Jackie Paterson and Rinty Monaghan. And all three knew the power behind Stewart's fists—and the endless courage in his heart.

Who knows how Tommy Stewart felt when he saw the three men he had been in close contention with in the square ring become undisputed World Champions? One can imagine him watching *Pathé* or *British Movietone* newsreels of these fights in some of the local cinemas like the Classic or the Imperial. He must have wandered home heavy-hearted.

Kane became a world champion at the age of 20 after beating Jackie Jurich. Who knows how things would have gone had Stewart been allowed to continue the remaining two minutes (or less) left of their classic bout and perhaps produce a punch to turn the tables? Either way Kane didn't look for a rematch.

Jackie Paterson was born in Scotland on 5th September 1920. He turned professional in 1938 and in July of that year came to Belfast and knocked out Rinty Monaghan in five rounds. In September he returned and was held to a draw by Tommy Stewart who was unlucky not to get the decision. He—like Kane—made sure he didn't meet Stewart again.

At 23, Stewart was five years older and went on to defeat Monaghan on points. These results should have compelled those in charge of Stewart's destiny to guide him in a more restrained and professional manner. Perhaps a more selected type of opponent, or a manager with an eye to seeing him on the road to the big time, instead of just another meal ticket, might have seen the York Street man in a better position in the league of British and world class flyweights. It could also have been his bruising, hard-hitting, no-surrender type of boxing that ensured the good ones, with the exception of Rinty, didn't come back for a second helping.

How often he must have pondered on that result as he watched Paterson climb to the very top.

Rinty Monaghan could indeed have been deemed as a cruel turn of fate by the unlucky Stewart. To be successful against all manner of flyweights, bantams and sometimes featherweights and then to be beaten twice by a young man born almost in his own backyard must have given him many sleepless nights.

The records show he was never decisively beaten by Monaghan and only a sliver of difference separated them in their last two fights. Monaghan, however, turned out to be a crowd-pleaser and a world beater.

It's said Rinty's potential was really recognised after the war—Rinty had spent the war as a merchant seaman and in the army entertaining the troops—when he beat the brilliant young Belfast flyweight, Bunty Doran. The fight was for the Northern Ireland title and Monaghan won decisively by knocking Doran out in four rounds. The fight was in Belfast in November 1945.

Two bouts later, he stopped Paterson in seven in Belfast and went on a winning streak marred only by the disqualification against Dado Marino.

Monaghan was the first boxer in the history of the game to defend four major titles on the same night. He retired undefeated in September 1949 still holding the World, European, British and Empire Flyweight titles. I'm not sure whether or not he sang 'When Irish Eyes Are Smilin'' on the night, but I do know he kept them smiling for many years during and after his fight career. I well remember the night he beat Marino. My father, a keen boxing fan, suffered a stroke whilst listening to the fight on the radio in our home in Earl Street. He recovered most of his faculties except his speech, and died in January 1948 without being able to describe his joy and pride at the very special achievement of a very special York Street man.

Stewart may have looked back in disappointment at his last Rinty bout. Monaghan had fought technically—and who could blame him? His advisers knew the safest way to defeat Stewart was to stay away from those lethal punches. Perhaps he fought as ordered—cautiously, knowing if they went toe-to-toe he could have been knocked out. Stewart, on the other hand, probably entertained the same thoughts, but was still prepared to fight.

What if ...? What if ...?

AFTERWARDS

Rinty Monaghan died on 3rd March 1984 after a long illness which he had borne with tenacity and good humour. Both he and Stewart had outlived the factory chimney which had poisoned their lungs and took years off their lives. Stewart retired in 1940, and the Germans put the Mill and its chimney out of action about a year later during one of the many air-raids on the area.

The York Street Flax Spinning Company had lived a lot longer than both of them, but it would no longer continue to destroy the lungs of those who dwelt beneath its shadow.

The Henry Street of that period has changed dramatically. The mill houses were torn down and rebuilt with indoor bathrooms and toilets. The street is tree-lined and looks out at a York Street Tommy Stewart and Rinty Monaghan would find hard to identify. Gone are the public houses both men liked to sup a jar in with their many supporters.

The White Lion, The Toddle Inn and The Bowling Green, where a large portrait of Tommy Stewart hung in an honoured position behind the bar, have now been designated to history and the memory of those old enough to remember them. The industrial area once covered by the Mill and later Gallaher's tobacco factory has also been rebuilt and designed in an environmentally friendly manner with a multitude of greenery that transforms the once drab scenery. The dockside of York Street is also tree-lined and a modern motorway swathes its way through Great George's Street, Lower Henry Street, Trafalgar Street, Earl Street, North Thomas Street, Dock Street, Fleet Street, Ship Street, Whitla Street, Duncrue Street. The sky-high gantries of the shipyard of Harland & Wolff which cast a giant shadow across the Sailortown of Tommy Stewart's era have also vanished along with the shipbuilding dry docks which were the envy of the western world. Only the giant cranes Samson and Goliath now dominate the skyline, straddling a dry-dock which is now as obsolete as they are.

The old LMS railway has been rebuilt and modernised and the halt is now called Yorkgate. Trains glide across a track about forty feet up in the air, travelling across the centre of what was once the hub of a proud city.

A handful of bored commuters dot the landscape as they head home to the outlying estates. They do not blacken the streets as did the doffers, spinners, rovers, carders, spreaders, oilers, sett boys, bobbin boys, overseers, spinning masters and doffing mistresses as they hurried home mingling with Gallaher girls, shipyard men, dockers and carters as they all rushed through the cobbled streets to the ugly terraced houses they called home.

Tommy Stewart could have been among them, making his way home from a timber yard in Duncrue Street. He'd run all the way, weaving and sidestepping to evade the crowds that moved in the opposite direction. Using his ring expertise he would avoid physical contact with the milling throng. He was more than proud of the fact that one local newspaper reporter had named him 'the Billy Conn of Irish Boxing'. Conn, to the uninitiated, was an Irish-American who became Light Heavyweight Champion of the World back in the 30s. An example of his dazzling footwork can be seen in an Errol Flynn film *Gentleman Jim* which was based on the boxing career of James Corbett who became the first Heavyweight Champion of the World under the Marquis of Queensberry rules. Conn was knocked out in the 13th when he tried to take the heavyweight crown from reigning champion Joe Louis.

Reaching home, Tommy would wash the sawdust from his body at the 'jaw-box' in the scullery. He'd tap pensively at the newly-healed scar line across his left eye and silently pray that it would hold long enough to allow him to get close enough to the opponent of the night and enable him to administer what his legion of fans referred to as a 'good night's sleep', doses of which he carried in either hand.

Perhaps he ate a hurried piece of toast and rushed round the table, kissing his little ones in turn as he moved to the kitchen door, pausing only to lift the bag that contained his boxing equipment. He stopped for a moment at the door, and smiled at his wife.

"Wish me luck girl. It's Peter Kane tonight. He's hot stuff. If I beat him we're all on our way to Easy Street."

THE WEAKEST INK AND THE STRONGEST MEMORIES

When it comes to facts outside his boxing career there are few things we can take for granted in the life of Tommy Stewart. We know he was born on a Monday (22nd February 1915) and died on a Tuesday (31st March 1964). Between that particular Monday and Tuesday Tommy lived 49 years and 37 days. Half of that time would be spent in good health with great expectations, but the remainder would see him constantly struggling to regain the strength and vigour that had made him a force to be reckoned with in the hard-nosed industry of professional boxing that flourished in his hometown of Belfast, Northern Ireland. In a whirlwind career that lasted seven years, he fought all comers and retreated from no one. He always gave value for money, even when he was hiding the illness that would eventually force him to retire from the sport into which he poured so much and received so little in return.

The year he was born saw the defeat of the first black heavyweight champion, Jack Johnston, by a white farm-hand called Jess Willard. It was reportedly a shock result which was shrouded in mystery. The fight took place in Havana, Cuba, and has been a talking point ever since.

In the year of Tommy's death a similar upset would occur in the heavyweight boxing world. It concerned a 22 year old African-American called Cassius Clay who sent shock waves around the world when he defeated Sonny Liston, a feared and respected champion in seven rounds. As with the Johnston fight the words 'fix' and 'sell-out' were in the air when people met to talk of these unexpected results. Clay became Ali, arguably the greatest champion of all.

In an article in the *Belfast Telegraph*, Malcolm Brodie revealed a conversation with Rinty Monaghan's manager, Frank McAloran, six months after the popular World Flyweight's last title fight. He told Brodie he was retiring Rinty. When the reporter asked why, McAloran said, "Rinty has difficulty breathing—and if he can't train, he can't fight." Even in death Monaghan and Stewart suffered the ill same health and ill luck.

At this stage it becomes difficult to separate the fact from the myth that has built up over the last half-century about the man and his times. It is said the weakest ink outlives the strongest memory and whilst the people I spoke to were confident of their statements, some don't hold up to examination in the records. In one instance an acquaintance of Tommy's warmly remembered an incident when the boxer was pencilled in to meet a cross-channel boxer. The guy in question was good. He told Stewart he would attend to him quickly as he wanted to catch the boat train home that night. Stewart listened, then said drily: "I'll make sure you do," and knocked him out in the first round.

It's a good story but according to the ring records available, Tommy lost the fight on points over 10 rounds. This doesn't mean the informant was wrong. The fight could have taken place. There were so many fight venues and contests in those days and not all of them were recorded. However, the record says Stewart fought this guy once and lost—and that's the way it is, however good the anecdote. It's also said that he substituted many times. If a boxer didn't show up on the night they sent for Stewarty, who was always prepared to fight anyone. He had a large family at that particular time and needed extra cash to support it. It's said he got £7 for his battle with Kane although another source claimed it was £70. Either way it was hard earned as Tommy engaged in a 10 round war with a young boxer who went on to be a legend in the game.

Fights like this would eventually undermine his health and cause concern for his well-being. He was hospitalised a few times with a lung condition, but this did not stop him boxing in exhibition bouts with up-and-coming young hopefuls or acting as sparring partner to fighters like the legendary Jimmy Warnock. On one such occasion he was allegedly summoned to Warnock's training camp at Bangor to act as sparring-partner and was sent as quickly home when he reputedly floored the Irish champion during sparring exchanges.

I was interested to know why the two never fought for real and was told they had a respect for each other that bordered on fear.

Warnock had a colourful career and was knocked out in four rounds by Peter Kane in an eliminator for the World Flyweight title. He was still campaigning as late as 1948 when he knocked-out Jamaican Pincie Thompson in six rounds on the undercard of the Monaghan/Paterson fight. His manager tried to persuade Maurice Sandeyron to fight the Shankill Road man but the Frenchman declined. Sandeyron had been present to substitute for Paterson in the eventuality of the Scots champion not making the weight.

On the subject of drink, it was said Tommy drank little and not before a fight but liked a few in the company of his cronies afterwards—win, lose or draw. One anecdote concerned Rinty who called into the White Lion during a session. He ordered a brandy and was met with groans of disbelief from the frugal pint drinkers. It was quickly set-up when he explained it was for his eyebrows. However, no one could explain or shed light on this cryptic comment.

Stewart's condition worsened, although he would be fit enough to fight exhibitions in places like the Buff Club, if he felt inclined to turn up. One young prospect called Sammy McKee told me he was thrilled at the opportunity of sharing a ring with the Belfast Battler. Tommy, however, didn't show up.

According to those who knew him he continued to box in exhibitions up until 1950. Most of the young men saw it as an honour to share the ring with him whilst one or two sparrows would attack the old campaigner in an effort to ingratiate themselves with the watching promoters. This didn't happen often as Stewart generally dug deep and came up with the armoury that caused them to regret their arrogance, before the bout ended.

Apparently, he stopped drinking about this time in an effort to salvage his health. His last years were spent operating an overhead crane in the shipyard. Bobby Officer, a mine of information concerning boxing in the 30s and 40s, spoke highly of the little man with a big punch from Henry Street. He told me Stewart had the heart of a lion and in his opinion could have boxed for a world title had he been handled and managed properly. Incidentally, Bobby had his own theory for the early retirement and bad health syndrome.

He believed it to be fact that many of the fighters, no doubt caught up in the euphoria and excitement, did not remain long enough in the dressing-rooms after the fights. This meant they weren't properly rubbed down. They would then go out in the night air with their pores open and their bodies still sweating profusely, thus provoking the chest and lung problems that blighted their careers.

Bobby mentioned some boxers of the same era who lived long and healthy lives because their trainer refused to allow them to leave the dressing room whilst still wet with sweat.

He told me he was also responsible for passing on the news of Stewart's death to Jack MacGowan, sports editor of the *Belfast Telegraph*. The newspaper produced a short obituary under a photograph of the boxer:

> Irish boxing lost another of its great stalwarts this week with the death of Tommy Stewart, an ex-flyweight champ. The picture above should bring back many memories to his fans. It was taken in his younger days.

Other newspapers picked up the story, and a further headline, dated Wednesday, 1st April 1964, says:

STALWART STEWART DIES AT 50

> Irish boxing has lost another of its great pre-war stalwarts with the death in a Belfast Hospital of Tommy Stewart. Tommy fought just about every top-ranking flyweight of his day, Jimmy Warnock excepted. He won the Ulster title by knocking out Jim McStravick, prior to which he had beaten Rinty in an eliminator. Monaghan later took his revenge before going on to win the World Title. Stewart's fights with Jackie Paterson, Peter Kane, Kid Tanner, and Al Sharpe will always revive memories of a wonderful era in Irish Boxing.

The *Ireland's Saturday Night* is a very popular newspaper with the sporting fraternity of Northern Ireland. In the edition after Tommy's funeral, Jack McGowan's story runs:

BUSY TOMMY

> Tommy Stewart's death came as a shock last week to his many friends. It seems like only yesterday since Tommy was battling it out with some of the brightest names in the flyweight division. Names like Kane, Paterson, Tanner, Monaghan and Brady. Stewart held only an Ulster title, but by today's standards he was good enough to win a British title.

This fond and affectionate tribute was dated 4th April, 1964 and was probably the last constructive comment about the York Street Battler of his short but explosive career among the flyweights and bantams. Incidentally, he had not reached the age of 50 as reported, and was in fact 49 years and 37 days old when he died.

In later years, boxing historians would touch on his name as the man who fought the well-loved Rinty Monaghan three times.

When I wrote to Fred Heatley, a fellow York Street man with an avid and wide knowledge of its places and people, for his opinion of Tommy Stewart, he very graciously gave me permission to use his reply. Fred is indeed an autodidact of the sweet science and had this to say about Stewart and his contemporaries:

> Tommy Stewart's boxing record has not, to my knowledge, been published. His early bouts are really untraceable as there were in Belfast at that period so many small halls (some in the York Street/North Queen Street area) which never got a mention in the press. But the first fight I have for Stewart was sometime in 1933 when he lost to the late Al Lyttle in a bantamweight competition. Al showed me the medal he won for winning the competition but was unable to provide the date, and my search through the various newspapers failed to uncover it.

Fred goes on to mention the many fighters Tommy swapped punches with and continues:

> Altogether, from what I have assembled, he won around 60 per

cent of his contests which, considering the standard of those he met, is certainly nothing to be ashamed of.

Fred continues his reflections with his own assessment of the flyweight contenders of the period:

For my money the best flyweight we ever produced was the Jimmy Warnock of the late 30s, when at his peak. The McStravicks were both quality lads and, of course, Rinty went all the way after the war by beating the best men then around. But there were so many wee men active in boxing all through that era that to reach the top meant exceptional ability and a dedication to training, which for many reasons, some were reluctant to do.

Tommy Stewart averaged 15 fights each year of his career (in a couple of years having 20) and gained experience the hard way. He must surely have had a lot of natural ability to mix with the company he did. I trust this will assist you in your tribute to the wee Henry Street man. He was not the greatest flyweight/bantam produced in Ireland, yet there were not many better.

In a later telephone call, Fred revealed he has over 130 recorded fights for Tommy Stewart. Unfortunately, I have only been able to find 109, and most of these (104) were given to me by Bobby Officer who sat up for two nights copying them out in pencil from the various books he has accumulated through the years. Denis Smyth, that perennial searcher after all things concerning York Street/Sailortown, beavered his way through reams of dusty long forgotten newspaper copy in the Linen Hall Library and eventually came up with photocopied reports of long forgotten fights which Stewart engaged in.

Without the input of people like Bobby Officer and Fred Heatley, the story of this extraordinary York Street man could not have been told. Indeed, it would not have been recorded by this particular scribe had he not been told by Denis Smyth (in no uncertain terms) that it was his duty, as it was for all other working-class writers, to record the deeds of exceptional people who came before and lit the sky with their achievements. As Denis has so unselfishly given of his time, his talent and his life to embroider the richness of life in the docklands area of Belfast, who am I to say no to such a persuasive and single-minded person.

Mr. 'Gleek' McLaughlin gave me his memories of the man he termed his greatest mate. Gleek's recollections were important in the reconstruction of Tommy's life and, as such, are invaluable.

Perhaps the last word should go to the family who loved him. Tommy Stewart's wife and family were not mentioned often in this chronicle of his boxing life, but they figured greatly in his hopes and expectations. His sudden and early death threw a large burden of responsibility on the shoulders of his loving and grieving wife. Possessed with the fortitude and love of a working-class mother, Tommy's wife, like many before and after her, assumed the mantle of both father and mother and served her children and grandchildren until her own much regretted death.

The family notice of Tommy's death, in the *Belfast Telegraph*, dated 31st March 1964, perhaps says it all:

You left us quietly, your thoughts unknown.
You left a memory we are proud to own.

With respect to the family, it's a memory everyone who came from the proud area of Belfast known as York Street would agree with. Almost non-existent today, except in the hearts and minds of those who dwelt in its tight and narrow confines, York Street will always be remembered by boxing aficianados as a breeding ground for a school of gloved gladiators—second to none—who plied their hard-earned, hard-learned skills and expertise in the oft-times white-hot atmosphere of the roped square.

Some, like Tommy Stewart, gave more than their all. I sincerely hope this tribute is worthy of his memory.

TOMMY STEWART, BELFAST
FORMER NORTHERN IRELAND FLYWEIGHT CHAMPION
Born 22nd February 1915. Died 31st March (Easter Tuesday), 1964.

BOXING RECORD COVERING YEARS FROM 1933 TO 1940.

1933

10th March: Jim THOMAS (Belfast), WON (Points), Belfast 6.
4th April: Pat FINNEGAN (Belfast), WON (Points), Belfast 6
28th May: Al SHARPE (Belfast), LOST (Points), Belfast 6.
22 October: Jack MUSSEN (Belfast), WON (Points), Belfast 6.
15th December: Al SHARPE (Belfast), LOST (Points), Belfast 6.

1934

14th January: Pat MCSTRAVICK (Belfast), WON (Points), Belfast 6.
9th February: Ted ROSBOTTOM (Belfast), LOST (Points), Belfast 6.
25th February: Marvin HARTE (Belfast), LOST (Points), Belfast
8th April: Pat KELLY (Belfast), WON (Points), Belfast 6.
22nd April: Marvin HARTE (Belfast), LOST (Points), Belfast 8.
6th May: Jackie CAMPBELL (Belfast), DREW, Belfast 8.
27th May: Ted ROSBOTTOM (Belfast), WON (Points), Belfast 8.
30th June: Jack HARVEY (Manchester), WON (KO. Round 3), Belfast 8.
18th July: Jim LAMONT (Belfast), WON (RSF. Round 2), Belfast 4.
21st July: Roy FITZSIMMONS (Blantyre), WON (KO. Round 4), Belfast 6.
22nd August: Johnny BASHAM (Belfast), LOST (Points), Belfast 8.
30th September: Dick HILDITCH (Oldham), LOST (RSF. Rd 6), B'fast 8.
28th October: Jackie SAUNDERS (Manchester), WON (KO. Rd 3), B'fast 8.
4th November: Jackie CAMPBELL (Belfast), LOST (Points), Belfast 4.
12th December: Billy WARNOCK (Belfast), LOST (Points), Belfast 4.

1935

13th January: Jack STUBBS (Congleton), DREW, Belfast 6.
19th January: Mick MCADAM (Airdrie), WON (RSF. Round 7), Belfast 10.
3rd February: Young MCMANUS (Glasgow), WON (KO. Rd 3), B'fast 6.
10th February: Paddy DOHERTY (Glasgow), WON (Points), Belfast 6.
17th March: Matt GRIFFO (Dumbarton), DREW, Belfast 6.
31st March: Gary ROACH (Wexford), WON (KO. Round 5), Belfast 6.
7th April: Pat MCGOLDIE (Glasgow), WON (Ret. Round 5), Belfast 6.
23rd April: Jim BRADY (Dundee), LOST (Points), Dundee 10.
20th May: Joe BRADLEY (Edinburgh), WON (KO. Round 7), Belfast 10.
30th May: Jack MUSSEN (Belfast), WON (Points), Belfast 6.

14th June: Jackie RYAN (Hamilton), WON (Points), Belfast 6
18th June: Freddie TENNANT (Dundee), LOST (Points), Dundee 10.
4th July: Teddy O'NEIL (Dumbarton), LOST (Points), Belfast 6.
13th July: Johnny BURKE (Kilmarnock), WON (Points), Belfast 10.
2nd September: Paddy DOHERTY (Glasgow), WON (Points), Belfast 8.
24th November: Joe HARDY (Manchester), LOST (Points), Salford 15.
5th December: Al SHARPE (Belfast), LOST (Points), Belfast 6.
15th December: Tut WHALLEY (Hanley), LOST (RSF. Rd 9), M'chester 12.

1936
18th February: Tommy HIGGINS (Manchester), DREW, Belfast 6.
2nd April: Tommy HIGGINS (Manchester), DREW, Belfast 8.
9th May: Jackie DAVIS (Manchester), WON (RSF. Round 6), Belfast 10.
23 May: Charley CURRY (Wheatly Hill), WON (RSF. Round 8), Belfast 10.
23rd June: Jim MAHARG (Glasgow), LOST (Points), Glasgow 10.
9th July: George MARSDEN (Nottingham), LOST (RSF. Round 4), B'fast 8
22nd July: Mick MCADAM (Airdrie), WON (RSF. Round 3), Belfast 10.
8th August: Tommy BODELL (Oldham), WON (KO. Round 8), Belfast 10.
27th August: Peter KANE (Golborne), LOST (RSF. Round 10), Belfast 10.
19th September: Tommy ATHERTON (M'chester), WON (Points), B'fast 10.
9th November: Pat MCSTRAVICK (Belfast), LOST (Points), Belfast 6.
28th November: Bob BATES (Coxhoe), LOST (Points), Belfast 10.
5th December: Bob BATES (Coxhoe), WON (Points), Belfast 10.
30th December: Tiger DENTON (Sheffield), WON (Points), Belfast 10.

1937
11th January: Jack MUSSEN (Belfast), LOST (Points), Belfast 10.
[Eliminator for Northern Ireland Flyweight title]
23rd January: Ted GREEN (Sheffield), WON (Points), Belfast 10.
6th February: Bob BATES (Coxhoe), LOST (Points), Belfast 10.
24th February: Peter MILLAR (Gateshead), WON (Points), Belfast 8.
10th March: Ted GREEN (Sheffield), WON (Points), Belfast 10.
29th March: Charley CURRY (Wheatley Hill), LOST (Points), Belfast 10.
12th April: Charlie CURRY (Wheatley Hill), LOST (Points), Belfast 10.
21st April: John KELLY (Glasgow), WON (Points), Belfast 10.
12th May: Abe TWEEDIE (Wishaw), LOST (Points), Belfast 10.
7th June: Ginger EBBITS (Glasgow), WON (Ret Round 5), Belfast 10.
26th June: Leftie MCKIE (Middlesborough), WON (KO. Rd 4), B'fast 10.
5th July: Leftie MCKIE (Middlesborough), WON (KO. Round 7), B'fast 10.
14th July: Abe TWEEDIE (Wishaw), WON (Points), Belfast10.
19th July: Tommy BROWN (London), LOST (Disq. Rd 3), B'fast 10.

9th August: Hughie WOODS (Glasgow), WON (Ret. Round 4), B'fast 10.
26th August: Tommy ROSE (Liverpool), WON (Points), Liverpool 8.
4th September: Tommy HAMILTON (Middlesboro), WON (Points), B'fast 10.
15th September: Willie LEGGAT (Glasgow), LOST (RSF. Rd 3), B'fast 10.
2nd October: Pat MURPHY (Jarrow), WON (Ret. Round 6), Belfast 10.
13th October: Willie LEGGAT (Glasgow), WON (Points), Belfast 10.
22nd October: Al DYER (Wigan), WON (Ret. Round 5), Belfast 10.
30th October: Bob BATES (Coxhoe), WON (Points), Belfast 10.
9th November: Joe TIERNEY (Manchester), WON (Points), Belfast 10.
22nd November: Tommy MCNEILLY (Middlesboro), WON (Ret. Rd 3), B'fast10.
3rd December: Young SIKI [Andrew Devine] (L'pool), WON (Points), B'fast 10.
18th December: Al SHARPE (Belfast), WON (Points), Belfast 10.
20th December: Stan WOODBURN (Barnsley), LOST (Points), Belfast 10.

1938
1st January: Joe SKELLY (Barnsley),WON (RSF. Round 7), Belfast 10.
10th January: Mickey CLARKE (Rochdale), WON (KO. Rd 4), B'fast 10.
13th January: Joe TIERNEY (Manchester), WON (RSF. Round 8), B'fast 10.
26th February: Joe SKELLY (Barnsley), WON (Points), Belfast 10.
14th March: Tommy NAUGHTON (Burnley), WON (Ret. Rd 4), B'fast 10.
2nd April: Ginger EBBITS (Glasgow), WON (KO. Round 6), Belfast 10.
7th April: Kid TANNER (British Guiana), LOST (RSF. Rd 7), L'pool 10.
22nd April: Jim MILLAR (Leeds), LOST (Points), Belfast 10.
14th May: Young TULLY (Manchester), WON (Points), Belfast 10.
20th May: Billy HODGSON (Lancaster), WON (RSF. Round 6), Belfast 10.
4th June: Willie SMITH (Margate), WON (Points), Belfast 6.
11th June: Billy TANSEY (Middleton), LOST (Points), Belfast 10.
20th June: Taffy JONES (St. Helens), WON (KO. Round 4), Belfast 10.
29th June: Artie SMITH (Burnley), WON (Points), Belfast 10.
9th July: Colin WARREN (Hanley), WON (Points), Belfast 10.
19th August: Jackie PATERSON (Glasgow), DREW. Belfast 10.
2nd September: Rinty MONAGHAN (Belfast), WON (Points), Belfast 10.
[*This fight was an eliminator for the vacant Northern Ireland Flyweight Title.*]
22nd October: Joe TIERNEY (Manchester), WON (Points), Belfast 10.
23rd November: Jim MCSTRAVICK (Belfast), WON (RSF. Rd 10), B'fast 15.
[*Won vacant Northern Ireland Flyweight Championship*]

1939
17th February: Joey DIXON (Macclesfield), WON (Points), Belfast 8.
3rd March: Billy NASH (Clerkenwell), WON (Points), Belfast 8.
20th March: Pierce ELLIS (Manchester), LOST (Points), Manchester 10.

28 March: Billy TANSEY (Middleton), WON (Points), Belfast 8.
4th June: Willie SMITH (Glasgow), WON (Points), Belfast 6.
10th June: Al SHARPE (Belfast), DREW, Belfast 8.
28th June: Rinty MONAGHAN (Belfast), LOST (Points), Belfast 8.
9th December: Joe BARRETT (Liverpool), WON (KO. Round 2), B'fast 10.

1940
6th January: Pat O'TOOLE (Liverpool), WON (Rtd. Round 4), Belfast 8.
4th March: Rinty MONAGHAN (Belfast), LOST (Points), Belfast 8.
22nd April: Jim BRADY (Dundee), LOST (Points), Belfast 8.

Key to abbreviations
KO = Knock Out; RSF = *Referee Stopped Fight*; Ret = *Retired by corner*; Disq = *Disqualified*

Summary:
Contests 109. WON 67. DREW 7. LOST 35.

Local historian Fred Heatley puts the real total at around 137. Boxing expert Bobby Officer sees it nearer 150. Tom Stewart junior remembers reading somewhere that his father had 200 bouts, losing 50. Another family member swears Stewart had over 300 bouts during his short career. The above is an honest and substantiated record gleaned from old newspapers and boxing magazines, and as it stands it is a credit to the wee man who gave so much to the fight game and got so little in return.

HALCYON DAYS
Henry Street Boys' Amateur Boxing Section

IN the austere days following the end of the Second World War there was little in the form of amusement for the schoolboys of York Street. Granted, Hitler's air force had left them many pieces of wasteground where they could play football until dusk but this recreation didn't suit the mothers of the area. Many of them were newly made widows as a result of the conflict, who frowned at a leisure that took soles and heels from hard-to-replace footwear. The rain was another enemy of the open-air games. Apart from a reading session with *The Rover* or *The Hotspur* there was not much else to do in those pre-television days.

The opening of a new Boys' Club in Henry Street, caused some interest but there was a limit to how many players a football team could have. The lads who fell between the stools of schoolboy and youth were not old enough to play on the snooker tables or enjoy a game of table tennis.

In the winter of 1947, John Bradbury, an ex-amateur boxer and a barber by trade, with a shop in North Queen Street, was approached by the club's leader, Jackie Montgomery, to start a boxing section. After refusing a few times, Brad, as he was known to all, was eventually coaxed into an undertaking which literally ran his life for the next decade or more.

The word got around and a few lads moved tentatively into the sparsely equipped gymnasium. Within weeks, the trickle of would-be pugilists became a stream as boys from nearby streets and others from the Shore Road and the Crumlin Road arrived to be taught the art of self-defence by the wise-cracking hairdresser, who discovered he had a natural flair for the instructional side of the game.

As mentioned, these were the days before sports equipment was manufactured wholesale in Hong Kong or Taiwan. Tracksuits were almost non-existent and any boy with a dressing-gown had to be a good scrapper. Some lads trained for weeks in vests and underpants. When the mothers thought it wasn't going to be a nine-day wonder, some pieces of cloth would be purchased from the local remnant shop. This fabric would be then run-up into a passable pair of boxing shorts by a friendly aunt or sister, lucky enough to own a sewing machine.

It was much the same with footwear. Most boys worked-out in stocking feet, until the Co-Quarter came and allowed the purchase of a pair of white mutton-dummies. If he fell by the wayside, these could be used for running the streets in the summertime. Those with headier aspirations and a few actual fights under their belts could look forward to a prestigious pair of boxing-boots, bought brand new, courtesy of a Provident Check. Others, whose parents weren't fully convinced of their offspring's dedication to the noblest art, had to make do with a secondhand pair, finely bartered for at the local pawn shop. A sad few remained in vests and underpants and had to borrow gear when competing. No matter; clothes do not make the man and likewise kit did not make the sportsman. Brad painstakingly sought out the boys with something to offer and set about moulding them into boxers.

From these humble beginnings and under Brad's excellent tuition, the lads brought back many hard-fought-for trophies and honours to the small York Street clubhouse. Locals, exiled elsewhere when the area was demolished during the 70s, still wax lyrical when they talk about the titles gathered by the young but capable fists under their trainer's shrewd and sometimes unorthodox methods, in that era long-past but still remembered.

In 1950, three years after its completion, the club was able to boast a total of 43 champions. The Boys' and Youth Club and junior and senior Ulster titles were wrested from sometimes stiff opposition, in smoky, sweaty, backstreet gyms or in the hallowed roped-off white square under the blinding arc-lights of the Ulster Hall.

The supreme testimonial to Brad's selfless devotion and his pupils untiring enthusiasm came in 1949, when John took local lad, John Wilson, to London to fight in the British Gold Star Championships. Outside the ring, Wilson or Pee-Wee, as he was affectionately known, was in modern day terms a pussycat. Shy and somewhat withdrawn, he hid behind the nearest obstacle when changing into his skip. Once inside the ring, he became a wicked and ruthless fighter. He never gave or expected quarter. His punching was lethal and he was beaten only once in his short but explosive career. Even in sparring sessions, he cut down opponents with remorseless accuracy and venom. Such was his killing instinct, Brad refused to put a junior in with him for instruction. He didn't know how to pull his punches and many fighters of note refused to share a ring with him.

The venue was the Empire Pool in Wembley. In the semi-final and final the 7 stone 7lb Pee-Wee stopped both his opponents, both in the second round, returning in triumph to the adulation of the Belfast boxing fraternity and Sailorstown. Sadly, his obvious potential was never fulfilled. A few months after his victory he took a job as a cabin boy on a cross-channel coaster. The ship collided with an aircraft carrier and sank within minutes. Pee-Wee was lost along with many of his shipmates and his body was never recovered.

Paddy Graham, a deadly ring enemy but devoted friend of Wilson remembered the great little fighter's death in the memoriam columns of the *Belfast Telegraph* for many years after his tragic death. Paddy later became an Irish Champion.

The following year, perhaps to show he wasn't a flash in the pan, Brad took the road to Wembley with another battler. Tommy Campbell, an Ulster Youth Champion, was tall and lean with a knockout punch in both hands. A close friend of the departed Pee-Wee, he lacked Wilson's killer instinct. Brad had tremendous confidence in this boxer who weighed in at 8 stone 7lbs.

Campbell, a veteran at 16, did not let him down. He stormed through the contests, winning both semi-final and final in jig-time and gave Brad another British champion to come home with.

Tommy Campbell, like his pal, took to the sea. He joined the Royal Navy and continued fighting, winning quite a few naval titles during his service. He died in 1981, as a result of gunshot wounds inflicted six years earlier. He was 47. The bullet that eventually killed him had entered his spine and left him constantly in pain and in a wheel-chair for the rest of his life.

The energetic little trainer, now in his seventies spoke wistfully about his two British champions who had both died tragically, when I talked to him recently about his club's remarkable record.

"They were the best," he stated, the memory making him uncharacteristically solemn.

Jackie Reeves, another of his exceptional fighters who were present and had seen both boys perform, agreed wholeheartedly. Jackie had been selected as the third Henry Street boy to make the trip. When they arrived, it was found he had been billed at a different weight and was unable to fight. He was allowed to take part in the opening ceremony and says it was an occasion he would never forget. As I talked to him, I could see the bond of affection between boxer and trainer had not diminished one iota during the entire passing years.

When I asked Brad if he had any favourites, Reeves answered quickly: "He treated us all the same," he remembered, "In fact a loser got more consideration than a winner. He always had a comforting word for a loser. With a winner he would simply shrug and tell them they were lucky. A master at the put-down Brad reckoned it kept the lads from becoming too cocky."

"I always allowed the boys to fight one round on their own initiative," he explained, now and again jumping to his feet to compound the point with his fists flaying the naked air.

"Whilst they fought I watched the opponent and figured out his shortcomings. When my boxer returned to his corner I dictated the strategy for the rest of the fight. If they didn't fight or box to my orders, they didn't fight for me again. I never watched my own boxer—why should I? I knew what he could do. I watched the other guy, spotted his mistakes and exploited them."

The lads understood this and there was never a cross word between tutor and pupils. Most of the boys were glad to be under his expert eye, learning to take care of themselves. Besides that, fierce competition was rife in the game and every boy had to be in tip-top condition to survive, let alone win.

Down the street was the St. John Bosco club, run by Jimmy McAree, who was later to steer Freddie Gilroy to a World Bantamweight title shot. There was also The Star, The Newsboys, The Windsor, Lower Shankill, St. George's and The White City, run by York Road man Sammy Wallace. There were others, including a host of thriving clubs outside Belfast.

John's problem was ambitious fathers, who, when their sons became popular, wanted them to turn professional. Brad was wary of such ventures and most of the lads took his advice. He reflected grimly that only one lad turned pro against his advice and was thrown to the wolves.

The club continued to turn up exceptional little warriors. Jackie Lyttle from Trafalgar Street was a four stone, All-Ireland champion and was known as 'The Bouncing Ball' and beat almost everyone put in front of him. His orders from Brad never differed. "Jump in, throw a left hook to the head, a right cross to the body and move clear." Lyttle had this down to perfection and was beaten only once, in a long and prestigious career, by a boy whom he had beaten five times previously.

He was a natural—a courageous young scrapper who actually punched above his own body-weight. Brad had great plans for him but when John 'Pee-Wee' Wilson died, Lyttle hung up his gloves. The death had come as a great shock to him as he had idolised Wilson, who was also his cousin. Lyttle never fought in the ring again.

Reeves himself, now a supervisor for a Life Assurance firm, was no slouch at the punching game and his class was such that once, whilst a Junior Flyweight champion, he boxed and beat a Senior (against Brad's advice). The fight lasted one round and the shame-faced loser left the ring in silence. He was later taken to hospital with a broken jaw. Reeves campaigned for a long time in the flyweight division and remembers fighting four hard contests to win a medal, no bigger than a penny-piece. In another instance, he recalls boxing three times, in two nights, just to reach a semi-final. His display of trophies and prizes is impressive but he explains, without rancour, that a lad fighting today could amass the same amount in a lot less time than it took him. Ten years to be exact.

He also boxed on the first Ulster Select ever formed. This team which included the great Terry Milligan, fought a Liverpool side in the Guildhall, Londonderry, on the 16th January 1953. The fighters never received any momento to celebrate the event and perhaps the only proof of its happening is the faded programme, still in Jackie's possession.

The contests were a mixture of four and six two-minute rounds. Reeves fought and beat an opponent named Kearns, an Englishman, who went on to become an ABA finalist. Jackie's retirement, at the age of 18, was due to the pressures that fall on most lads of that age—courting and studying for his City and Guilds. He went back two years later as a Bantamweight and beat a youth whose previous result was a narrow points defeat by the then up-and-coming Freddie Gilroy. Another victim of his heavy punching was Eddie Shaw, who found fame as Barry McGuigan's trainer. Reeves stopped him in the third round. He was tempted to turn professional but honoured a promise made to his father never to do so.

Tommy Stewart, from York Road, was, according to Brad, the best prospect he'd had in a long time. A Junior title-holder, he was taken to Dublin to fight in the All-Ireland Finals. According to Brad, Stewart won the match hands down but the decision went against him. The normally partisan crowd booed the result. The victor, an Irish soldier, received the winner's cup and promptly handed it over to the Ulsterman.

Stewart then fought an Irish International, called Harry Perry and known as 'The Wonder Boy'. He was 17 years old, still at school and had recently beaten a Golden Gloves Champion and a European champion in Dublin. Stewart, also 17, gave the wonderboy a terrific fight and lost narrowly on points. This form enhanced his already growing reputation and he would have become an international star of the future but some months later he gave up the game and never returned.

Ronnie Currie was another excellent craftsman who won lots of honours for the club. He became an international and boxed many times for his country, before turning pro under the watchful eye of ex-Irish champion, Jackie Briers. The highlight of his career was a points win over Jake Tuli, a former Flyweight Champion of the World.

Davy McClean, another Ulster champion, came close to International honours. His greatest achievement was beating Scotsman Bobby Neill at Edinburgh in 1954. Neill later fought for the British Featherweight title.

Other names spring easily to mind: Jim Neill, the bald-headed southpaw, who caused a minor sensation when he defeated Olympic Champion Jim McCourt in Canada. Neill, who visited Northern Ireland more than once as the trainer of the Canadian boxing team, has since come home to stay. His older brother, Gil, was an Ulster Youth Champion.

Billy Cord won an Ulster Junior title in 1954. Billy is now living in Long Island, New York, according to Jackie Reeves, whose son had a million-to-one encounter with the exile, whilst visiting New York.

Jackie, Ray and Sam, the Bond brothers from York Road, also deserve a mention. Jackie was a Junior Lightweight holder, whilst Ray, a tough, southpaw tearaway, held an Ulster Junior Welterweight title. Sammy, the youngest, joined the club in its closing year and moved to the White City club, where he won Irish Titles and boxed numerous times for his country. Jim Brown was a Senior Light-Welter, who later had a career in the paid ranks.

The list of title-holders goes on: Tommy Marlin, a native of Cookstown, stayed in digs in Belfast to receive tuition from Brad and was rewarded with a Junior Middleweight title; Davy and George Watson, Jackie Trimble, J. Herron, Ray Lindsay, D. McQuade, not forgetting Geordie Boyd, T. Emerson, J. Montgomery, Harry Stockman, Jim Smith and last but not least, Eddie Crawley, who had the distinction of winning the club its first title before going on to greater honours with the Sea-Cadets.

For the record, Brad's last fight was at the age of 39 and against a 20-year-old. The venue was a Butlin's camp and Brad had to suffer the indignity of a trial match with the camp trainer to see if he was up to the task. He won the man's breathless approval by stopping him in a few seconds with a crashing blow to his breastbone. His opponent in the final was dispatched in the second round by a similar punch. The out-foxed loser was no pushover. He later fought his way to the Northern Ireland finals. Incidentally, over three thousand people watched the fight at Butlin's.

Brad's love for the game is legendary and he tried to instil in his charges a sense of fair play and decency when competing. The club was ousted from its premises in Henry Street and took up residence in North Queen Street, in a building behind the now vanished Duncairn Picture House, in the Duncairn Gardens. The name was changed to Duncairn but most people still regarded it as Henry Street. Brad left for a while to gather his thoughts but didn't remain away for long.

Henry Street was arguably the most popular boxing club in Belfast. Hundreds of hopefuls passed through the hands of Brad and his able assistants, Tommy Neill and Tommy McKendry. He would dearly love those still alive who have lost touch to contact him or Jackie Reeves with a view to a giant reunion.

In its short but noble existence the club amassed over one hundred and thirty titles. Brad's reputation grew with every contest. He was Chief Whip for the prestigious Ireland versus The Golden Gloves in 1953. These talents were appreciated by the press in the clippings he provided to verify his statements.

His greatest thrill came one night in Ballymena. Brad was in a corner, with one of his fighters, when an official entered the ring to read out the selected Irish team to box Scotland. He finished the announcement by turning in Brad's direction and saying, "Ladies and gentlemen, in this corner—The Irish trainer for 1953—John Bradbury." No amount of money could buy the smile on his unmarked features as he savoured the memory.

Long retired but still as fit as a fiddle he can often be seen striding along York Road with the jaunty swagger most ex-boxers seem to acquire. Still wisecracking and bubbling with enthusiasm, he loves to talk about the old days but refuses to take an ounce of credit himself. "It was all down to the boys," he says, "Without them I could have done nothing." Most people who remember the era, including many respected sports journalists and the boxers themselves, would tell you it was the other way round.

MEMORIES OF A FORKLIFT TRUCK OPERATOR

APART from the firm's handcart, used in my early days to transport cargo-handling gear from the store in Nelson Street to the ship we were detailed to work at, the first vehicle I had the privilege of operating was a Ransom Rapier Lift-truck. Although not new, it was, without doubt, the largest forklift truck in Northern Ireland. Because of its colour the dockers immediately christened it 'The Green Goddess'.

The year was 1964 and the owner of the firm I worked for had travelled personally to England to purchase the unique machine. He was stevedoring a Continental General cargo ship, which arrived regularly in the port of Belfast to be discharged and then reloaded with freight from local firms. Included on its manifest were tanks of Tuborg lager, each weighing about three ton. The smaller Hyster trucks were not wide enough in the carriage to allow their forks to enter the slots provided and thus carry the tanks safely from the ship's side to the area where they were stacked or loaded onto lorries. The Rapier was purchased because her carriage was wide enough to allow her to perform this task.

It was also fitted with a portable extension beam, which transferred the truck into a reliable mobile crane. There was only one drawback: most of the cargo was perishable and had to be off-loaded inside the cargo sheds. As they filled up, the Rapier's length and bulk became a handicap. A hired Hyster 80, less than half her size and capable of lifting the same weight, literally ran rings around the aged Goddess. Eventually, she was scrapped and replaced by two spanking new Hysters.

I was detailed to drive one of these vehicles and was operating it at a timber boat in York Dock C when the boss asked if I would go, with the machine, to the new factory being built by the ICI, in a place called Kilroot which was on the outskirts of Carrickfergus. My ignorance was such that I didn't know where Kilroot was! I went the following day and the contract, which was originally for two weeks, lasted, with a few intermittent breaks, for almost eight years.

The machine and myself were seconded to a squad of riggers but it soon became the workhorse of the entire site, doing all the chores it was built for and quite a few never dreamed of by its designers.

I returned to the docks in the 80s to find decasualisation had decimated the casual workforce. My employer had become stevedore to a fledgling shipping company named Unit. This ship carried loaded containers and flat-racks from Liverpool to Belfast. When these were off-loaded, the ship was filled with full or empty flat-racks and containers.

A giant machine was needed to implement this service and a Hyster 620 was purchased and brought to Belfast. Capable of lifting 25 tonnes and weighing a massive 45 tonnes, she was more than three times the size of the last machine, purchased initially to lift empty containers.

Whilst there are heavier and larger trucks operating on Belfast Quay, these are technically container-handlers and employ hydraulic spreaders which lift the loaded boxes from the top instead of the slots on the bottom. Efficient as they are, they are not as versatile as the lift-truck, which was the biggest forklift truck in Ireland.

The Hyster could also lift from the top as well as the bottom and the method of operation, whilst perhaps primitive, was simplicity itself. A 30 foot by eight foot steel frame with lifting wires and ISO shoes attached to each corner allowed the operator to hoist and move loaded containers and flat-racks with safety and speed. The driver added the beam to the machine by driving the forks of the truck into the slots provided. After use, he would reverse out of the lifting frame and resume normal working mode.

Vision was almost 100 per cent as the truck was not equipped with a cab. This did not unduly worry me, as I specifically wanted to be able to see clearly where I was going at all times. I made do with a heavy coat over my legs, much in the manner of the old carters, who had disappeared with their flesh and blood horses around the same time the diesel powered substitutes hit the quay.

Through hard-earned experience, I had learned to watch out for telephone poles and wires, overhead power lines and other such inanimate but dangerous objects. The machine itself commanded respect from me, as I gradually became aware that I was in sole control of a metal monster capable of knocking down brick walls or anything else of substance that cared to argue with it.

It could roar like a lion or purr like a pussycat. Either way, she was worth her daily drink of fuel when it came to clearing up the work.

The arrival of this truck revolutionised cargo handling and rendered many of the old methods obsolete. For instance, coils of steel weighing up to 25 tonnes were, at that period, lifted from the ship by a fixed harbour crane and left to the elements of the open berth. Mobile cranes found it difficult to operate between the roof-trusses of the harbour sheds and those large enough to lift such a weight would find it difficult to even enter the shed. The additional cost of hiring lorries to transport the coils from the ship's side to the shed made the scheme too expensive for the stevedore to contemplate.

The Hyster, with specially made lifting wires, was able to pick up the coils from the breast of the quay and carry them quickly and safely into the shed. This also saved the stevedore the worry of rust-causing rain and the cost of hiring expensive tarpaulins, some of which were often stolen or blown into the dock.

Steel plates each weighing one tonne, with dimensions of 20 feet by 8 feet and a thickness of two or three inches, were loaded, in that period, one at a time by mobile cranes with two slingers, using wire ropes and cumbersome plate-dogs for lifting. The lift-truck was able to slide its forks beneath 18 of these (which was the legal limit for a lorry load) and deposit them on the back of the trailer in a matter of minutes. Reinforcing wire, used in the manufacture of concrete beams, came in two-ton bundles, about twenty or thirty feet long and were loaded just as quickly. The list was endless and the truck and operator were very much in demand.

Other chores included the odd errand of mercy into Whitla Street, to pick up containers and flat-racks thrown from lorries when their unsuspecting drivers failed to manipulate the tight curve of the new road between the lower end of Duncrue Street and Garmoyle Street. The local police got to know me by name as they came for me many times to rescue these unfortunate drivers, who were later booked for careless driving.

Sometimes, the machine would be sent to uplift unattached loaded trailers that had crushed their dolly wheels and crashed to the ground, making it impossible for the tractors to engage and pull them ashore. Containers would also be overturned in the bowels of a ferry if it crossed in rough weather. Work would be at a standstill until the Hyster appeared to clear the bottleneck.

These acts of mercy would be performed in between her principle duty of keeping the Unit Shipping traffic moving. Such became the dependency on this particular piece of equipment that a breakdown, however brief, took on the hallmarks of a catastrophe. Everything, literally, came to a halt, whilst the experts rushed to get her mobile again. The ballast quay boasted one fixed crane, and it could only reach so far. If the Hyster wasn't there to carry the cargo away then the area would become congested and the crane would be unable to empty the ship. As Preston, where the Guernsey Fisher steamed from, was a tidal port, it was imperative that the vessel was ready for sea at the correct time.

Management decided that a back-up vehicle was needed. The necessary arrangements were made and soon the Hyster had a big brother in the shape of a Clark 800 Container Handler. Sporting the colours of the old Green Goddess, she weighed in at a mammoth 60 tonnes and could stack 40-foot containers three high with absolutely no effort. She was 20 metres long from front to stern and travelled on six wheels, two on each side at the front and two on the back. They were shoulder-high to a six-foot tall man. The power-assisted steering was so light the operator could turn the steering wheel with the index finger of one hand. A spacious cabin protected the driver from the elements and falling pieces of cargo, but it took away a lot of his vision.

Its capabilities were enormous. Whilst the Hyster sometimes strained with an overloaded container, the Clark could hoist anything up to 30 tonnes from ground to lorry or vice-versa in under two minutes.

In earlier days, dockers had scoffed at the idea of putting cargo in wooden or tin-boxes. 'How can 30 feet long steel pipes or 45 gallon oil drums be stowed in a box?' they asked, firmly dismissing the whole idea as a gimmick. Today, almost everything we wear, eat, need or use, including 30 foot long steel pipes and 45 gallon oil-drums are carried on flat-racks or in containers of which there are over 20 different types to choose from. They are clean, efficient, and minimise pilfering and damage. On the debit side, they were a deathblow to an already ailing industry.

After almost two years of blistering activity, a Clark with just a little more muscle reluctantly replaced the Hyster 600. Unlike the container handler, it was fitted with forks and like the Hyster, could double-up as a handler by using the portable lifting beam. The forks were heavy and had to be moved from inside the cab by pressing a button. Thus, it could hoist literally anything. It was ideal for lifting and moving, from the crane area, large slabs of granite that weighed anything up to 25 tonnes. These would later be loaded onto lorries for destinations in the Republic of Ireland. It also handled enormous pieces of machinery, carted by heavy-haulage vehicles from the GEC factory in Larne. These were off-loaded in the Stormont sheds until the vessel they would be loaded onto arrived at the 200 tonne crane. Any piece of cargo too big to be put in the shed was left in the open berth within range of the crane. Expensive and sometimes irreplaceable articles like these had to be handled with extreme care and caution. A reckless or inexperienced operator could lose a valuable load simply by travelling at the wrong speed. Men on the ground were also at risk, especially older dockers, who were unaccustomed to the vehicle's speed, noise and ability to turn in its own length. The drivers had to be extremely wary of pedestrian dockers, when working at close quarters.

One horrifying experience of my own will never be forgotten. At the end of a long day we were loading the ship with her return cargo of laden and empty containers and flat-racks. The flats were stacked in nests of six and lashed with chain lengths to make them one secure unit. Because of the noise that came from the machine's heavy engine, normal speech was out of the question. The checker and myself had developed, over the years, a hand-signalling system that allowed us to work as a team. He would position himself where I could see him and point at the lift he wanted placed beside the crane.

A nest of 30 foot flats had a pair of tensed chains over it and looked ready for shipping. The checker was of the same opinion as myself and waved me into the lift. I noted the bottom flat was without pockets, which would have allowed me to lift cleanly. The alternative was to coax the blades of the truck beneath the bottom flat and force them in below it thus making the lift secure. A 20-foot loaded container directly behind it would stop the flats from sliding away from the machine. On the run in to perform this not very difficult operation, I noticed that the forks were not as widely spaced as I would have liked. As this was the truck without the press-button movement, I had to dismount and adjust them physically.

Imagine my consternation when two old dockers ambled out from behind the flat-racks. Unfamiliar with the normal method of working from where they could be seen, they had thrown the chain-lengths over from the front and proceed to tighten them down at the back on the blind side, placing themselves out of my sight in the narrow space between the flats and the loaded container.

Had I continued the first time I would have shoved the flats against the container and crushed both men to death. The fact that only a split second change of thought saved these men from a horrible demise has always served to remind me that the danger of accidents, major or minor, to man or property, is only a heartbeat away at any given moment.

Another man wasn't so lucky. I had been lifting down unloaded containers for him to examine in his engineering yard most of the day and he'd been telling me of his plans to go on holiday at the end of that very day. I had dropped the last box for him to examine and was ready to drive the small truck to base when I was detailed to leave it and proceed with the Clark container handler to the Stormont Wharf, where a full container was waiting to be loaded onto a lorry.

An inexperienced man was detailed to bring the other truck back to base. As he was leaving, he was asked to move one of the boxes I had lifted down. As he reversed, the truck drove over the man who was checking the container's number on a piece of paper. He was badly injured and died a few days later.

Enthusiasm is no substitute for experience and familiarity can only breed the most dangerous kind of contempt. The kind that causes over-confidence and tempts the driver to take the short cuts he can sometimes live to regret. In the final analysis, the machine will only do what the operator's hands and feet urge it to. To stay out of trouble, he would need the neck of a giraffe, the eyes of a hawk and the luck of the devil.

On a lighter note, a long association between man and mechanical beast can create an affinity between flesh and inanimate metal. After all, the machine has taken the place of the mate with whom he generally worked before becoming a truck operator.

I experienced such a feeling of camaraderie with the Hyster 600. Like the Clark 800, I was its first operator and often wonder where it is now. My only regret was that I couldn't take it into the pub with me for an end of the workday drink it so richly deserved.

In retrospect, there would not have been a big problem getting it into the public house but I don't think the owner and the customers would have been amused at the method of entry.

first published in *Export and Freight Magazine* (1986)

THE JOHN HEWITT I KNEW

ONE of the most agreeable experiences of my life was meeting, and getting to know John Hewitt. I won't pretend I knew him well, or for long, yet each time I had the honour to be in his company, either socially, or otherwise, I came away richer in knowledge. The wisdom he passed on so freely was priceless.

More importantly, it was neither condescending nor patronising. It was man to man, scribbler to scribbler over a nip of scotch or a glass of ale. I was not in any way unique to this treatment. John Hewitt gave freely of his time and expertise to many of us who strove to express our thoughts and feelings through the written word.

I first met him in 1981, when he graciously sent me an invitation via a young female student of English literature who was collecting material for a thesis. A radio producer, who had expressed an interest in some poems I had written, had given my name to her. Needless to say, I was thrilled. I knew of his work and his tremendous standing in the literary world.

On the specified night I arrived at his home clutching a selection of what I thought were my best efforts, plus a half-bottle of Black Bush. He met me at the door and shook hands warmly before ushering me into his study. After some tea and biscuits, prepared by his niece, Jean, we then broke out the whiskey. After a few appreciative sips we then began to talk, or rather, he talked and I listened. He seemed genuinely pleased to receive the poems I had brought him. After a moment or two silently browsing through it, he nodded approvingly and placed the slim booklet along with the vast array of books that sat on shelves lining the walls of the room. In return he gave me an audio cassette of some of his poetry, read by himself, as well as a Blackstaff edition called *Poets of the North of Ireland*, which, at my request, he signed and dated. Needless to say, I was moved by this gesture.

Then, like the walrus, he began to talk. He spoke of Thomas Carnduff and the Rhyming Weavers. He gently criticised me for making do with unpure rhymes and implored me to treat every effort with all the ability I could muster, before making it complete. He urged me to continue to record the trials and tribulations of the working-class people of York Street and Sailorstown, quietly assuring me that no-one else, to his knowledge, was writing poetry on these themes. I enjoyed his company that night. It was the first time anyone of note had discussed my writing and I resolved to remember everything he had told me. An impossible task perhaps, but from that night I never used an impure rhyme no matter how great the temptation. I also took on board his advice on other methods of writing poetry, like free verse. However, I had decided early in life never to work or to present work in this idiom. If it's poetry or verse, I believe it has an obligation to rhyme; if it doesn't, it's prose. A sweeping statement perhaps, but I'll stick to it.

A year or so later, I was pleased to see him at the launching of my Blackstaff collection called *Saturday Night In York Street*. During the proceedings he congratulated me warmly and asked me to sign a copy for him. Sometime later, he invited me back to his home. This time he provided the whiskey. He had made himself familiar with some of the poems in *Saturday Night In York Street* and seemed a little troubled by the emphasis on violence in some of the contents. I told him I was equally opposed to physical aggression and tried to explain it was a way of life in some areas. I didn't glorify it but simply recorded it because it was and is a sad basis of fact in most working-class communities. This was due to circumstances, which in many instances included poverty and neglect.

We shared a table more than once at the annual 'Poets and Pints' Night held at the Laganbank Social club in the Markets area.

There, he received adulation more befitting a god than a visiting poet from the Malone Road. When he took to the stage, the normally boisterous crowd would fall silent the moment he began to speak. Leaning on his walking stick, he looked them in the collective eye and told them he was an Ulsterman and nobody was going to chase him from the land he loved. They approved his defiance and respected him for it. When he left the rostrum, it was to tremendous, prolonged applause.

During one of these sessions I invited him on a tour of the fast disappearing bars of Dockland which he and his niece, Jean, accepted. Most of the district had already fallen to the demolition crews. Only a fraction of the dwelling houses remained tenable and only a few of the public houses were open for business.

He asked for and received no preferential treatment. We squeezed into one of the packed bars on the North Queen Street peace-line in the Protestant district before making our way to Pilot Street in the Docks area. Blending into each company I introduced him to, he sipped stoically at his occasional half-pint of ale. He was extremely interested in his surroundings and most of the journey was spent in silence as he took in the desolate landscape.

Sometime later, we met at the launching of John Gray's marvellous *City In Revolt* on the steps of the Customs House in Donegall Square. He spoke of his pleasure at the earlier trip and asked if we could do it again sometime. I was a little apprehensive. The marching season had started and I didn't relish taking him into Garmoyle Street during that time. His wide, mocking grin seemed to say I wasn't as tough as I thought I was. Without further ado, we arranged a meeting on the 13th July. Perhaps I was being overly cautious but it was a sensitive period in the calendar. The sound of fifes and drums, which heated the blood of most Protestants, had an adverse effect on the Catholic population. I needn't have worried. In every bar we were treated with friendship and cordiality. Our last stop was the Rotterdam Bar in Pilot Street. It had just been newly renovated and I thought John would be interested in the decor. I wasn't disappointed. He sipped and smoked as his eyes wandered appreciatively around the low-ceilinged barroom. Now and again he would allow his chin to rest pensively on the head of his walking stick.

During the proceedings, I noticed a group of young men at another table eyeing us with considerable interest. My built-in hassle detector went into top gear when one of them rose and moved quickly out the door and into the street. Naturally, I assumed the worst. Most of the Catholics in that community were broadminded but generally they didn't get an influx of Prods during the marching season ... not socially anyway. John and his niece remained blissfully unaware as I exchanged concerned glances with the other member of the party who was doing the driving. After what seemed an eternity we rose to leave. The young men watched our exit with muted interest. We were all in the car and ready to depart when the lad who had left the bar came running to us. As he approached the car he dug his right hand into the inside pocket of his jacket. Our worst fears were unfounded when the hand came out clutching a book, which turned out to be a copy of John's latest publication. He reached it in through the open window.

"I thought I recognised you in the bar and rushed home for the book hoping to get back before you left," he said breathlessly, adding, "I was wondering if you would sign it for me, Mr. Hewitt." Needless to say my companion and I heaved a sigh of relief as John happily autographed the book, blissfully unaware of our apprehension.

Our next stop was the Grove Tavern. A bustling bar on the predominantly Protestant York Road, it was packed with drinkers recovering from the rigours of the Twelfth. Again, John sat shoulder to shoulder with the locals. We had just finished our first drink when one of my friends, slightly under the weather, approached our table. For a moment, he gazed with what I took to be awe at the imposing figure of the poet. Then he spoiled it all by leaning forward and playfully tugging at John's grey beard. "What about ye, oul han'," he grinned affectionately.

"Cut that out," I growled angrily, rising to my feet. John Hewitt removed the tension by laughing as loudly as my friend. I was outraged. "Bouncer," I chided, addressing him by his nickname. "This gentleman is one of the finest poets in the whole of Ireland. His name is John Hewitt." Bouncer, suitably chastened, lowered his head and muttered an apology. John gave me a sidelong glance that implied I was making a mountain out of a molehill but I continued, loud enough for the rest of the bar's occupants to hear. "Earlier today I took this gentlemen into a few of the pubs in the Dock area. He was treated with the respect and admiration a man of his standing is entitled to and on one occasion was asked for his autograph. Then I bring him to this fountain of life and what happens? Bouncer pulls his beard".

By now, Bouncer had retreated, shamefaced, to the rear of the bar, convinced he had committed the crime of the century. However the comparison I was at pains to make wasn't lost on the other customers. During the drive home I asked John if he had enjoyed the outing. His eyes glinted as he answered in the affirmative, adding, "especially when that fellow pulled my beard." I think he was tickled by the irreverence. Such was the man in my company at least; no airs, no graces, just, dare I say it, one of the boys.

I received word of his death with sadness. Over the years I had tried not to presume on our relationship but would, now and again phone him, when in need of advice. Now, the oracle was dead. In terms of education and upbringing, John Hewitt was light-years away from most of the would-be writers and poets he had helped to enlighten. Yet, as stated earlier, he had a unique way of blending into whatever environment he found himself in. He seemed to be as equally at home with the punters in the American Bar as he was with the academics of Queen's University.

Sometime later, I received a letter from the management of the Laganbank Social club, asking if I would read two of his poems at a memorial service they were arranging. I readily accepted the chance to pay homage to the man I had greatly admired. On the night I read from the book he had given me years earlier, the poems, 'A Father's Death' and 'Sonnets for Roberta.'

Others present who contributed to the moving tribute were Roy McFadden, James Simmons, Damian Smyth, Martin Lynch, Sam MacAughtry, Denis Grieg, Padraic Fiacc and Tom Morgan—each, I'm sure, with their own personal memories of the man and his work. Dixie Gilmore, the then Lord Mayor of Belfast also put in an appearance. During the homily, John's remarkable likeness looked down from an excellent painting commissioned by the management of the Laganbank club. The artist was local painter Joe O'Kane.

Through the years I knew him, John Hewitt showed me kindness. He didn't have to and wasn't obliged to, yet he gave selflessly of his time and wisdom. The esteemed author of many books and poems gently tried to ignite the flame of a lesser light. I thank his memory for his patience and understanding. In my own humble opinion, he was a poet beyond par; a tremendous talent, who underplayed his own eminence. His voice may have been silenced but his poetry and prose will continue to stir and delight humankind, until the light of the world flickers out. As fine an epitaph as any, for one who could truthfully claim to be the poet of all the people. May he rest in peace and long may his praises be sung. I, for one, was proud and honoured to have known him.

THE MAGIC BOX

DETECTIVE Inspector Alan Delany of the Belfast Harbour Constabulary entered the guardroom of the Tomb Street station and sat down at his desk. The long, low but audible sigh that escaped from his pursed lips caused the other occupant of the room to glance in his direction.

"You feeling okay, sir?" asked the uniformed sergeant, who up to that moment had been painfully typing a statement with the index finger of his right hand.

The inspector seemed not to hear him. He was gazing intently at a small piece of white paper, which he had just drawn from the top pocket of his tweed sports jacket. The other officer shook his head and returned to his typewriter.

Delany unfolded the piece of notepaper and read the contents, before placing it carefully under a glass paperweight on his desk. Leaning forward, he put both elbows on the desktop and began running the fingers of his right hand through his long, dark hair.

"C'mon," he muttered, "logic is logic, fact is fact. There's got to be a logical, factual answer."

"To what?" stated the sergeant, thinking the remarks were addressed to him. Delany looked up, visibly startled. He had not been aware of the room's other occupant. He smiled wanly, "Didn't know you were there Joe," he murmured.

He opened the top drawer of his desk and fumbled for his

beloved pipe. An unseeing finger checked that the bowl was full and the next instant saw the stem clasped between his teeth. Only when the smoke cleared from the first inhalation did he seem to relax.

"It's the proverbial long story, Joe, but if you've got a few minutes, maybe you'd like to hear it."

The typewriter was completely forgotten as the sergeant watched his superior rise from his chair and walk to a large, grey filing cabinet. Grabbing the handle of a drawer that had his name and rank neatly typed on a small white card, he jerked it fully open.

He hoped the watching sergeant didn't notice his hand shaking as he dug his searching fingers into the back of the drawer. He himself felt different. His mood had changed. He was now experiencing a tingle of excitement, a thrill of satisfaction, that usually came after weeks, even months of intensive inquiries; the painstaking series of eliminations that took a file from the 'unsolved, left open' section to the 'matter successfully dealt with, file closed' category.

It didn't happen often and detective work or forensic evidence had not brought about the conclusion of this case. Like more cases than the inspector would care to admit, this one had been solved by the passage of time and coincidence. He drew forth a buff-coloured folder from where it had lain hidden and forgotten for over twenty years and walked back to his desk.

Taking the pipe from his mouth, he carefully knocked the hot ash into a large ashtray, before returning it to the drawer. Leaning back in his chair, he clasped both hands behind his head and smiled over at the bemused sergeant.

"Would you come here a minute, Joe, I've something I'd like you to read." The sergeant duly obeyed and was handed the buff-coloured folder. Delany once again ran his fingers through his now dishevelled hair, before saying, somewhat desperately:

"Read that statement aloud for me. I've got to get a second opinion on this."

Joe pulled out the faded pages and placed them on his knee.

"Forget about the official crap," muttered the inspector. "Just read from the day and date taken."

The sergeant nodded dutifully, but looked up with an inquiring glance when he read the date as the 9th July 1966.

"That's thirty years ago!" he stammered. He was waved on by the inspector and continued: "Statement made by Patrick Hilton aged 64 and 2 months, after caution, by Constable A. Delany, in Ward 4, Mater Hospital. Statement begins:

To tell you the truth, I was still half-drunk from the night before. The boys were finishing up for the Twelfth. I should have known better for I'd work to go to the next morning.

The inspector allowed a slight smile to cross his thoughtful features as the sergeant continued:

Andy Brunton and me had two dirty freight containers to wash. I work for Global Contractors away down there on the reclaimed land beyond the power station. That's my job. I wash out dirty containers. I'm sure you know what containers are, constable. They are big steel boxes that come off the boats and are loaded onto lorries that deliver their contents all over the country. They come in two or three different shapes and sizes and carry everything from coal and foodstuffs to television sets and tobacco.

The sergeant raised his eyes from the statement. "Bit of a prolific old goat," he laughed. Delany moved his feet and tugged at the creases in his chocolate-coloured slacks.

"That was my doing, Joe," he muttered, half-smiling at the recollection. "I fancied myself as a bit of a journalist in those days; besides, it was my first statement and I wanted to record all the facts." He moved his chair backwards and stretched his legs. "Maybe I'm throwing you in at the deep end. Perhaps I should fill in a bit before you go on. Then you'll see what I was up against ... The more that oul fella talked the more absurd and far-fetched his story became. As you can see I got him to initial almost every paragraph to prove they were his own words, but I never did get the courage to show the finished item to my superior."

"Here's how it started," he continued, as he puffed from his pipe. "On the day in question I was on mobile duty in the landrover with Billy Kyle. About 10:30 a.m. we got a call from base to investigate a report of an accident at a container storage depot down at the West Twins. It's all built-up now with factories and what have you, but in those days it was virtually deserted. A grass-covered wasteland inhabited by horses and ponies owned by local men who put them there for grazing purposes. There wasn't even a road to it. We followed the tracks made by the lorries that left the containers down to be steam-cleaned.

"Eventually we arrived at a wired-up compound containing a small wooden site hut and a few broken-down trailers. There were also a couple of forklift trucks, plus, of course, the containers that were to be washed. The perimeter fence was about 15 feet high, and at the entrance gate, which was equally as high, we saw a man bending over another man who was lying prone and motionless on the ground. The man on his feet identified himself as Andy Brunton. He told us the injured man had been trying to gain entrance to the compound by climbing over the gate and had fallen.

"Brunton, who had possession of the keys to the premises, had opened the gate and the door of the site-hut to gain access to a telephone. He named the man on the ground as a fellow worker called Paddy Hilton. Hilton was checked for broken bones before being lifted into the back of the landrover. I radioed base to say we would be leaving him in the capable hands of the men manning the fire brigade station in Whitla Street. This was okayed by base. I took a brief statement from Brunton as mentioned, and wrote the matter off as an industrial accident when I returned to headquarters."

He broke off and smiled at Joe's thinly-disguised look of boredom. "On the Monday, two days later, I returned to a right rollicking. I'd made a prime mistake and the chief was flaming. In our hurry to get Hilton to hospital we'd driven off leaving the gate and the door to the site hut open. Brunton, you'll recall had opened it to phone Base. Worse was to come," he added grimly, his face a mask as he relived the past. "When the staff checked the grounds they found a forty-foot aluminium container was missing."

"What was in it?" asked Joe, suddenly interested.

Delany rolled his eyes heavenward. "It was empty, thank goodness. One of the pair the oul fellas were to steam-wash."

"How could they have moved it? Sure those things must weigh about two ton," said his companion.

Delany flashed him a wistful smile. "There were a couple of forklift trucks lying about the yard. They could have lifted them onto a trailer without any hassle. The ignition keys were in the hut we'd left insecure all weekend. Anyway, when the boss cooled down he ordered me up to the Mater to get a statement from Paddy Hilton. He reckoned it wasn't beyond the realms of possibility that he and his mate were mixed up in the theft. Those boxes make great stores or site huts. Farmers have been known to keep livestock in them. In those days you'd have got five or six hundred quid in your hand for an an aluminium one. And there was little or no comeback. They'd disappear down about the border, or even over it ... never to be seen again."

Joe agreed with a nod of his head. "Did you get any joy from the oul lad?"

"Listen," answered Delany. "When I went into the ward he was sitting up in bed with two black eyes, a swathe of bandages round his head, and minus his top and bottom dentures. Not a pretty sight. Other than that, he was as right as rain, as the saying goes. That was when he made that statement. It's the most incredible document I have ever drafted; read on," he added, "and only stop when I tell you to. Y'know, before that man was finished, I wasn't sure who was mad. Him ... Me. Or both of us."

Joe lowered his eyes to the paper as Delany tugged gently at his briar, blowing sweet-smelling smoke towards the guardroom ceiling.

Joe began to read silently. Delany reached over and poked him with the pipe. "Aloud," he said. "Read it aloud."

Joe cast an embarrassed eye around him. Other officers, some coming on duty, others going home, had stopped in their tracks and were silently eavesdropping. Delany poked him again: "Get to it," he ordered.

"He's still going on about the usefulness of these container boxes," continued Joe, reluctantly.

Some boxes are made of steel, others from aluminium. They are lighter to transport and less prone to rust. On the day of the accident, the one we were supposed to wash ... They were Jumbos ... That's slang for the very large boxes ... Nine and a half-foot high and forty feet long. Towser, that's Brunton's nickname, and me decided to go down there early and get done early, but it didn't work out that way. As usual he was late and he had the keys of the gate.

It was a funny sort of a day. Warm, overcast. I sat there on my own for about half an hour, just looking round me. The big lake, just outside the compound was shimmering and shining like a tub full of razorblades. A boat was unloading bulk-sulphur a bit further down and the grass was covered with a yellow dust that was blowing everywhere. Smoke was pouring, black as your boot from the Power Station chimneys across the dock, and a big grey cloud was wafting away from the fertiliser factory. I got kind of afraid sitting there. There was so much chemicals in them clouds and hazes, all it needed to blow the world apart was a stroke of lightning.

Joe broke off and looked at the inspector. "Is this a statement or a novel?" he asked with an unbelieving grin.

"That was the third re-write of his original. I thought he was lying and made him go over it in an effort to catch him out."

Joe continued:

I climbed the gate because I was dry and wanted a drink of water. I knew the hut was locked but the standpipe we used for washing was out in the yard. Towser said he found me at the bottom of the gate. Mebbe he did, but I wasn't climbing to get in ... I was trying to get out.

Constable, I know you are not going to believe this, but at least listen. Write it down. Investigate it. I need to get it off my chest. I feel as if I'm caught between a pleasant dream and a nightmare.

Joe looked up and saw a group of his colleagues were as engrossed in the proceedings as the inspector was. Shrugging his shoulders, he returned to the statement.

When I came round, blood was running from a massive cut in the side of my head. I was groggy and could just about hear Towser chiding me for being a silly fool. I never told him the real story, but I've been lying here all weekend turning it over and over in my mind until I wasn't able for anything else. You want a statement, well you're going to get the full story and I demand an explanation into what took place.

As I said, I successfully scaled the gate and made my way to the standpipe. The water was lovely and cold. The sun was getting hotter and to be honest, I felt like stripping off and going for a dip in the lake. I wandered over to the first of the boxes to be washed. Out of habit I checked the number against the one in my notebook 'cause you don't get paid if you wash the wrong box.

Joe paused when the inspector indicated that he wanted to speak. "The number is written on the margin and I can tell you it was the serial number of the box that disappeared."

"Went missing," corrected Joe.

"Disappeared," repeated the other with a mysterious smile.

Joe lowered his eyes.

I decided to open the doors of the box and have it ready for when Towser appeared. I was almost choked by the strong smell of chemicals. White powder lay like snow on the ridged floor. I moved away quickly and walked towards the other container. That's when I noticed the red plastic bucket. It was standing under the tailboard of a derelict trailer, on which lay some rusted barrels, almost hidden by the trailer's high sides.

'It had lain there for more years than I could remember — damaged aboard ship, the trailer had been dumped and forgotten. The bucket contained a small amount of liquid soap. Some of the contents of the leaking barrels had also filtered down into it. I took it to the standpipe and filled it with water. Time was passing and as Towser still hadn't showed up, I thought I could make a start by sluicing the floor of the container. More than once I cursed him for not letting me have the keys to the site hut. With them I could have got the steam-washer to do the job properly and I wouldn't be lying here looking into your disbelieving eyes.

"Stop," thundered the inspector. His harsh tone caused the men around to gaze silently at each other. "Before you go on, I want you to visualise the scene. A rookie cop and a little man with a story straight out of *Billy's Weekly Liar*. Would you have believed him?" he added hoarsely.

"My bet is he was still suffering from concussion, and unable to distinguish from dreams and reality. No disrespect sir, but it's obvious you were taking a statement from an unreliable witness," said the sergeant.

Delany neither agreed nor disagreed. "Read on," he said curtly.

The watching officers were now observing him closely. His face was strained and agitated. He seemed to be back in time with the old man. Joe felt somewhat uncomfortable but obeyed. Again he took up the story.

Usually I walk halfway up the box, toss the water against the rear bulkhead and let it sluice backwards to carry some of the dirt and dust with it. However the stench of the chemicals was too great to enter the box, so I stood at the door and threw the water up as far as I could.

The sergeant stopped reading suddenly, his face a mixture of mirth and disbelief.

"Go on," yelled Delany, harshly, triumphantly.

The room was silent as Joe continued. He tried vainly to suppress the laughter that threatened to engulf him.

There was no blinding flash to herald what happened next ... No thunderous crack from the skies, no smoke, and what was worse ... there was no container. Two tons of metal had disappeared before my eyes. I threw the bucket as far away from me as I could. I never felt so alone, so frightened. The hairs on my head felt as if they were standing on end and an uncontrollable shiver caused my body to shake visibly.

Delany looked at the men around him. "That old man is describing the symptoms of pure unadulterated fear. Pray you never encounter the same," he finished with a smile.

"Sorry sir, but it sounds like pure undiluted alcohol to me," answered the sergeant. The inspector accepted the titter of laughter that followed with a grim grin.

"Continue," he ordered. The sergeant obeyed:

Then I saw the container. It was perched between two blades of thick grass. Complete, intact with its doors still open ... But it was barely six inches long and about two inches high. Then I did the daftest thing. Had I left it there, had I not touched it, I would have proof of the greatest invention of the century. I'd have been swilling champagne with the big-timers instead of sitting here accused of theft.

But all that my brain would register was the fact that I had damaged an expensive item, so the first priority was to get rid of the evidence. I got down on my knees and picked it up gingerly, but it was solid to the touch. I peered at it closely. Everything was exact. Just like peering down the opposite end of a telescope. It scared me. I rose to my feet, and drawing my arm back, hurled it as far into the lake as I could.

It floated through the air like an empty cigarette packet and landed with a small splash. For a few moments the water surged and roared as if a bomb had exploded beneath the surface, then it fell silent and calm again.

I've thought of nothing else since I regained consciousness. I didn't steal the box. No one did. It's out there in the lake. Find it constable ... Find it and I'll split the proceeds with you. Better still ... Get the bucket, get somebody to examine it. We'll make a million.

As I said, when Towser found me, he thought I'd fallen gettin' in, but it was the other way round. I was trying to get away from a nightmare. Constable, get them to drag the lake. I know the article is small, but if they were to find it. Just imagine, containers you could carry in your pocket, and they'd be damned easy to wash.

The watching men were openly grinning as Joe looked up and said: "Statement ends."

Almost immediately their eyes turned to the inspector, who was smiling like a poker player who knows he possesses the best cards in the game.

"I read and re-read that statement," he said impassively. "Rookie or not I knew there was no way I could take it to my boss. He would have had me locked up for wasting police time and the old man committed to an asylum. But I continued to ponder what had happened to that container. I wondered if maybe the men who stole it had attacked the old fella. Some drivers could have entered the compound and been surprised by Hilton. Remember it was the beginning of a holiday week and they didn't expect to see anyone.

Keys were not needed for the lift-trucks. I later learned they could be started by a screwdriver.

"I thought about his mate Towser maybe being in on it. Providing the keys and staying away purposely. Outlandish or not, fairy tale or truth, these were the factors I had to wrestle with. One thing was certain; the container, which had been checked in on a Friday night, had disappeared without a trace. Could two tons of hard metal vanish into thin air? What if the old man's rantings were true? We're taught most of the world's greatest inventions have been discovered by accident. What if a container the size of a cigarette box is languishing at the bottom of the lake?" He lifted the piece of paper from under the paperweight, grinning sheepishly as a titter of laughter followed his last sentence.

"Okay," he admitted defensively. "An officer has to investigate every source open to him. My immediate duty was to take his statement to the chief and ask him to have the lake drained or dragged in an effort to prove or disprove the old man's story. But I didn't. Self-preservation prevailed and that's why I'm a Detective inspector and not still a constable. I threw the statement to the back of my drawer where it lay until now. I told the chief the old man was delirious and couldn't remember anything.

"Hilton recovered and went back to work. He told all and sundry about his magic box. People told him a cigarette box wasn't much good as a freight container, but he continued to search for the red bucket he had used that day. He earned himself the nickname of 'Buckets' because he kept looking for it until they retired him some years later."

"Did you ever get to the bottom of it?" asked the sergeant.

Delany's face was pensive, unsure. He lowered his eyes and stared at the page in his hand before looking directly at Joe.

"Just one more page to read, sergeant," he whispered before handing over the piece of notepaper. "Read that and tell me that fact is fact and logic is logic."

Joe took the piece of computer paper and glanced at the small paragraph in the centre of the page.

"Unbelievable," he muttered, before reading the words aloud to his now hushed audience.

"Gotto Wharf 09-30 hours Wednesday. Message to Police Office

Harbour Estate. Foreman in charge of squad draining large stretch of land-locked water adjacent to Global Container yard has uncovered forty-foot container approximately 40 metres from the perimeter wire. The box is aluminium and is lying on its side with its doors open. Would ask if any such item has been reported missing recently. Also would seek advice on how to remove it as it is well outside the radius of any crane jib known to us.

"Message ends," said the sergeant quietly.

"Read the serial number Joe," coaxed Delany quietly, "and you'll see it's the same as the one in the statement."

"But it's the full-size," gulped Joe.

Delany rubbed his head slowly.

"I can think of nothing else since I went down there to see it. It would have put you in mind of a ditched moon rocket or an unidentified flying object. The Ganger on site still can't believe it. They are still scratching their heads as to how it got there.

"Remember in the statement where the old man mentioned the explosion in the water. That must have been the sound of it regaining its full height and length. Just think had I listened to that oul fella's plea, instead of engaging in policeman's logic, I'd be a millionaire now.

"That oul fool, through a mixture of chemicals and coincidence, had stumbled onto a potion that had caused the reaction. You could transport them in your pocket if need be, then when you reached your destination, a swish of the hose would enlarge them to their proper height and length. We're talking empty boxes, but who's to know if the same principle wouldn't apply to the loaded ones. That would revolutionise shipping and make ships and lorries obsolete."

He rose to his feet and made a wild dash for the door. "Where are you going, sir?" cried the concerned sergeant. Delany flashed him a wild stare. "Where do you think?" he growled harshly, "I'm going to look for that bloody bucket!"

AN OLD HAND GOES BACK TO THE CLASSROOM

AT half-past nine, on a Monday morning, some weeks ago, I walked into the reception area of a large, impressive building which houses the training ground and classrooms of the Industrial Truck training branch of the Road Transport and Industry Training Board of Northern Ireland, situated about twelve miles from Belfast at a place called Nutt's Corner. Perhaps, an appropriate name for such a place.

A pretty and cheerful young lady listened intently as I explained to her that I was there to do a two-and-a-half day course on industrial truck driving. To the uninitiated, 'industrial' is government jargon and simply a collective name for the many types of lift-trucks now in use in industry.

The smiling receptionist marked off my name and gave me a pink-coloured 'Code Of Conduct'. This was a list of dos and don'ts to be obeyed during one's stay. It was obviously meant more for young tearaways than a staid 48 year-old like myself, who wouldn't dream of loitering in the toilets or playing cards.

She pointed me in the direction of Room 2, first right at the top of the staircase. It was a typical classroom with tables and chairs for the pupils and a large desk, presumably for the instructor. A large blackboard on a three-legged easel stood beside the door. Opposite it and alongside the desk was a small overhead projector. It faced a white screen on the wall behind the desk.

A large film projector housed in an aperture behind the pupil's seats gave the room the appearance of a small cinema. I wasn't the first to arrive; five men were already seated at various tables. A few pretended to read out-dated magazines, whilst others stared pensively at the swirling rain that beat against the windows. The atmosphere was similar to that found in a dentist's waiting room.

At 8.45 on the dot, a tall white-coated instructor wearing a blue safety hat entered our lives. With a friendly smile, he introduced himself as Jim Devanny. A badge declaring this was attached to the breast of his coat in case we forgot.

Still smiling, he proceeded to call out our names. Establishing everyone was present he marked a piece of paper accordingly. After observing us for a few moments, he asked each man what, if any, experience they had in the operating of industrial lift-trucks.

It was the moment I had been dreading. Most of the answers were predictable, ranging from a week to a fortnight or a month. Finally his enquiring gaze fell on me. "A long time," I muttered to the unspoken question. He sensed a secret. "How long?" He persisted. "About twenty years," I replied sheepishly as the other men turned to gaze at me like an exhibit in a museum. My reluctance to answer was understandable. The last thing I wanted was to be separated from the anonymity of the flock.

He held a sheet of paper across his lower face as his eyes twinkled in mock astonishment. He was undoubtedly thinking of all the bad habits I had accumulated over that lengthy period.

A no-nonsense Ballymena man, attending a Pedestrian Truck course, began the inevitable banter. "What are you doin' here?" He asked, not unreasonably, as the others added their comments. He had asked a good question.

Back in 1964, I began to drive forklift trucks, intermittently, until I became a constant operator for a stevedore on Belfast Dock. Over the years as the need for larger capacity trucks became greater, I graduated, via experience, from a four tonne capacity machine to a forty tonne container handler weighing itself almost sixty tonnes. Almost every working day from that time, I have been in the driver's seat and can honestly say I have handled hundreds of thousands of tonnes of material with comparative safety and efficiency during that period.

Being employed by a firm, which until recently had hired out a truck with an operator, I have worked all over Belfast and in many of the outlying areas. My employer had many machines of various capacities and sizes and a working day could have found me anywhere, from the computer rooms of Queen's University to the whiskey stained vaults of a bonded warehouse. On the toes of trucks I have carried many cargoes. An injured cow was carried from a frozen field in Kilroot to the comparative warmth of a grateful farmer's byre and, on a lighter note a piano was carried from one club to another along the esplanade at Whitehead. Nothing odd in this except that the pianist, sitting on a stool, was also on board, playing and singing as we moved slowly along the sea front. A second passenger was standing on the footplate nearest the kerb with his upturned cap stretched out towards the people who stopped to watch and listen.

Sometimes, a sad cycle can be completed. In 1970, when the man-made fibres industry was thriving, I unloaded the giant machines that spun the fibre and helped place them into position in the ICI factory at Kilroot. In 1984, with the giant plant long shut down, a lot of machines were sold and transported to Belfast for shipment overseas. It was my job to carry the machines to the ship that would take them to their new place of toil. Speaking of the Kilroot factory, our original contract there was originally for three weeks and stretched into an incredible eight years.

So, the Ballymena man was entitled to be curious as to why I should be attending a class of instruction on lift-trucks, after all this time driving them. The answer was simple. I was about to be made redundant and despite all the previous experience, I had never attended a course of instruction.

At my age, the prospects of work were slim—without the pass certificate, infinitesimal. Little wonder, I was somewhat apprehensive. I had worked in front of an audience many times but this would be the first time I had presented my skills before a person capable of assessing them. Twenty years of bad habits would have to be erased completely during the two-and-a-half day period.

My mind returned to the lesson as Jim explained that the small class of six would be split into pairs, each with an individual instructor. Two men from Carreras and the *Belfast Telegraph*, on a five-day sojourn, were transferred to another room. The two Ballymena men worked in the local Gallaher factory. They were on a two-and-a-half day course for pedestrian trucks and remained, as did the man and myself from Telecom, who was for the same instruction as myself.

Another tutor, Mr. Joe Buick, a pleasant soft-spoken man (whom I'd met briefly when he came to Belfast Dock to assess the duration my training should take) joined us. The Telecom man and myself were placed in Joe's charge. His unassuming manner put us at ease and our first lesson began.

The subject was a load capacity centre. Jim cut through the verbiage and simplified the theme by comparing a truck to a seesaw with the front wheels being the point of balance. Trucks were built to lift a specific load (he explained) and to attempt to lift more than that amount was unprofessional and highly dangerous. A small metal plate was fixed to every truck in a position where the operator could see it. This stated the machine's safe working load and other information useful to the owner and driver. He likened this to a Plimsoll line on a ship and warned each of us not to disregard it.

The room was darkened and a very useful and informative film was screened. Its theme was the hazards created by what the instructor called 'Cowboy' drivers and exposed the industrial truck to be a fearful weapon in the hands of ill-trained and thoughtless operators. A similar film was shown about the pedestrian truck.

After the harrowing performances, Jim continued on the theme of safety at all times. Faults should be reported immediately. A truck with a major defect such as bad brakes should be immobilised. He was very precise in his wording and repeated each sentence slowly. Unsafe machines must not be driven. Any man who knowingly operated a faulty machine could be liable to a jail sentence.

With the aid of the blackboard, he went on to quote statistics of death, injury and destruction to property. A third of industrial accidents were caused by forklift trucks and of these, 45 per cent were caused by operator error. In a series of slides on the projector, he showed the grim facts in black and white. Every year, in industry, trucks kill twenty men and injure over five hundred.

It was a dangerous environment in which we had chosen to work, and it was up to us to make that place as safe as possible for ourselves and our fellow workers. The instructor elaborated, at large, on how an accident can change a man's life. His standard of living and expectancy of further work is drastically minimised, if he is seriously hurt and dependent on state benefits.

This lecture, though informal, was intimate and serious as Jim hammered home the absolute necessity of proper recognition of safety procedures, in all places, at all times. It caused me to think back with a shiver, on the many times I had cut corners in an effort to beat a clock or a tide.

After a welcome break, Jim equipped us with safety hats and took us on a tour of the training area. It was fenced off into three sections, with warehouse-type stacking shelves in each section. The pedestrian truck, the electric reach truck and the gas-powered counter-balanced truck waited patiently in their respective segments.

Joe introduced us to our mechanical beast of burden. It was a 3000 gas-operated, counterbalance truck, with 24-inch load centres. He carried out the pre-operational checks all drivers are supposed to do, before putting the truck to work. Lifting the bonnet, he inspected the battery and the radiator, before checking dipstick levels on the engine, hydraulic and transmission oils. Tyres, lifting chains, forks and fork faces were examined for visible damage. He then climbed carefully onto the machine and switched on the ignition.

He exaggerated the action of looking all around him before releasing the handbreak and driving the truck a few paces forward. He braked sharply, thus testing the foot brake favourably. Continuing to follow procedure, he checked the ground behind him for tell-tale signs of oil or water leaks. Satisfied, he then applied the handbrake and began to test the hydraulics by first checking the tilt, back and front. Taking the forks as high as they would go, he then lowered them to the recommended position for travelling, which is approximately six inches from the ground with a slight back tilt.

The rest of the morning was spent getting the feel of the machine by driving it carefully around plastic bollards, which Joe had placed strategically on the ground.

At lunchtime, he provided us with a voucher and pointed us in the direction of the site canteen, where we were served a nice three-course meal. When the half-hour break ended, we returned to the training area and spent the remainder of the day driving around the cones, under the watchful eyes of our instructor. A ten-minute coffee break was our only stoppage until four-fifteen, when we were released for the day.

On Tuesday morning, at 9 a.m. sharp, we began to practice the art of stacking and destacking loaded pallets. These were taken from racks on both sides of an aisle about six metres wide. A strict code of movement was observed during the operation, which could be termed 'driving to a pattern'. Each lift contained a series of movements and to stray from the tight programme was forbidden.

I will not explain the procedure constituting the test proper, (which we were now practising) as it could spoil the spontaneity of other aspiring truck drivers. I would liken it to a dance. A series of choreographed movements for a lifting machine. This may sound absurd but as I've stated, each act had a definite arrangement, from which nothing could be omitted or added to. In the well-versed hands of our instructor the truck travelled through its chores with flawless precision.

A cynic may see driving to numbers as unimaginative and view the exercise as robot-like and boring. However the safety standard of such driving was undeniable. Joe informed us that failure to include each move would incur a loss of marks during the test. Some mistakes were deemed more serious than others and brought a penalty of five marks, whilst lesser infringements caused a one point loss. 60 per cent was the lowest to be awarded as a pass. Joe didn't help our confidence when he told of seeing men lose 40 points during the first lift.

He continued to ply us with helpful advice, until the noon break. Half an hour later we returned to find he had rigged up another nightmare for us in the shape of a chicane, built by placing empty pallets on their ends. This was to simulate a narrow aisle or passageway. Picking up a loaded pallet with the machine, he reversed into the man-made bottleneck. After negotiating safely in and out again, he invited us to try and warned that fouling the chicane with either truck or load would cause a loss of points.

We practised this movement diligently, until the 3 p.m. tea break, after which we moved back into the classroom for another film on safety. The operators in this excellent and hair-raising movie were all stuntmen but the staged accidents were lethal and thought provoking. I shuddered at scenes involving larger trucks, for in the course of my work I had seen most of these accidents happen for real.

Another lecture followed on the evils of 'cowboy drivers' and defective trucks, with questions being asked by the instructors and answered to the best of their ability by the pupils. The instructors explained those we were unable to answer in full. This exercise brought the second day to a close.

On Wednesday, we returned to the practising area, where Joe let us train a little more, before fully explaining the dreaded test to us. He made sure both of us knew exactly what we had to do before taking us back to the classroom for a written test.

The questions covered all we had been taught and the questionnaire was straightforward. Each question had three possible answers in boxes marked a, b and c. We were asked to place what we thought was the right answer in the appropriate box. At completion, the instructors marked these accordingly. We were then presented with our test marks and received further instruction on questions some of us had answered wrongly.

We then adjourned for a welcome cuppa, before returning to the test area, where we would this time do the test for real. I wasn't exactly biting my nails but I must admit to a feeling of unease. I didn't mind being overseen by Joe Buick, bearing in mind I had more practical experience of large trucks than any of the examiners had at that time.

However, Joe had proved to be an expert in his field and like it or not, I was in his field.

I opted to go first and the other man was sent back to the classroom to bite his nails. Onlookers were prohibited in the area during a test.

Joe gave me one chore at a time, explaining fully and precisely exactly what he wanted done. The whole operation was completed in an eerie silence, marred only by the purring of the truck's engine. The test itself lasted just over thirty minutes.

I parked the truck, removed the key and awaited my fate with a certain amount of trepidation. A genuine smile of pleasure crossed Joe's face as he looked up from the page and congratulated me. I had made four minor faults but he was more than pleased with my overall effort under the circumstances. I thanked him for his patience and consideration before moving back to the classroom.

The Telecom man moved out to his fate and I found myself giving solace to the Ballymena man who had failed. We small talked until the other two, complete with passes, returned. Armed with vouchers, we moved to the canteen for our final meal together, before going our separate ways. The food was excellent and rounded off the day. Afterwards, as I walked pensively towards my transport, I pondered on the events of the last three days. I had just been adjudged capable of operating an industrial lift-truck after twenty years of continual lift-truck driving. The type of truck I'd passed the test on was the kind I had cut my teeth on all those years ago. I had since moved to much larger truck and container handlers. However, it was time well spent. I came away with the feeling I had learned something valuable. Overall, we'd been taught that common sense, care for the material and consideration for the pedestrian must be the order of the day. All in all, sentiments with which no serious-minded operator would disagree. I looked around the vast area for the last time and wondered, wryly, had anyone served a longer apprenticeship?

FOOTNOTE

I was made redundant at the end of March 1985. I drove a gas-operated machine for a large garage on the Holywood Road for about five weeks. During that time, I applied for and secured a job at Queen's University. I have never operated a lift-truck since.

first published in *Export Freight* (1986)

STRANGERS IN THE NIGHT

THE phone-call from Rainbow Hagan came as a surprise. I hadn't seen or heard of him since the night he told the newspapers that Frank Sinatra had visited his public house, in the depths of Belfast's Sailorstown and sung a duet with a barmaid. Hagan had been in the process of carrying out a series of auditions for a 'Search for a Star' on his Friday night karaoke show when the alleged happening had occurred. The fact that that particular 'Search for a Star' week was the aforementioned Mr. Sinatra caused the hack who visited the bar to be more interested in Rainbow's renowned hospitality than he was in the incident. The reporter got drunk but his newspaper never ran the story.

This could have stemmed from the fact that people were spotting celebrities all over the place when Hagan ran one of his talent shows. During the Elvis search, he had minions ringing the local press with reported sighting of the late Mr. Presley walking along York Street taking in the sights or cruising the Queen's Bridge on a Harley Davidson motorcycle. Rainbow would then phone the newspapers and explain that the people concerned were contestants heading for his auditions. The hard-pressed editors, no doubt thankful for the opportunity to print some light-hearted copy, in a period when most news stories told of murders and explosions, went along with the scam and gave him the free publicity he was after.

After a series that saw the search for Tom Jones, Patsy Cline, Michael Jackson, Tammy Wynette and Elton John, the enthusiasm of the local press to boost these clambakes began to wane. Rainbow decided to end the series with a search for Ireland's answer to Frank Sinatra. This was a pretty good way to end it because, on that very week, the famous crooner would be in Ireland, doing a show in Dublin with a few supporting stars. This was Mr. Sinatra's first appearance on the island and, as such, had created a lot of local media interest.

Hagan advertised his show as the alternative main event. His underlings fly-posted every vacant space in Belfast. The poster advised those unable to travel to the real show that this would provide not one Sinatra but at least ten and also stated that only the best would get through his very tough series of auditions. Of course, unlike the giant stadium where Mr. Sinatra was performing, Rainbow warned the public that his seating space was limited and advised the punters to get there as early as possible. What Mr. Sinatra's administration thought of this blatant hijacking of the title of their sell-out show has gone unrecorded. It was the last presentation Hagan did in the area. Shortly after the show, he sold the dockside bar and bought premises on Belfast's 'Golden Mile', and started on his way to becoming a reputed millionaire.

I hadn't been in when he rang and received the message from my wife. I immediately phoned the number he'd left. I dialled with a twinge of curiosity—after all it wasn't everyday a millionaire called.

His voice hadn't changed, only his accent. When I identified myself, he dropped the Americanised drawl and answered in his familiar backstreet Belfast brogue. After the usual homilies he got down to the matter at hand. "Lissen," he growled with a sincerity I knew he was faking, "I'm throwin' a wake in the celebrity lounge for poor oul Belle an' I'm inviting all her oul buddies an' pals. I thought you'd maybe be interested in comin' over. I'm gonna give her a send-off she won't forget."

My baffled silence prompted him to explain further. "You remember Belle, don't you? She was my senior barmaid in the old place. The one who caused the commotion the day after the Sinatra contest."

Of course I remembered. "Yeah, she was the one who swore the real Sinatra turned up to audition for the show ... "

"No," he broke in impatiently, "He came into the lounge the next morning with an entourage of two men. He identified himself as Frank Sinatra and introduced his colleagues as his musical director and bodyguard. She thought they were wise guys I'd sent in to wind her up."

"Yeah," I replied vaguely, "It's comin' to me now ... "

"Lissen," he interrupted, "I need to talk to you anyway so come on over an' pay yer last respects, an' hear what I've got to say. I'll send a car for you."

"But look Rainbow, I didn't really know the woman," I replied lamely.

"Shure you taped her story an' always said there was something in it. Didn't you actually write it up and show it to her one night?" he countered.

"That's true, but we couldn't find anyone to substantiate it except when the garage mechanic came forward and that looked, well, something like you'd set up. Belle's story was genuine enough but remember, she wasn't a Sinatra fan and wasn't familiar with his act or his voice. I liked the idea, however fanciful, of Frank Sinatra singing a duet with a barmaid but it just didn't ring true," I replied.

"But she also said he looked a little like the Sinatra she remembered from her schooldays and when he did sing, he gave her goose-pimples," he cut in triumphantly.

"Well, we'll never know for certain, now she's dead," I replied, trying to think of a good reason to turn down his invitation.

"Come over anyway," he said with a trace of urgency in his voice. "You never heard the finish of the story ... Neither did she, God rest her. So come on over while I'm in the mood to finish the tale, an' boy will you have an endin'."

I realised he was drunk. It wasn't that his words were slurred or his breath was heavy. There was seriousness in his voice that I'd never detected in all the years I'd known him. Although it was intuition on my part, he agreed with a muffled sigh when I put it to him.

"Shure I am," he growled a little hoarsely, "otherwise I wudn't be revealing my true feelin's. But I owe it to her to set the record straight. She put me where I am today an' I never even thanked her. The car'll be there in twenty minutes," he said, before putting the phone down.

Puzzled as to his behaviour and intrigued by the conversation, I decided to search out the manuscript I had written up of Belle's version of the events on the day in question, as I waited for the car to collect me.

Belle had been a middle-aged barmaid when I first met her. She had an open face with quizzical eyes and an inscrutable grin. This was the mechanism she used to get her day in and seemed to be steeped in her own thoughts as she dutifully pulled the pints and poured the spirits. Only when accepting your money and returning the change did she seem to appear on the same wavelength. She also had a pleasing figure and must have been a very attractive girl in her day.

Unfortunately, as earlier stated, she had only one witness to the coming of Sinatra, and this was the owner of the local garage at the bottom of the street. Sadly he didn't corroborate the story until the next day and many people thought Rainbow had coaxed him into the plot to give Belle's story more meat. He did, however, stick to his version that Sinatra's limo' with his musical director and his bodyguard, had called into his garage, when the chauffeur had informed his boss that the car's engine was giving him cause for concern. When questioned as to why the singer was in Belfast the night after a hectic concert in Dublin, the garage owner said he'd been told Sinatra's private jet had been unable to land at Dublin airport and had been ordered to the Belfast Harbour air terminal, where the Sinatra entourage would join it as soon as possible. An accompanying car, carrying the singer's wife and several more of the party, had continued on to the airport. He said Mr. Sinatra had personally asked him not to mention their visit until they were out of town and he had agreed.

Locating the handwritten details, I settled down in a chair by the living-room window, awaiting the arrival of the car. It was a first draft I had later shelved as unworkable. Her story went like this:

I'd slept in an' got to the bar an hour late. So I was rushin' to get finished before Rainbow came in. My head was still sore from the night before. All those skinny guys an' a few not too skinny givin' it 'My Way' an' 'New York, New York' an' 'Strangers in the Night' ... If I ever hear that particular song again, I think I'll throw up over whoever's singin' it. The noise was terrible. Worse than that, some of them had themselves believing they were Sinatra. Rainbow had brought in a dozen bottles of Jack Daniels, a whiskey that the singer is supposed to favour. Well I didn't know that an' when the first ones asked for Jack Daniels, I said there was no-one of that name drank in the lounge, but maybe if they tried the bar. Well that got a few snickers, until I realised what they were talkin' about. They drank the lot! You shuda seen the toilets afterwards. It was a terrible night for me. Some of them had photostatted American money an' were tryin' to pass it as real coin over the bar. I was on my own an' I can tell you I really earned my corn.

Anyway I got stuck into the gents an' was workin' away when I heard a polite coughin' coming from the direction of the bar. I could hear it clearly as I'd left the toilet door ajar. I always did this since the day I went in and found an oul fella asleep in one of the cubicles.

I realised I must have left the lounge door open and walked out slowly in case it was someone who had come to burgle the place. But it wasn't. It was three men, the youngest of whom was middle-aged so the fear left me. Two of them were dressed in business suits and one of them was built like 'Ructions' Toal who used to be a hard man round here before the start of the troubles. But it was the wee one who caught my eye. He was a chubby man and wore one of those baseball caps all the kids seem to be wearin' now an' one of them shiny jerkins the Yankee sailors like so much. His skin was the colour of mahogany, the same colour oul 'Slicebar' Christie used to be when he came back after a long foreign trip, an' his eyes, well they were as blue as the dinner plates my granny used to keep in her china cabinet. I remember he had them full on me when he asked if they cud get a drink, adding, the guy who runs the garage down the street told them they could spend an hour there until their car was repaired.

He also told me his name was Frank Sinatra and would I oblige him by not notifying the media. Needless to say I had a good laugh at that.

"Okay Frank," I said—I was convinced Rainbow and Dessie who owned the garage had set me up, so I went along with it.

He doffed the baseball cap and smiled apologetically. "Thank you ma'am', could we have a drink?" he asked. "It's my pleasure Frank," I answered, tryin' to keep the sarcasm out of my voice. I'd had a hard night an' was in no mood for tricks. Deciding to forget the toilets I moved to the bar. Rainbow didn't approve of ejecting paying clients an' he was probably close by, laughing his bloody head off.

"Well Frank," I smiled from behind the bar, "Jack Daniels?" He seemed agreeably surprised and said "Yes sir, ma'am," in that perfectly adorable voice that was beginning to grow on me. I gave him a big smile and said, "Sorry chum. Your colleagues drank it all last night and then proceeded to throw it up down the toilet."

I expected some reaction, but their faces were blank and quizzical, whilst still smiling. I suddenly though they might be American sailors. Quite a few of our foreign customers couldn't understan' me if I spoke too quickly.

The one built like 'Ructions' Toal came up to the bar from the door where he'd positioned himself. He put a crisp twenty-pound note on the counter. "Three whiskeys, and keep the change," he ordered with a flat American drawl.

I nodded pleasantly and set up the drinks, carefully placing the change into the pocket of my overall.

With a tip like that, they could be whoever they wanted to be. Skipping along the bar, I scooped some ice from the fridge an' put it into the coolbox on the bar beside his drink. I noticed the younger of the other men had joined him at the bar, whilst the one built like a house had returned to the lounge door.

He declined the ice and the water jug nearby and tossed the drink down his throat in one go. I swear to Heaven, he never even blinked before fixing me with a hard, amused stare. He raised his right hand and clicked his fingers lazily. The guy at the door raced forward with another twenty-pound note and instruction to keep the change.

I must admit I felt like a hustler, but if he wanted to play the big star, why should I care.

As I poured the drinks, I studied the hand holding the empty glass. It was long and slender and deeply bronzed as I imagined his whole body would be. A heavy gold ring adorned the little finger, matchin' a *thick gold bracelet that hung loosely at the base of his wrist. I looked at the two guys an' wondered how much he was payin' them to keep up the act. I suddenly felt ashamed; perhaps the old guy was a pensioner who'd come to take part in the contest, and was now spending money he couldn't afford.*

I set down the drinks and decided to level with them. "Luk," I says, "the Frank Sinatra competition is over. It was last night, an' it was won by a wee skinny fella from Mount Vernon who spent all his time listening to his da's records an' learnin' from them. At least that's what he tole the men from the BBC who interviewed him at the end of the night. There was a whole lot of wee fat men who looked like you, but the crowd went for the wee skinny fella."

When I finished, they looked at me as if I was from another planet and I realised they hadn't understood a word I had said. I was about to repeat myself when the guy at the lounge door ambled up with a poster of the event he had taken off the wall. The man with the baseball cap smiled showing teeth that were unbelievably white.

"Pity we're a day late. I could have entered," he said. They all laughed heartily at this before the doorman wandered back to his seat.

The sound of a motor-horn signalled the arrival of Rainbow's car. I folded the notepaper and lifted my jacket, before walking out into the street. Opening the car door, I was swamped by the sound of Frank Sinatra's voice blaring from the four speakers of the Mercedes as the singer swept through the haunting strains of 'Strangers in the Night'. I smiled a little, remembering Belle's aversion to the same song.

"Do you like Sinatra?" I asked, conversationally, as the driver pulled away from the kerb. He looked over his shoulder.

"Before my time, mate," he laughed, "but the boss loves him so he's always in the machine."

I pulled out the draft and settled back to more of Belle's recollections. The noise of Sinatra didn't faze me as most of my interviews were done in noisy pubs and I'd long since learned to cut through the buzz and concentrate on the person I was interested in. Anyway, it seemed somewhat appropriate for Belle's story to blend with the Sinatra soundtrack.

I read on:

Ruction's double had just bought the fourth drink and I'd just pocketed the change from my fourth twenty, when I realised I really wanted him to be Frank Sinatra. Don't ask me why, because as I'd said earlier, I wasn't really a fan. I'm not musically inclined.

But at that moment I wanted to believe the guy was a superstar. It might have been the time when he looked up from the poster and fixed his eyes full on my face. They were blue, so clearly blue. It seemed as if someone had cut two circles from a cloudless summer sky and placed them in his eyes. They looked so young, so vibrant, and so out of place in his tired and world-weary face.

"What's this about auditions," he asked, slowly, as if under the impression that English wasn't my native tongue. As if you didn't know, I growled under my breath, but I thought of the change nestling in my smock an' went along with it. "Well Mr. Sinatra," I explained civilly, and slowly, "the man who owns this place runs contests to bring ordinary people who sing like stars to the notice of the public."

"Sounds interesting," he smiled as he toyed with the whiskey glass, adding, "and are there many budding Sinatras in town?"

"Hundreds," I replied, "an' I think they were all in here this week."

"Yeah, that musta bin somethin," he conceded with a mumble, reaching me the empty glass as the big guy rushed forward throwing another twenty on the bar. As I set up the drinks he swivelled on the barstool and looked toward the rostrum.

"Is that where they strut their stuff?" he asked. When I nodded, he walked slowly over to the stage and studied the Karaoke machine for a moment. Suddenly he raised his right hand an' clicked his fingers.

His companion at the lounge who hadn't uttered a word since entering the bar, leaned in his direction. After a few whispered moments, he said, "Dad wants to know if he can use the stage. He'd like to sing to you," he added with a grin.

"No chance," I snorted, "Rainbow wud sack me if anythin' happened to that machinery. Ack, tell him not to touch anything." He deciphered this outburst as a no and passed the message. Both men returned to the bar.

'Dad' locked eyes with me, and I swear I shivered. That long lingering look made me feel like a young girl—loved, wanted an' desired. It seemed as if an age had passed, and I was convinced I was in the presence of the real Sinatra. I almost succumbed to his sexual

aura when I realised I was being romanced by a man old enough to be my grandfather. It was as if he had imitated the real thing so long that it came naturally to him.

He took out his wallet, brought out a crisp new banknote and placed it on the bar top. His companion quickly produced a pen and the little man signed the note with a flourish.

He reached it to me sayin' "Let Junior get the machine goin' an' I'll sing for you alone."

"I'm sorry," I stammered. He stifled my protests by folding the note and placing it in my hand. The feel of the money made my mind up. "As long as he knows what he's doin'," I said wearily, pushing away a touch of guilt that said I was as mercenary as the other two.

Junior stepped forward quickly and a flashing of lights above the rostrum indicated that the machinery had come to life.

The driver coughed politely. "We've arrived mate," he said apologetically. I pushed the pages into my pocket and climbed from the car and onto the busy pavement.

Hagan had certainly come up in the world. I squeezed past a bouncer who looked like a mountain wearing a bow-tie. He eyed me suspiciously when I asked for Rainbow.

"Is the boss expecting you?" he growled whilst towering over me. When I nodded mutely, he went to a phone on the wall whilst keeping a baleful eye on me. His scowl changed to a grin and he suddenly looked likable. "Right sor, this way," he purred warmly, adding apologetically, "just tryin' to keep the riff-raff out."

I smiled and went in the direction he pointed. When I opened the door, the air was immediately filled with the drone of human chatter. At least fifty people, mostly middle-aged women, were in the large room. A coffin, presumably containing Belle's remains, sat at a huge ornate picture window, through which the sun shone, lighting up the casket and its occupant.

I walked respectfully to the spot and looked at the peaceful face that was swaddled in white lace. The coffin was a rich, dark, mahogany colour with brass handles that shone like gold in the light of the sun.

"Oul Rainbow did her proud, didn't he?" said a voice at my shoulder. A petite, middle-aged woman, dressed in a style much too young for her, sipped at a sherry, before continuing. "It wasn't outa turn. She worked hard all her days for him. She had to. Her husband dropped dead in the city centre at the start of the troubles. They had two wee childer an' she had ta put in them an' on them. Still, there's thousands like her," she concluded, with a muffled sniff.

"But I have to admit he's done her proud," she continued, "Do you know he brought in one of them beauticians to do her face and hair before he allowed the coffin to be opened ... an' luk at that coffin. It wouldn't be outa place on the Malone Road."

A silence reigned as we both gazed at the corpse. The woman took another sip and looked into my eyes. "She was niver the same from the Frank Sinatra episode."

"*The* Frank Sinatra? Did she know him?" I asked innocently.

"She sang a duet with him in Rainbow's oul pub," she answered primly. "Of course Rainbow wud tell you she had too much to drink an' imagined the whole thing. But I went to school with Belle an' she niver told a lie in her life. Some people say Frank Sinatra an' not Rainbow is payin' for all this. Others say the singer had an affair with Belle an' tole her not to mention it."

"In the bar?" I inquired.

"Where else?" she answered grandly before gliding off to the drinks table.

I located Rainbow at the other end of the room. He was alone and sipping a beer. He motioned to a white-coated waiter hovering dutifully close to him.

"Get my friend a drink, Sam." Sam dutifully obeyed and seconds later I was sipping the beer and surveying the scene.

"Not a bad send-off, eh?" he muttered. Rainbow had changed since I had last saw him. The straw-coloured hair was no longer shoulder length and the full beard that had accompanied it had been reduced to a straggly moustache that trespassed, surreptitiously, into his beer glass, when he took a sip from it. He wore a tailored, grey-coloured business suit and a white, silk shirt with a black necktie. His chubby features were relaxed, although his brown eyes seemed now and then to be preoccupied. He wasn't a tall man but he had wide shoulders and a square jaw that made him look rather formidable. He sported at least three gold rings on each hand. Large and vulgar and probably very expensive.

I decided to cut through the flannel. "Okay Rainbow. There's somethin' goin' on here. Has it anything to do with the Sinatra sighting?" I asked.

He smiled to himself and studied the beer in his tumbler, before turning his head to look at me. "Do you know why they call me Rainbow?" he asked, with an amused grin on his face. Before I could answer, he continued, "From I was no height I was a hustler, always lukin' to become a millionaire overnight. I can't tell you how many schemes an' scams I set up in an effort to break into the big time."

He was obviously enjoying the recollection, which was more like a soliloquy than a conversation. "My Ma," he continued, "christened me Rainbow because I was always lukin' for the pot of gold. Thanks to Belle I eventually found it."

"Are you tryin' to tell me Sinatra really did visit the bar in York Street?" I asked, in a tone that requested the truth.

He straightened up. "Tell me what she told you an' I'll fill in the rest. Remember I tole you I'd finish the tale—well I will."

The excitement that rose in my breast was cut down by the emergence of reason. "I hope you've got more than hearsay" I added.

"Much more," he giggled drunkenly, "much, much more," as I began to relate Belle's story, that was fresh in my mind from the recent reading.

When I'd reached the point I'd got to in the car, I pulled out the script and began to read the remainder of the barmaid's story.

He stopped me abruptly. "You've filled me in on what I didn't know. I can follow it on from there myself."

He paused only to order another drink before continuing, "They certainly shared the stage alright. What did she tell you they sang?"

I glanced quickly at the notes. "Belle says Sinatra made a bet with his musical director that he could sing any song word perfect after hearing it once or twice. She reckoned this sprang from the musical director saying Sinatra had muffed a few lyrics during his performance at the Point and that the singer should pay more attention to the teleprompter.

Sinatra asked her to sing her favourite song to him once or twice and bet the musical director he'd sing it along with her on the third go. Belle told him she only knew one song. She sang it haltingly and sure enough on the third go the singer joined her and was word perfect."

"What did they sing?" asked Rainbow, looking intently at me.

"'When Irish Eyes Are Smiling'," I replied.

He shook his head slowly from side to side. "Back in the 60s Sinatra campaigned for John F. Kennedy in the American Presidential elections. He must have heard that song sung a thousand times. There'd be no need for anyone to teach it to him."

He paused to allow me to accept his point, which I did with a slow nod of my head.

Rainbow continued: "It was shortly after that they left. Belle continued to clear up and was there when I arrived.

"I knew something was wrong and eventually coaxed the story from her. She omitted telling me about the tips he had given her, so the till showed nothing other than the price of a few drinks. I went to the karaoke machine but it was as clean as a whistle. Whoever had operated it had made sure there was no recording of the session. I even looked for the cigarette butt he had squashed out on the podium, but super-efficient Belle had already cleaned that up and dumped it in the bin with a million others .

"It was only when Dessie out of the garage came in and told about the car that I began to believe her story. I rang the Telegraph. They sent a man down, but he was cynical from the start. I guess it was a case of me being the guy who cried wolf too often.

"The reporter arrived and questioned Belle and Dessie. He was looking for hard facts and of course, there were none to give. Dessie had been paid in coin of the Realm, as had Belle.

"The newspaperman tried hard to look interested, as he sipped pensively at a glass of Irish whiskey, on the house, of course. 'Why didn't the garage owner ring us as soon as he knew it was Sinatra's car? We'd have had a camera down in double-quick time. I'd a give my eye teeth to do that interview,' he added wistfully.

"When Dessie said he respected customers' right to privacy, the journalist shook his head just as I did. He asked Dessie why the great singer had not ordered a taxi and continued with his journey.

Dessie couldn't answer that, but forcefully argued that he had repaired a superstar's limo and would be putting a plaque up outside his garage that would state that point.

"I was gutted as well. Think of it. The great Sinatra in my bar, drinking my drink and singing without payment." Rainbow took another sip of his drink and couldn't resist the urge to wax lyrical. "They came and went like strangers in the night."

"That would make a great song title," I muttered sarcastically, adding, "get on with the story."

He nodded in sad agreement and continued: "At that point Belle broke in. 'He was here, mister,' she told the reporter. 'It was nobody else. At first I thought it was an impersonator, but there was something about him, like a presence that none of the other people at the auditions and show ever produced. And the thing is, he sang to me. To me alone. I don't care what you say or think. I'll never forget it for as long as I live.'"

Rainbow paused for a drink, before going on: "The reporter wasn't impressed and who could blame him? We rang the City Airport to confirm the plane was there. They wouldn't comment on private plane movements," he sighed.

"'It sure is a swell story and it might be true, but I couldn't go to my editor. He'd sack me if I made a claim that the Voice was in Belfast based on the evidence you've presented. I'll give you a write up in tomorrow night's column and say the contest was so good some people imagined the real Sinatra had been present.'

"But that's not the finish, is it?" I said. I was extremely impatient to hear the ending but knew Rainbow would take his own sweet time before reaching the conclusion—if there was a conclusion.

He paused to call another drink, making me wait for the pay off. I looked around the room whilst the waiter set down the drinks and realised I had been so engrossed in Rainbow's story that I had shut out the buzz of conversation that now attacked my ears as people continued to come and go in a steady stream.

"She certainly was popular," I remarked.

"Yeah," agreed Rainbow, adding sceptically, "so is free food and drink. Anyway," he continued with an added seriousness, "she deserves every minute of it. But for her I'd still be hustling down in York Street."

My own impatience erupted with this remark—"Well then," I replied, "cut the cackle and get to the point."

He grinned and continued, "The first break came the following day. I'd given Belle the day off, as she'd been under pressure the whole of the week before, because of the contest. As per ritual I visited both toilet areas to check for burst pipes or anything else out of the ordinary. In the ladies I came across a crumpled piece of paper that looked suspiciously like a bank note. I opened it up and saw it was funny money. Some guys had photocopied American currency just as Belle said and tried to pass it as the real thing during the Sinatra auditions. I was about to bin it when I noticed the writing.

"It was almost unreadable, but seemed to say 'Thanks, Francis Albert Sinatra.' My interest increased when I noticed it was a thousand-dollar bill. I was puzzled as to how any of our contestants would have access to a bill of this value in order to photocopy it."

"Is that the note he gave her for allowing him to use the karaoke?" I whispered to Rainbow.

"It would seem that way," he countered, "but I wasn't aware it was given to her until you mentioned it in your story. She either lost it from her pocket or threw it away when she saw it wasn't coin of the realm."

"Maybe she dumped it when the reporter failed to believe her story," I suggested.

"Whatever the reason she never mentioned it to me. Probably happy with the amount of genuine dough she'd got in tips," he replied.

"Was the bill genuine?" I asked.

"Yessiree," he said without emotion, "I took it to my bank and it was real American currency."

"Did you mention it to Belle?" I asked.

"Didn't see no reason to," he answered, "but maybe I should have."

"Did you cash it?" I continued relentlessly

"No. I had an expert analyse the handwriting, and yes, it was a genuine Sinatra autograph, endorsed on a genuine thousand-dollar bill. I later learned this was his way of saying a personal thank you for services rendered."

He took a sip from his drink and paused for a moment. I wanted to ask him a million questions, but stayed silent. He put the glass down and began again.

"But that was all in the future. As I stood in the Ladies' studying the note, I heard a key turning in the door downstairs, followed by footsteps. A few moments later the lounge door opened and in walked Billy Totten, a local Mr. Fixit who did odd electrical jobs about the bar. I had given him his own key for the lounge. This was to enable him to work on the intricate disco system at any given time. As the system usually clocked out late at night it meant neither me nor the staff would have to remain on the premises whilst he repaired it."

Rainbow smiled vaguely at the remembrance. "I automatically looked to see if he was carrying anything, as he only called to see me when he'd something to sell, or was looking for payment for services rendered. He was an easy-going guy about thirty-five or so. He had a mop of unruly blond hair and a perpetual grin. He generally wore an old navy overall and a checkered shirt, but today he was dressed in his best suit and an open-necked shirt.

"Reaching the bar, he plopped heavily onto a barstool and grinned warmly at me. 'Well was it a success boss?' he asked, with a quizzical stare.

"'Yeah,' I replied, 'we even got a visit from the real Sinatra.'

"He burst into laughter and threw his arm around my shoulder. 'Rainbow,' he says, 'you'll niver get into Heaven. Shure everybody knows Frank Sinatra died twenty years ago. Isn't he buried beside Elvis?'

"'Yeah,' I answered dryly, as I poured him a drink. As you can guess my bar wasn't exactly a watering-hole for intellectuals.

"'The video camera,' he asked, 'Did it do the job?'

"'What video camera, what job?' I replied vaguely, wishing he'd leave, so I could study the thousand-dollar bill in private.

"'Ach, I meant to leave you a note to say I'd installed it, but I was in a hurry to git finished because she wanted to go to Donegal, so I forgot. Here's the account,' he finished apologetically.

"'Are you telling me you fitted a video camera at the entrance of the bar?' I asked.

"'No,' he grinned, taking me by the arm and guiding me

towards the rostrum. When we were both behind the microphone stand, he pointed toward the wall facing. 'I fitted it there,' he said.

"I peered in the direction, but didn't see anything and said so.

"He smiled knowingly. 'Look closer,' he said, 'it's behind the flower arrangement, peeking through the shrubbery. I knew if the wannabes seen it it might make some of them nervous,' he added.

"'Well it's too late now,' I murmured. 'How does it operate anyhow?'

"'It's automatic,' he replied. 'Once you switch the karaoke on it records whatever happens on the rostrum.'"

Rainbow paused, expressing delight at the incredulous look that covered my features. I started to speak but he interrupted. His voice was harsh and triumphant.

"Suddenly the burning question. The question on which everything I longed for rotated. The question that would decide whether I had found the pot of gold or a lifetime of regret.

"'Did you load a tape in it, Billy?' I said hoarsely, and almost swooned when he replied in the affirmative.

"'But I'm sorry I didn't let you know,' he continued. 'I know your main reason for buying it was to video the auditions and study the performances at your leisure. They are all in there for posterity an' you didn't know. My fault. So just say the word an' I'll take it down.'

"'How long is the tape?' I enquired.

"'Six hours,' he replied, 'but it turns itself over and will record every time the machine is turned on. It's definitely a state of the arts job, but I won't charge you the full whack,' he added hurriedly.

"'So you're telling me that the last act that performed on the rostrum has been videoed?' I persisted.

"'No problem,' he replied confidently, 'if they sang through the mike they're in the can.'

"I hugged that odd-job man so warmly that he began to get worried as to my intentions. Looking hurriedly at the clock he said. 'Make up your mind Rainbow, I've another job in the pipeline.'

"Needless to say I allayed his fears and sent him packing. When I heard the door slam behind him I climbed on a barstool and removed the tape from the camera. From there I went to the video player with the large screen in the downstairs bar. My hands were shaking so much I could hardly fit the videotape into the slot. Putting it in fast reverse I watched the images flicker swiftly across the screen. I slowed it down to normal and there they were, large as life. Frank Sinatra and Belle Todd sharing a microphone and singing their hearts out in my pub ... "

He stopped and added mysteriously, "And they weren't singing 'When Irish Eyes Are Smiling'."

"What the hell were they singing?" I thundered.

He rose and finished his drink. "C'mon up to my office and see for yourself." I barely contained my excitement as I walked with him through the mourners and up the back stairs. Entering the office he motioned me to sit down on a soft leather chair. Going to a large desk, he unlocked a drawer and pulled out a videotape. I watched silently as he walked across the plush carpet and loaded the cassette into a recorder. He picked up the remote from the top of the large and expensive television before walking back and sitting down in a chair facing me.

He pressed a button and the screen lit up. The picture showed a man adjusting the microphone on the raised dais.

There was no doubting the location. A large banner on the wall behind said, 'Welcome to Rainbow's End!' "What's it to be, boss?" he called as he fiddled with the knobs and buttons on the consul.

The boss walked to the microphone and studied a pamphlet containing the numbers and titles of each song. I leaned forward in my chair. It certainly looked like the famous crooner.

"Make it number 11—I feel a little bluesy," he answered, drawing heavily on his cigarette and letting the smoke cascade down through his nostrils. It filled the rostrum with a purple haze before floating lazily towards the ceiling.

Suddenly the room was full of music. He tapped his foot in time with the slow beat and blew more cigarette smoke towards the rafters. He looked in the direction of the bar with a roguish smile. "This is my favourite song of all time," he purred, "an' I'm singin' just for you."

I was entranced from the very first word. His voice blended perfectly with the lush yet tender strings that complemented the wistful and muted horns featured in the orchestration.

It was a smokey voice; an old voice, hurt and bruised and battered by life. His face twisted occasionally as he reached for a note or lingered on a word from the lyric, but his eyes were alive and alight with a magnetism that almost hypnotised me. I found myself hanging onto every note as his voice caressed the music with an urgency that made him seem frail and vulnerable, yet strong and immortal. The theme was sadness and he brought that feeling into a room which seemed to grow smaller with every word he uttered. Rainbow had disappeared in the darkness and my eyes glistened with appreciation as he took the song into a grandstand finish.

When the music simmered to a close he threw the remains of the cigarette onto the floor before crushing it savagely with his heel. I recognised the song immediately. He had co-written the lyrics during the time of his tempestuous and ill-fated marriage to actress Ava Gardener. I had heard him perform it many times on radio and disc, but there was no comparison to watching him doing it for real in a bar in York Street, Belfast.

As we watched, another tall, balding man stepped onto the rostrum and spoke to the singer through haze of blue tobacco smoke.

I managed to speak for the first time since the tape had begun. "That's his son," I gasped, "that's Frank Sinatra junior. Okay Rainbow, you've convinced me. You could maybe have fooled me with a Sinatra clone, but no way could you fake the son."

"That's exactly what the bookie said," he replied with a grin as he stopped the video and went to a cabinet behind the television set. When he opened the doors, the inside lit up with a muted glow to reveal a number of bottles and glasses.

"What bookie?" I enquired curiously.

He returned with two brandies in large crystal balloon glasses.

"The very rich bookie from South Belfast who bought the original tape and the autographed thousand dollar bill," he answered smugly, reaching me one of the drinks. "Yeah, my friend," he continued, "the pot of gold me old mum talked about finally landed in my lap."

I was sceptical. "It surely is a collector's item, but I couldn't see it bringing in a pot of gold."

"Of course you're a Sinatra fan, aren't you?" he asked, with the ghost of a smile.

I nodded, "Along with another fifty million people on the planet who appreciate good music. However and with no disrespect, despite my earlier burst of enthusiasm, that snip you just showed could have been taken from any of the early Sinatra television shows."

He grinned widely. "You're not very smart are you?"

"Excuse me?" I replied a trifle affronted.

"When did Sinatra make those early TV shows?" he continued remorselessly.

"The late 50s," I replied confidently.

"Would Junior be a middle-aged man?" he teased, "would the transmission be in glorious colour? Lastly, and most importantly, what about the backdrop saying 'Welcome to Rainbow's End?'"

I sunk into my chair and made no answer, deeply embarrassed, my stupidity equalled only by my astonishment. "Why didn't you tell the world?" I shouted. "Why have you kept this a secret?" I demanded to know.

He looked at me. "I thought of it," he admitted slowly before turning his gaze to the brandy glass he was swirling lazily.

"Then I began to think what it meant in terms of commerce. If I told the world, I'd be in the papers for a week or two then Mr. Sinatra's lawyers would claim copyright and I'd lose or have to destroy the tape." I looked at him as a glimmer of a smile crossed his serious features. "The fat bookie," I whispered.

He nodded "But it wasn't the solo that brought in the dough. It was the duet. Belfast barmaid sings along with the world's greatest vocalist. Now that line-up gave the price tag a hefty lift towards the clouds, but the song shot it into the stratosphere where it landed at the foot of the rainbow. Had it been released commercially it would have soared straight to the top of the hit-parade, at least here in Northern Ireland."

"Then for Heaven's sake play it," I yelled hoarsely.

The screen flickered again and we watched as his son joined the celebrity.

"Perfect," said the young man, "you didn't fluff a line."

"What's that supposed to mean," replied the singer with an icy edge on his voice.

"Nothing," replied Junior guardedly.

"Listen, kid," said his father, "I have a photographic memory for songs, and I'm not in the habit of fluffin' lines."

"Sorry dad, I'm just tired from being on the road so early."

"Yeah," growled the legendary singer, "I'm gonna sack that agent when I get back stateside."

"Forget it, dad. It's a 10 million dollar deal we're going back to sign with the networks. We'll have plenty of time to catch up on our sleep."

"Never mind that," came the curt reply, which showed he was still smarting from the earlier remark, "get the old girl up here and I'll prove my point."

Junior left the rostrum obediently and returned on camera a few moments later with a bemused and bewildered Belle.

"Did she do a show in the late 50s?" smirked Rainbow, as we watched the singer give Belle, an affectionate hug.

I didn't answer. I was mesmerised by what was happening before my eyes.

Sinatra pushed the baseball cap to the back of his head. "I just bet my son I could sing any song word for word once I'd heard it three or four times. Now it would need to be a song I don't know and there aren't many of them around. Perhaps there's a local song; y'know a folk-song you learned at your mother's knee. Familiar in Ireland, but little known elsewhere."

Belle looked as if she was about to faint. After a moment or two she said in a strained voice, "What about 'When Irish Eyes Are Smiling'?"

Junior laughed. "He's sung that a million times."

"'The Mountains of Mourne'?" said Belle in quiet desperation.

"Jack Kennedy taught that to me along with dozens of other ballads like 'Phil the Fluter', 'I'll Take You Home Again, Kathleen' and 'The Boul Fenian Men'," laughed the singer. "I probably know more Irish songs than you do." He added softly, as if remembering a pleasant period in his life.

Belle looked perplexed as she searched her brain. "Here's the only folk song I know," she said a moment later and nervously launched into a halting rendition of the chorus of 'The Sash My Father Wore'.

> It is oul but it is beautiful
> an' its colours they are fine,
> It was worn in Derry, Aughrim,
> Enniskillen an' the Boyne.
> Shure my father wore it when a youth,
> In the bygone days of yore,
> An' it's on the twelfth
> I love to wear the sash my father wore.

She sang another two verses a cappella in a quavering voice, each time repeating the chorus, as the singer looked on. He listened intently whilst tapping his feet to the tune.

I gazed in astonishment at Rainbow.

"Sinatra singing 'The Sash'?" I whispered with amazement.

'That's where the money is," he smiled, as I returned my eyes to the screen.

When Belle finished, Sinatra applauded and turned to his son pensively.

"Never heard the Kennedy clan sing that number, but that's an old Tin Pan Alley tune from the turn of the century, it's original title was 'The Hat My Father Wore.' I remember Ted Lewis featured it in his club act. It probably originated here and came over with the immigrants. What's a sash anyway?" he murmured as an afterthought.

Junior replied with a shrug of his shoulder, "Dunno. Maybe a cummerbund of some description."

"No matter," replied the singer triumphantly, "I know the tune, so I've got it half-licked." He turned the famous smile on Belle. "Go ahead ma'am, let's hear it again. This time I'll hum along."

I sat spellbound as the great Sinatra voice changed key to accompany Belle's trembling pitch as she once again gave a spirited version of the old Orange folk song.

"Why did she say she sang 'When Irish Eyes Are Smiling'," I whispered.

"I'm a Catholic. She probably thought I would have sacked her for singing a party song in the bar. If she was here now I'd kiss her to death," laughed Rainbow.

I returned my eyes to the screen and grinned with pleasure when Junior pulled a harmonica from his pocket and accompanied the singers with a fair rendering of the tune.

On the third try they gathered around the microphone like a barbershop trio and did it again. Belle got into the swing of things and began to dance backwards and forwards, lifting the hem of her skirt up over her knees, showing shapely legs and thighs.

Sinatra joined her and they both locked arms and twirled around the rostrum as Junior really went to town on his harmonica.

During all this Sinatra's voice came through strong and clear and word-perfect.

They finished and continued again when Sinatra, caught up in the euphoria ordered them to 'go one more time'. As they danced around the rostrum, Sinatra did a makeshift jig and Belle tried her hand at an impromptu piece of Irish dancing whilst Junior blew up a storm and stamped his feet to the infectious beat. The overall result was something I could have watched forever.

Unfortunately, a heavily built man, who entered the picture and pointed in the direction of the door interrupted them. Junior stopped playing and put the harmonica into his top jacket pocket. "The car's arrived, dad," he said.

The singer waited until he got his breath back before speaking to Belle. "Thanks for your hospitality, ma'am. That sure is a good song. I'll maybe record it when I go back and send you a copy." He put his arm around her neck and hugged her as his son gently coaxed him off the stage.

"Goodbye ma'am and God Bless," he said warmly before leaving the vision of the camera. Frank Junior returned to the consul and presumably turned off the power as the video ended at that moment.

"Now you got your story," said Rainbow. "Now you know why I owe Belle a debt of gratitude."

"It's a pity you didn't let her see the tape before she died," I answered drily. "She must have felt terrible when no-one believed her story."

"I'd loved to have done that, but she'd have blown the whistle. Like most barmaids, Belle couldn't hold her own water, and pretty soon she'd have told someone who'd have sent the newspapers," replied Rainbow, defensively. "Even so, she knew it really happened and she might have been embarrassed to know I knew it wasn't 'When Irish Eyes are Smiling' she sang with Frank."

"Can I write this story?" I asked in a level tone.

He didn't answer, but rose and lifted my empty glass and refilled it. His features were deep and purposeful as he returned from the cocktail cabinet.

I took the proffered drink from him and watched in silence as he sat down and drank deeply from his glass.

"Not until I'm dead," he answered impassively.

I knew the signs. "Are you in trouble?" I asked.

"I got too greedy," he said. "I copied the tape four or five times and sold each one as an original." He shook his head. "Definitely unethical, but very profitable."

"What happened?" I asked.

"Wouldn't you know," he replied with a drawn-out sigh. "One of my customers had a party and decided to show the tape to his friends. Needless to say one of them had the same 'original' stashed away in his safe at home. I also had the thousand-dollar bill counterfeited a dozen times. I know a guy in that business and he copied it on beautiful paper in exchange for a few copies of the original. I also provided him with the authentic letter from the handwriting expert who stated the signature was genuine. He copied that as well and I sold the lot as a package to some wealthy men."

"You mean each one got a tape, an autographed thousand dollar bill and a letter to say the bill was genuine?" I asked, knowing what would come next.

"The hard men came looking for me last week. A couple of shooters were produced. I told them I'd sell the bar and make good what I owed their clients. I asked for a week ... " he concluded.

"What are you going to do now?"

"The bar's already sold," he replied with a forlorn grin. "A guy I know in Dublin came down yesterday and gave me cash in hand. I lost a few thousand in the deal, but half-a-loaf's better than a hole in the head so I signed it over there and then."

I sensed the meeting was over, so I rose and headed for the door. "What about Belle's funeral?" I asked.

"It's tomorrow. I've set up a fabulous amount of food and drink for the mourners when they return. Me, I'll just drive on to the International airport from the cemetery. I'll stop over in London, then on to places unknown. The tape and the banknote will sell anywhere there's a strong Irish connection. The Prods will love it and the Catholics will see the funny side of it. I won't be daft enough to sell more than one in any city or town. Needless to say I'll pick a big country, with plenty of room to get lost, if I have to," he added, with a parting smile.

We shook hands at the door. "The car's at the front. I'll phone down and get him to take you home." As he spoke we made eye contact and at that moment, I sensed I would never speak to him again.

The mourners were still eating and drinking as I walked through them. Belle's body lay in the comfort of the luxurious coffin, her pale, unseeing features looking contentedly at the ceiling. On an instinct, I leaned over and lightly kissed her stone-cold forehead on the pretext that any friend of Frank Sinatra was a friend of mine. Punching my hands into the pockets of my jacket I headed to the door. The bouncer smiled as if I was an old friend. "There's your car, sir. Goodnight."

Deep in thought I climbed into the back of the Mercedes and was driven home to the strains of Mr. Sinatra singing, 'Didn't We Almost Make It, This Time?' How appropriate, how apt, I thought as the car purred its way through the town and onto York Street. We passed the site of Rainbow's old bar, which had been blown up by one of the warring factions some weeks after he had sold it. The garage was still there with cars parked all around it. Dessie had reneged on the plaque, thinking, quite rightly, that people would laugh at him.

Belle's funeral was a grand affair. I went as a mourner and got a final wave from Rainbow as the Mercedes sailed through the gates of Carnmoney cemetery and up towards the Antrim Road, presumably heading for the Belfast International Airport.

I never saw him again, but six months later I was told by his mother that he'd been killed in Melbourne, Australia. Apparently his car had blown a tyre and went off the road in a remote part of the country. It had plummeted down a disused mine shaft and would have been lost forever had not a couple of hitchhikers been drawn to the spot some hours later by the sound of a woman singing. The man and woman had just built a campfire and were about to settle down for the night when the voice suddenly came out of nowhere and blared all over the countryside.

The campers recovered from their initial fright and set about tracing the source of the voice. As they moved forward nervously, they heard a man's voice joining in song with the woman. They hesitated, thinking they'd maybe came upon a party of drunken Hell's Angels or some other team of nomads.

They discovered Rainbow's car lying on its roof at the bottom of the quarry. He had been thrown through the windscreen and was dead when they found him.

Police officers investigating the accident confirmed that the wreckage might never have been found if the car's radio/cassette player had not continued to play after the impact. They added that the audiocassette found in the machine had only one song on it, and became silent whilst the expensive audio system continued to roll both sides of the tape until the song emerged again. The female had sung solo twice before being joined by the male voice and a musical instrument in what could be loosely termed a duet. They reckoned the top of the range equipment would have played the duet once every ninety minutes until the car's battery ran down.

The hitchhikers related the story to the local press because they believed the male voice sounded like that of the well-known American popular singer Frank Sinatra.

However, when the press investigated the story, it was found Frank Sinatra had never recorded the song that had brought the hikers to the scene of the fatal accident.

The reporter lost interest in running the story after checking with the singer's recording and business manager in the United States.

The recording was a fake, probably the work of a gifted impersonator, said the representative, after it had been played to him over the phone. His last words sealed the fate of the story, which was deleted from the reporter's notebook. "Never, to anyone's knowledge had the legendary singer recorded a song called 'The Sash My Father Wore'."

As the reporter withdrew the cassette and threw it into the wastepaper basket, the Sinatra representative, thousands of miles away in New York, put down the phone and looked across the room at his secretary. "What the hell's a sash anyway?" he asked with a puzzled grin.

At his mother's request, Rainbow's body was cremated and his ashes sent to Belfast. I received a letter inviting me to a simple Service where the ashes of the deceased would be spread over what remained of the dockside pub he used to own.

I arrived to find quite a crowd there. We watched as the Parish Priest performed the ceremony. He was finding it difficult to make his words heard over the constant roar of the passing traffic and smiled gratefully when a local police officer took a bullhorn from a waiting Land Rover and passed it to him. The police had been asked to the scene to stop traffic going up the narrow street adjacent to the bombed-out public house but were powerless to halt the heavy goods vehicles that roared along the nearby motorway.

The officer returned the smile and touched his cap before walking back to his colleagues with a rolling gait that suggested he would be more at home in a country lane than a city street.

Rainbow's mother emerged from the crowd and proceeded to thank the officer. A petite wisp of a woman, she opened her handbag and reached him an audio-cassette. She spoke to him and he bent down to hear her over the noise. He straightened up, looked at the cassette in his hand and walked to the landrover and climbed inside.

Some moments later the sombre tones of Frank Sinatra drowned out the roar of the traffic as the song 'My Way' floated from the speakers on the roof of the police vehicle. Seconds later, a long hydraulic arm stretched tenuously from a red fire tender. We watched as the arm, operated by two helmeted fire fighters, standing on a covered platform, moved slowly toward the large gable wall.

We heard the rasp of an electric drill and saw one of the men screw a brass plate into the wall about thirty feet above street level.

The priest raised the bullhorn and spoke into it. "Mr. Hagan was very generous in his donations to the Brigade. As a tribute to this generosity they volunteered to construct and erect a plaque in his memory. It's big enough to read from the ground if you're close enough. For those not that close I can tell you it contains two words: 'Rainbow's End'. A fitting tribute from our brave friends in the Fire Service."

"Shud have also said Frank Sinatra sang here," growled a voice in my ear. I turned and recognised Regan, the garage owner.

He had changed out of his oily rags for the occasion. I was somewhat surprised to see he was an elegant dresser, with a brown trilby pulled down over gold rimmed glasses.

His suit and shoes matched the colour of the soft hat, as did his fashionable shirt and what looked like a silk tie. His long face was as sharp as a hatchet as we watched the fire fighters guide the mechanical arm back to its base.

I didn't answer but had to suppress a smile when a dock-worker walking by recognised the garage owner in all his splendour and called out to the muted merriment of the crowd.

"Hey Regan, whose car are ye fixin' this week? Humphrey Bogart's?" Regan squashed his cigarette with his foot.

"It was him," he muttered. "It definitely was him," he repeated, before being swallowed up by the crowd.

I moved across the waste ground that was once a public house to pay my respects to Mrs. Hagan. The family priest joined me and we both watched as the frail old lady was put into the back of a funeral car and driven to her home. His shoes were muddied and some of Rainbow's ashes had blown back onto his shiny, well-worn, navy blue suit. He was a small, gaunt man with a careworn face that beamed out hope and mercy when he looked into my eyes.

Smiling up at me he reached for my hand and shook it warmly. "Mr. Hagan was a great fan of Mr. Sinatra, as I believe you are," he said in a voice as warm as his grip. "Many's the night I nipped into the little room at the top of the house and whiled away a few hours with Rainbow whilst Mr. Sinatra whirled on the turntable ... " His voice drifted off as if he was reliving a favourite moment.

"Yes," I replied, "I've spent a few hours in the same situation. Frank Sinatra certainly can sing."

The priest looked up into my eyes and studied my face for a moment. An impish grin covered his features as he put his arms around my neck and whispered into my right ear ...

"He does a fair rendering of 'The Sash My Father Wore', doesn't he?" he whispered.

He stood back and savoured the astonished smile that immediately crossed my features.

"Good luck with the story and don't spare the rich bookies," he added with a grin.

He shook my hand again and winked knowingly before walking off quickly and jauntily in the direction of a Presbyterian clergyman, who had also come to pay his respects to York Street's best-loved and sadly missed entrepreneur.

I looked, reflectively, at Regan's downcast features as I moved toward my car. He would soon know the truth. Now that Rainbow was dead, I could write the story; but would anyone believe it?